DEATH ᴏF THE ANCHORITE

A TALE OF MEDIEVAL MURDER, MYSTERY
AND SKULDUGGERY. BOOK THREE OF THE
DRAYCHESTER CHRONICLES.

M J WESTERBONE

FREE BOOK OFFER

Get your free copy of Death Of The Messenger

The Prequel to the

Draychester Chronicles

Visit www.westerbone.com to get exclusive discounts, news on upcoming releases **and a free copy of *Death of the Messenger*,** the prequel to the Draychester Chronicles series.

OTHER BOOKS IN THE SERIES

Available Now

Book 1 of the Draychester Chronicles

Death Of The Official

Available Now

Book 2 of the Draychester Chronicles

Death Of The Vintner

.

THE ANCHORHOLD AT SNERTHERHIDE

It wasn't the smoke that woke her first, nor was it the heat or flames, although they would soon become ferocious in the confined space. It was the unearthly noise that roused her, almost as though a bag of hissing cats had appeared in the sparsely furnished cell. The small ceramic pot had landed right next to her. It had been thrown via the hole in the outside wall of the anchorite's cell where she lay on the straw filled sleeping pallet. Before the choking smoke had taken hold she'd seen a face at the opening. It had grinned at her and shouted over the noise from the pot. "Don't mind if I watch do you? It's been years since I've seen one of these in action."

She'd had no time to answer as the pot had suddenly exploded with unbelievable force and splattered the stone cell with burning liquid fire. Engulfed in roaring flames, she sought no means of escape. She knew well that the stone cell had no door. The walling up had taken place twenty years before, at the end of a solemn ceremony. Old Bishop Thorndyke himself had laid the mortar for the last block. He'd watched as two of the local parishioners had heaved the heavy stone into place and her voluntary confinement had begun.

Her attacker was thrown backwards by the blast, away from the opening and into the damp undergrowth of the night time churchyard. Apart from two singed eyebrows and several nettle stings, he was unharmed. He stood up and hastily backed further away from the inferno that was greedily sucking air through the opening. It was like looking into a blacksmith's furnace, he'd forgotten how potent the mysterious mixture was. The pot being thrown in the open during battle he'd seen before, but never observed the effects in such a confined place. He chuckled to himself. After the last few months he felt he deserved some entertainment. It would be surprising if there was anything left of the old crone by morning. If the church itself survived, which was doubtful, they'd probably put it down to divine intervention. Not that he really cared either way, he'd be miles away before first light.

Fortunately, the thick stone walls confined the fire to the anchorite's cell. The room had been so sparsely furnished that there hadn't been a lot to burn, other than the anchorite herself and the contents of the pot. It had been enough to consume and reduce her to ashes in the initial minutes. The fire hadn't penetrated through the internal opening into the main church, although the smoke had filled the simple interior of the building.

The priest, Geoffrey Scrope, in his little shack on the opposite side of the church, had slept through the entire thing. Perhaps a consequence of the several hours he'd spent the previous afternoon at the local alehouse. His head was still pounding when he staggered out into the cool morning air. He leaned on the wall for support as he made his way along to the front of the building. Father Geoffrey pushed open the sturdy oak door and a billow of foul, sulphur smelling smoke hit him in the face. Eyes watering, he staggered away, bent down and retched over his own feet.

When he'd recovered sufficiently to move again, with some foreboding he made himself put his head through the open doorway. In the smoke-filled gloom of the interior he shouted towards the anchorite's cell.

"Joan, are you all right old woman?"

There was no response. The smoke made him cough and splutter, but he inched his way further inside.

"Christ's bones woman. What have you been up to? If you've been cooking for yourself in there I'll never hear the last of it. You know it's not allowed. Joan?"

Father Geoffrey could stand the smoke and stench no longer and he hastily made his way back out. Standing at the doorway, he drew in great lungfuls of morning air. Making his way around the opposite side of the church, he hurried along the wall to the opening into the cell. There was a black stain all around the hole. He placed a hand on the stonework, peered in and gasped. The room was completely covered in soot, the whitewashed walls were black and oily. On the floor was a pile of grey-coloured ash and what looked like pieces of broken pot. The few things the old anchorite had kept in her cell were gone, as was she. He stumbled away from the opening, and as the sense of what had happened hit him, he retched for the second time that morning. How this had come to be he couldn't under-stand. Perhaps it was a sign from God. With the back of a soot-stained hand he wiped the vomit away from his lips and then crossed himself. Some divine punishment had been visited on the village. Perhaps their sins had finally caught up with them.

As word spread, a small crowd of villagers converged on the humble church at Snetherhide. The news upset many, Joan had been popular. One after another they peered into the anchorite's cell. Their interest was either a morbid curiosity or to satisfy themselves old Joan hadn't just given up her vows and taken off. She would have needed to demolish a stone wall to escape, but the parishioners had suspicious minds. The reeve, Adam de Charnok stuck his own head through the outside opening to check. He nearly retched at the stench, but satisfied himself the walls were intact. No one had got out of the inferno. He grabbed hold of the priest's arm and pulled him away from the crowd. He whispered, "This isn't good Father. We can't keep this quiet. There'll be questions asked, and the coroner will have to be informed."

The priest shook his head. "The coroner doesn't have any authority Adam. Not over an anchorite on church property. It's not the coroner we must deal with but Jocelyn Gifford, bishop of Draychester."

Charnok glared at him. "The bishop? It's an accident, that's all. Why even tell him? The old woman must have set something on fire in there. She's not been right in the head since I was a boy. No need for the bishop to know. Why cut off the hand that feeds us?"

The priest hissed, "No need for him to know, are you mad? That we've been taking half the funds she should have been getting is one thing. She was a simple soul, never asked for much, but this ends it. We can't pretend she's still alive, you'd be a fool to think otherwise."

Charnok tried to justify the years of deception and theft, more to himself than to the priest. "It would have been a waste to give her more Father, we both agreed that years ago. The old maids tended her for nothing and the villagers fed her. The funds were better spent elsewhere."

The priest freed himself of Charnok's restraining hand. "It was good while it lasted Adam. Be satisfied with what you've had, I am. This bishop isn't like old Thorndyke, you can't pay him off or make some ham-fisted bargain." He gestured at the blackened hole in the wall. "With the manner of her death, I'll wager he'll know the old crone is dead by this time tomorrow, whether we send message or not. Trust me, we'd better send word, it'll look suspicious if we don't.

2

THE BISHOP'S PALACE

J ocelyn Gifford, bishop of Draychester, had been out hunting all day. They'd started by shooting a fine stag in Pilkington Park. The deer park lay to the west of the city of Draychester and the cathedral held exclusive licence to hunt there. From time to time the bishop liked to invite the more prominent citizens of the city to join him there. In the afternoon the bishop and a smaller number of friends had ventured beyond the park. They'd cornered a boar in some woods. Having brought down the ferocious beast himself the bishop was tired but in an excellent mood.

As he made his way towards his private quarters in the bishop's palace he stuck his head into the adjacent hall. His friend Scrivener, who was also his chief clerk and secretary, sat at the far end in his usual spot near the fire. Before him was a small desk.

The bishop shouted, "You missed a big old boar this afternoon Scrivener. I took it down myself."

The other man looked up from the parchment strewn desk at his friend and master, concerned but not surprised that Gifford had tackled the wild boar himself. Once cornered such a beast could be both cunning and dangerous. His master had been a soldier in his youth and although heading towards middle age still had a warrior's build and strength.

With a straight face Scrivener asked, "An old boar my lord, I take it to be a beast rather than one of the good citizens of Draychester?"

The bishop laughed and walked over to warm his hands by the fire that was burning in an alcove behind Scrivener. "Well, I must admit old Gillibrand, the mayor, was droning on and on. Fell of his horse at one point. Thought he might have broken his neck but no such luck." He turned, grabbed a leather cup off the corner of Scrivener's desk and poured himself some wine from a jug that sat there. "And you my friend, what excitement have you found in your papers today?"

Scrivener shrugged. "Only that an anchorite has died at Snetherhide my lord. Normally I wouldn't bother you with the details."

The bishop looked at his secretary curiously. "I don't suppose we have a shortage of anchorites my friend? If I'm not mistaken old Bishop Thorndyke was something of an enthusiast in that respect?"

"Indeed my lord, it prompted me to do some research in the archives. It seems we have inherited some forty anchorites across the diocese. The most famous of course is the venerable Dame Dorothy within our own cathedral precinct.

The bishop choked on his wine and spluttered, "God's teeth, forty? What was the man thinking of?"

Screener grinned. "I think foremost in his mind was the coin my lord. Even the most humble receives an annual

"8

stipend. Many had wealthy benefactors. In his later years Thorndyke was walling up one a month."

Shaking his head sadly the bishop said, "Well you know my views Scrivener. Between you and me, I find the whole process faintly ridiculous. Thorndyke's actions don't surprise me, the man was rotten to the core."

"You've spoken to Dame Dorothy yourself my lord?"

The bishop snorted. "Only when duty requires it. She just speaks in riddles. And that bloody pigeon she keeps in her cell, the Pigeon of Perception she's taken to calling it, I rather think she has lost her mind. Fearsome temper on the woman too; frankly she scares me."

Scrivener chuckled and poured himself a cup of wine. He said, "She's very popular with the city folk. She's also a great attraction with the pilgrims to the cathedral. Her fame spreads far and wide."

The bishop, warming to the topic, said, "Did you know Scrivener, one of our own canons, de Ward his name is, has wasted hours recording her manic ramblings over the years? He claims she's prophesied everything from the cook's love life all the way to our late king's fall from grace. Our new king himself took an interest in that one."

Scrivener nodded. "Indeed my lord, I'd heard as much myself and he's also made a generous donation to her upkeep."

The bishop grunted his verdict on their king's superstitious nature. "So what's so special about this woman who's died in Snertherhide?"

"The manner of her death was somewhat unusual. It appears she was incinerated in her cell within the church."

"God's teeth. I take it she was walled in?"

"Oh yes, twenty years ago I believe. The openings weren't big enough to allow her to escape."

"An accident you think?"

"Perhaps my lord, although from what I've heard the fire was of an unusual ferocity. We must establish the facts."

The bishop nodded. "I agree. Send Will, and Bernard of course. Oh, and that gloomy nephew of yours, Osbert the clerk. That lad could depress the very angels, it'll do him good to be out and about."

3

INVESTIGATION AT SNERTHERHIDE

The three bishop's officials came to a halt at a crossroads. It was a fine morning in late summer and they'd already made excellent progress, covering about seven or eight miles from Draychester. Whether that had been in the right direction was now debatable. Bernard, the sizeable man in the lead, patted his horse fondly, then stroked his stubbly chin, trying to decide which route they should follow. The thin-faced lad on the horse behind snorted and said, "Thought you knew the way like the back of your hand? Admit it, we're lost."

Bernard sighed, turned in his saddle and said, "Osbert, I've said it before and I'll say it again, you're never happier than when moaning about something. Can't you just enjoy the ride lad? Look around you and appreciate what a fine morning it is."

Will Blackburne, a red-haired young man only a few years older than their gloomy clerk, edged his horse past Osbert and came up beside the older man. "So we are lost then?"

Bernard shrugged. "What I said is that I knew the place, which I do. It's just been awhile."

"We could ask someone." said Will.

They looked around. There wasn't a soul on the road in either direction. The open fields on either side of the track were deserted. To the right, in the far distance, there was a smudge of smoke rising above a small thicket of willow.

Osbert said, "I say we go left. I'm sure that's the road to Iver, and that's in the right direction."

It was Will's turn to snort. "On that basis we'd better go right. We always head in the opposite direction to that which you suggest my friend. Hasn't let us down yet."

Bernard grunted his agreement and with a squeeze of a knee he gently urged his horse to the right. Will grinned at Osbert, who glared back. After a few minutes riding, the track narrowed and turned down towards a stream. They rode along the stream's bank to a small wooden bridge that comprised a few rickety planks laid side by side over the water. In the distance they could see the low turf roofed cottages that marked the edge of the village of Snertherhide. Thin trails of smoke rose from holes in the roofs. Further back they could just make out the top of a squat stone tower that belonged to a church.

Bernard nodded. "This is the place. Must be two or three summers since I was here last. It doesn't look to have improved much."

"Who's the lord of the manor Osbert?" asked Will.

The young clerk pulled a scrap of parchment from under his tunic. He studied it for a moment and said. "A Walter Fitzgerald. Not that you'll find him here. He has a fine house in Draychester near Eastgate. Spends his time gambling and whoring."

"Your uncle Scrivener tell you that did he?" asked Bernard.

"Amongst other things," answered Osbert darkly. "A man called Charnok sent the news to Draychester. He's the reeve."

They made their way down the single village street. The poorer houses at the edge of the village were built of cob and roofed in turf. Nearer the church lay a scattering of more substantial structures, some even boasting a second floor. The only mortared stone buildings in the entire place were the church and what they took to be the manor house that stood beside it. At the entrance to the muddy yard of the manor house they stopped as a nervous-looking figure emerged from a barn. He hurried over to them.

"Has the bishop sent you?" he asked anxiously.

Bernard gave him an appraising eye, "Are you Charnok?"

"I am, I'm the reeve."

Will said, "We've orders from the bishop to investigate the death of your anchorite. I'm Will, the big man is Bernard, and this is our clerk, Osbert. It was you who sent the message to Draychester, not the priest?"

Almost reluctancy it seemed, he nodded. "Yes, although it was Father Geoffrey that first discovered she was gone."

Berarnd said, "Gone? The report was that she's dead?"

"Dead yes, but there is no corpse to speak of. It happened yesterday morning."

"This doesn't look like a place that'd be wealthy enough to support an anchorite," said Will quizzically.

Charnok was offended. "We looked after our anchorite

well enough and better than most. Joan was her name, she was the lord's aunt and a blessing to the village."

Bernard said, "You say she was Fitzgerald's aunt? So he knows she's dead then, has he returned from the city?"

Charnok snorted. "Not him. He's not been here for a year, too busy in Draychester I gather. I've sent him word, though don't expect him to come. He was only a child when they first walled her up, he barely knows her. You'll want to see the church?"

Bernard nodded. "Course we will. Where's the priest?"

"He's in the church with some villagers."

"Then lead on," said Bernard.

Charnok led them across the muddy track and into the churchyard. They climbed down from the horses, and after tying them to a bush, followed Charnok to the side of the church. He gestured at the hole in the wall that opened into the anchorites cell. "She lived in there."

Will peered in through the square opening, the surrounding stonework was blackened. The anchorite's cell was about twelve feet square. Directly opposite on the far wall was another opening into the interior of the church. Neither was big enough for someone to climb through.

The cell itself was covered in an oily black soot, evidently caused by the intensity of the fire. It was almost bare; anything that had been in there, including presumably Joan, had been consumed by the flames. The ash and charred fragments that now lay on the stone floor were all that remained. There was a pungent smell over and above that of a normal fire. Will couldn't place it. It went right to the back of his throat and made him cough. He backed away from the opening. "Christ's bones, there's nothing left. No sign of a body or anything else. It's just ash. What sort of fire burns like that?"

Bernard stuck his head through the opening. As Will had said there was nothing but ash. The walls were intact. No normal person had left the cell alive that was certain. He ran a finger in the soot and rubbed it between finger and thumb. He brought it to his nose, the smell was vaguely familiar. He struggled to remember from where. A memory nagged him from years before when he'd fought the Scots with the king's army. Still, he wasn't certain.

He moved back and allowed Osbert to put his scrawny neck through the opening. They heard him gasp. The young clerk soon turned away, crossed himself and said, "It must be a miracle, her very body has been raised by God to the heavens. There's no other explanation."

Will shrugged. "It's strange, I'll grant you that, but there may be some more earthly explanation."

Bernard rubbed his stubbly chin in thought. "Have you ever seen the ceremony when they wall up someone like old Joan?"

Will shook his head. "Not me. I am not sure I'd want to. You?"

"Once. It was like watching a funeral. The bishop presided; It took bloody hours. They're supposed to be considered dead to the world when they're placed in there. Sort of like a living saint."

Will turned to Charnok. "She never left there? Everything she needed came in through the openings?"

"Yes, everything came in and out through there or the opening inside the church. We were all fond of her, she was a pious woman, an example to us all I dare say. Some women from the village looked after her needs both food and other things. "

"Other things?" asked Osbert.

Charnok looked at Osbert and smiled at the naïve question. "She still had to piss and take a shit lad, living saint or not. There was a pail for that which could be passed in and out. She even washed occasionally, at least twice a year I'd say."

Osbert reddened in embarrassment.

There were raised voices as they walked into the church. The smell of smoke and that strange something else was stronger inside the main building than it had been in the anchorite's cell.

His severe tonsure easily identified the priest. He was surrounded by a small crowd of his own parishioners who were arguing with him and each other with equal vigour. As they caught sight of the reeve and the bishop's men the angry voices turned into a sullen silence.

Charnok said, "Father, these are the bishop's men from Draychester." They introduced themselves.

Father Geoffrey gave a weak smile. "Welcome. We're sorry to have caused you a journey."

Bernard, always quick to get to the point, said, "Is there some disagreement going on here father?"

There were some scowls from the villagers, but no one said anything. Eventually Father Geoffrey, looking slightly uncomfortable, replied, "Joan was well liked. Her death has caused some shock. An accident most likely, as she was getting on in years."

Someone said, "Nonsense. Sharp as ever when I spoke to her last. She had nothing that'd make a fire like that."

There was a general murmuring of agreement.

Will said, "Someone took care of her needs day to day?"

A plump, plain faced woman with mousey brown hair

and a sharp voice said, "My sister and I have cared for her these last few years."

"You saw her the night before this fire?"

"As always. I passed a meal into the cell and she passed out the pail she used."

"From here in the church, or through the outside opening?"

"No, from here inside."

"You see anything unusual, either in the cell or here in the church?" asked Bernard.

The woman shook her head. "Everything was as it should be. Joan was a very pious woman, she ate little, and had even less in her cell."

Another woman stepped forward, she looked similar enough to the first who had spoken that Will took her for the sister. "Her needs were few. She was a simple soul. Normally she didn't even have a candle in the cell, although there was one usually burning here in the church outside the opening."

"So how did a fire start in there?" asked Will.

"I know not. An act of God? Perhaps it was just her time."

Bernard asked, "Did no one else see anything that night? Something out of the ordinary, either in the village or around the church?"

There was a sullen silence. Bernard sighed. He knew how the mentality of these people worked. Whatever they really thought, they would be reluctant to speak to anyone in authority. "We're not going to fine the village. This isn't like an inquest. No coroner will enquire into Joan's death. It happened in the church, so it's a matter for the bishop and church law."

From the back of the group a voice said, "We know how

these things work. Someone will be blamed. You can't promise otherwise."

Bernard shook his head in exasperation and said, "Then we'd better open it."

"Open what?" asked Charnok.

"The bloody cell of course, we need to see inside. Where was the entrance originally?"

Charnok gestured at the wall. "It was here. The opening you see is where the entrance was, they walled it up and left the top few feet. The stones have been whitewashed over."

"It shouldn't take that long then. So Reeve, you'd better get some men with tools and tear it down."

The priest looked shocked, "What now?"

Bernard even more exasperated turned to him and said, "Yes, right now."

Osbert hissed, "Is this necessary? The woman has obviously been taken by God. It's a miracle."

Bernard glared at the young clerk and Will said softly, "Don't be a fool Osbert. There's something not right about this. I for one want to see what's in there."

Bernard grunted his satisfaction at Will's common sense. He put his huge hands together, flexed his fingers and cracked his knuckles.

"Come on Reeve, we haven't got all day, or must I tear the stones down with my own bare hands?"

It took the blacksmith, who provided two chisels and two hammers, his apprentice and the miller to carefully chisel out the mortar and pry out the stone blocks. When the opening was wide enough Bernard held up his hand for them to stop.

"That's enough. Father Geoffrey fetch us a candle."

The priest quickly returned with a smokey tallow candle. He passed it to Bernard. With an outstretched arm the big man thrust it through the jagged entrance and carefully stepped into the anchorite's cell. He stepped to the left and with his back to the sooty wall inched away from the opening. Will followed him in. Behind them Father Geoffrey, Charnok and interested villagers all pressed close.

Will turned and shooed them back. "Give us some space. It's hard enough to see as it is without you blocking the light from the church. Osbert stand there and keep them back please."

The ash on the floor was about a quarter of an inch deep. Bernard tentatively stuck his foot out into the cell and stirred the remains. There was nothing much discernible at first. Then Will thought he saw something that might have been charred bone fragments. "You see that Bernard?"

"I see it. Could be what's left of the old women, hard to tell. Looks like bone to me. The fire burnt hot, that I can see."

He stirred the ash some more with his foot. There seemed to be some bits of broken pottery in amongst it.

He said, "You think you can get me a stick or something?"

Will turned and shouted to the reeve, "Can you get me a stick or a staff please."

It was the priest who answered. "Have you not done enough to disturb her remains? What do you hope to achieve?"

Will said sharply, "The bishop has tasked us to inquire what has happened here. Now get me what I asked for and be quick about it."

Bernard squatted down and began to probe the ash

nearest to him with a finger. He picked the pieces of pottery up and passed them back to Will who placed them just outside the cell's opening. Eventually a long willow stick was found.

Will passed it to Bernard. The big man grunted his thanks and used it to sift the ash further into the cell. A few more pieces of pottery turned up and were extracted. When he was finally satisfied Bernard said, "I'm coming out."

Will moved out of the opening as Bernard squeezed back out. He pointed at the broken pot piled against the wall.

"Osbert, collect that lot up lad, and put it in that bag of yours."

The clerk, mystified, did what he was told and carefully put the pottery into the leather bag he carried.

"We need somewhere to review the evidence," said Will.

Bernard nodded.

"What evidence?" said Father Geoffrey curiously.

Ignoring him, Will turned to the reeve and said, "You've got an alehouse in the village?"

The reeve said, "If you want a drink, come across the way to the hall." He added sarcastically, "I'm sure my lord, if he was here, would want me to offer you every hospitality."

They sat at a trestle table in the hall of the manor house.

"We need to speak of some bishop's business. Leave us for a moment will you Charnok?" said Bernard. His tone implied it was more an order than a request. The reeve scowled and then reluctantly left them to converse in private.

Will looked at Bernard and said, "The pottery?"

Bernard smiled and nodded. "I think I have an idea of what's gone on here, although as to why I'm at a loss."

Will said, "Osbert, let's have a look at that pottery. Empty it out onto the table."

The clerk carefully removed each piece from the bag and solemnly placed it on the table before them. "I really don't understand what we are looking for. Surely it was an accident, instigated by God."

Bernard gestured at the pottery, "What do you notice?"

Will studied the tabletop for a moment. He pointed to one piece and then to another. "There's at least two different pots here. One looks very much like pieces of a jug. Common enough I would think. She probably had it for water. The other, I'm not sure. A lot smaller, curved. Glazed as well."

Bernard nodded. "It was the smell I recognised, although it's been many years. Catches in the back of your throat. Sulphur and some other mixture bound together. Burns like a bastard."

"I think I'm beginning to understand. It was in this smaller of the pots?" said Will.

"Yes. My guess is it was thrown through the outside opening into the anchorite's cell when she was asleep. I've seen such a thing before. You know I fought the Scots in my youth with the old king's army?"

Osbert grunted. "You've bored us with your army tales often enough."

Ignoring him, Bernard continued, "The king had a special man with him, a Saracen. This foreigner had knowledge of Greek fire. You've heard of it?"

Will shook his head. Osbert said, "Surely it's just a myth?"

"Not so lad, I've seen it used. The mixture, Greek Fire, of

which this Saracen knew the secret, was placed in a pot. Something small enough to sit in your hand. You wrap a burning rag around it and hurl it at your enemy. Although some said you could just expose the mixture to air and it'd burst into flames itself, burning rag or not. The Scots were terrified of it."

Osbert snorted. "Sounds like something that would be more dangerous to you than the Scots."

Bernard shrugged. "I grant you, from what I saw, it was certainly dangerous to handle. Not that they gave a weapon like that to the likes of us you understand."

"So who used this Greek fire then?" asked Will.

Bernard rubbed a hand across his face. "We had some mercenaries with us. The king brought them specially from France. They were a bloody mean bunch, who kept to themselves most of the time. I saw them use the Saracen's weapon. When the pot broke, the mixture inside came out as a burning mass. You couldn't put the stuff out, even with water. It burnt with a fierce heat that you wouldn't believe and I'll never forget that smell."

Will picked some pieces up from the table. "You think this smaller pot is what remains of the weapon?"

"I do."

Osbert said, "Why in God's name would anyone do such a thing? The anchorite was surely harmless?"

Bernard smiled grimly. "Well, that's the real question isn't it lad?"

4

IN THE LIBRARY

I n the main body of the cathedral there was still a little light from the candles surrounding the shrines of Draychester's famous saints and from those in front of the altar. Elsewhere it was dark. After the night prayer had been said, and before the daily rituals began again in the early hours, there was a silence to be enjoyed. Ralph of Shrewsbury appreciated every moment of it, this being his favourite time of the day. His eyes were undimmed with age but even if he'd been blind, he could have found his way about with little trouble. Tonight he glided around the two sides of the cloisters with practised ease.

In old Bishop Thorndyke's time the north cloister had been divided into three studies overlooking the courtyard. They were made of wooden panelling with a lattice door. There was clear glass in the cloister screens to let in as much light as possible so that the more studious could study every day after dinner until evensong. In Ralph's experience they were also an excellent place to take in the last of the evening sun and catch up on some sleep. At this time of the day they were empty and dark. He glided through them without stopping.

The hooded black cloak Ralph wore made him practically invisible. He came to a halt by the entrance that led up to the library above the east cloister and produced a key from under his cloak. With hardly a noise, he unlocked the door that guarded it. Pushing it open just enough to slip through, he silently closed it again behind him and locked it once more.

The steps were narrow and steep, but fortunately there was only a short flight before he emerged in the dark space that ran the full length above the east cloister. The familiar smell of old documents and the lingering odour of the senior librarian's sweaty feet greeted his nose. He contributed to the aroma with a long drawn out, but mainly silent, fart. At his age farts were one of the few bodily pleasures he still enjoyed, and after climbing stairs were somewhat involuntary. He sighed contently and made his way between the reading tables. Some moonlight came through the windows set high in the walls and illuminated his progress. All along the back wall was a long run of shelving containing the cathedral's collection of valuable books each secured to the shelf by a long chain. At the far north end a partition separated the library from a small strongroom.

Ralph reflected that the strongroom was woefully insecure. The locks were so pitiful he'd be surprised if they couldn't be picked with a bent nail. Not that he needed to go to that sort of trouble, having long had a set of keys for most of the doors in the cathedral, including the strongroom itself. What it really needed was one of the cathedral servants to sleep up here in front of the door. A simple security measure, but not one that would ever occur to his fellow canons. They could scarcely imagine anyone would break the sanctity of the cathedral and steal. Not that he particularly wanted any of the silver and gold objects from the strongroom. The chests stored inside the room contained something even more valuable to him, knowledge. What he sought were the charters, grants and bequests made to the cathedral over the centuries.

He unlocked the strongroom door and made his way inside. There was a small desk and stool against the back wall surrounded by several trunks. He lit a tallow candle and placed it carefully inside a horn lantern that sat on the end of the desk. A pale golden light filled the room. Pulling the door closed, he debated which chest to open first.

Perhaps a little pleasure before business. The largest of the chests contained the library's prohibited books. With a boney fingered hand he selected from it a slim, battered volume, covered in wine stains. At least he hoped they were wine stains. Opening its mildewed pages, its author apparently one Howard of Warwick, a chronicler of times past, Ralph quickly became bored and threw it back into the chest. He sought something more salacious and lifted a heavy volume onto the desk. Ralph was amused to find it contained drawings of the female form. They were childish sketches at best but were deemed too shocking and inappropriate for the less worldly of the library's patrons. The hypocrisy of keeping the book hidden here in the chest wasn't lost on him. Even now he would wager at least half of his fellow canons were enjoying the carnal pleasures of their mistresses or a well-paid whore. In the city itself he knew of at least three properties the cathedral owned, which were rented out and used as brothels. The vellum pages of the book were well thumbed, the senior librarian evidently spent a lot of time shut in the strongroom.

There were other books in the chest that were more

interesting to him. The ones confiscated from those accused of practising the black arts. Ralph settled down on the stool and read with interest from a slim volume that outlined the ingredients required for various potions that could induce illness and lingering death.

After an hour or so, an almost inaudible tap on the door interrupted Ralph's reading. He sighed, closed the book on the desk before him and said, "Come in you fool, it's open."

Ralph's voice was startlingly loud in the deathly quiet of the library. There was a muffled cry and the sound of someone falling over, then the door slowly opened. The boy of perhaps fourteen or fifteen years, wearing a black cloak much like Ralph's, stood in the doorway. "I'm sorry master you startled me," he whispered.

Ralph beckoned him in. "Don't just stand there boy, come in. You're late."

"It was so dark master and I was afraid of making a noise."

Ralph grunted. "You'll learn your way about the place boy, dark or not, the first fifty years are the hardest."

The boy shuffled inside the strongroom and closed the door. Ralph pointed at one of the smaller chests. "Open that, it's not locked. Put the papers from inside here on the desk."

The boy did as he was bidden. "What are these master?"

"Details of property and money made over to churches in the diocese. Each to the benefit of maintaining an anchorite. You know what an anchorite is don't you boy?"

"Like Dame Dorothy here in Draychester?"

"Exactly boy. Although she's too well known for our plans. We need to take things slowly, a death here, a death there. Something to sow the seeds of confusion, then panic and finally desperation."

The boy's eyes gleamed in the candlelight. "Have you decided on the next one master?"

Ralph looked at the boy curiously. It always amazed him how the young were so easily corrupted. "Patience boy, I need to search the papers again. Do something useful and rub my feet while I find what I need. This cold floor pains them."

He thrust a boney arthritic foot at the boy who recoiled in horror and then tried unsuccessfully to conceal his emotions. Ralph chuckled softly.

As the boy sat on the floor rubbing the leathery old skin of his master toes, Ralph sifted through the papers on the desk. The more he read the more he came to realise how industrious old Bishop Thorndyke had been, even in his later years. Some of the bequests listed must make a lot of people very wealthy. He'd be surprised if much of it was spent as intended, namely to support the anchorites. Eventually he found something that appealed.

He took a scrap of parchment and in the golden light of the horn lantern carefully copied a place and name onto it. He wrote a brief message and folded it tight.

"Tomorrow you're to give this message to the man I sent you to before."

The boy looked up from his toe rubbing and took the note. "Yes master, the one with the strange mark on his face?"

"I believe it's a letter M boy. I'd advise you not to ask how he got it. It needs to be him, no one else. He has the black heart needed for the task."

"I'm not sure I understand master," said the boy concealing the note under his cloak.

"Don't worry about that, just do what you're told."

Ralph slowly eased his body up from the stool, breaking wind in a long drawn out fart as he did so. In the confined space of the strongroom the smell was overpowering and sent the boy scuttling to the door for air. Ralph chuckled happily.

The boy, as was usual for this day of the week, had been sent to buy trout at the Fish Stones. He had walked about two miles from the city along the road that ran alongside the river Dray. If you knew where to look a path could be found that led from the roadside down to the river. Set into the riverbank, three semicircular sandstone blocks, shaded by an old oak tree, gave easy access to the water. Here two friars would fish for brown trout. If they were lucky they would catch enough for a meal later in the day, the rest could be sold.

One of the friars caught sight of the boy carrying a basket coming down the path through the trees. He said to his fellow fisherman, "Here he comes. He's a strange one Brother is he not?"

The other friar regarded the approaching figure. The boy was small, dark-haired and scrawny, almost malnourished looking. "Aye my friend, the poor lad has something of the night about him that's for sure. Have you noticed he never smiles and I've hardly ever heard him speak a civil word."

He had just pulled a fish from the slow-moving waters of the Dray. Turning back to the task in hand, he laid the fish down on the top sandstone step alongside two others.

"You're early today boy. Still, the river has been kind, we've caught three already."

The boy scowled, and with no other greeting held out a coin. The friar took the money and the boy chose a fish. He placed it in the basket he carried.

One of the friars said, "I've got some bread to share lad and Brother James here has some cider."

The other friar nodded, "The bishop's favourite it is. Good stuff, put hair on your chest lad, on the inside that is."

They both laughed. The lad just scowled again and said, "I've need to get back, I've no time to waste in idle chatter."

Brother James shrugged. "Well, suit yourself lad. Don't say we didn't offer."

The boy turned and swiftly walked back up the path and was soon lost from sight. Brother James shook his head, "Mark my words Brother, there's something not right about that lad."

The boy slowed down once he was out of sight of the men at the waterside. The note given to him by Ralph of Shrewsbury was still to be delivered. It was a task he didn't relish. The excursion to buy a fish was the first opportunity he'd had to get away by himself.

The boy wasn't sure exactly where the meeting was to take place. Ralph had simply said the man would find him during the morning. The last time he'd been pulled by the hood of his cloak into a dark alleyway in Draychester. He'd been half strangled and his neck still showed the signs of the bruising. This time he was determined to conduct the meeting with more dignity. He scanned the trees warily as he made his way back to the road. He thought it more likely he would be intercepted in the city itself rather than on the way back, but it wasn't certain. Ralph had chuckled to himself, in that annoying way of his, when the boy had expressed indignation at the way he'd been treated. Ralph had said, "Be careful lad, he's not one to upset. He'd as soon as slit your throat as give you a straight answer."

The boy was inclined to agree. The man not only had a wicked-looking M burnt into his cheek, his eyes were as dead as any he'd ever seen. A shiver ran up his back at the thought of having to deal with him again and he slowed his pace. As he did so he was suddenly dragged off his feet by his hood and found himself dangling in the air, the basket with the fish dropping from his hands. He clutched at his throat and struggled to get free. Eventually he was released, and he fell to the ground. His assailant was sitting on the branch of a tree that jutted out over the path. The boy had walked directly underneath him and seen nothing.

The man smirked and said, "Not very observant are you boy? I could have been anyone. You need to be more careful, don't you know there are thieves about?"

The boy sat on the floor rubbing his neck and trying to get his breath back.

"I'm getting very curious about your master boy and I've got a mind to make you tell me who he is. I grow tired of the subterfuge."

"Subter... what?" the boy stuttered.

"Never mind, maybe I'll just hang you off this branch here until you tell me."

"There's a message." The boy hurriedly retrieved the note from under his cloak to divert the other's train of thought.

The man grinned and swung his legs backwards and forwards. "A message, how novel. Best give it to me then boy." He held out a hand to the boy, who strained on tiptoes to hand it up to him. As the man read it, balanced on the branch, he stroked a long finger over the wicked-looking welt on his cheek. The lad couldn't take his eyes off the M shaped scar. Whoever had branded the man had done a wicked thing, although he had no doubt it was well deserved. The man had tried to grow a beard, but it made a poor job of hiding the scar.

"Looking at something?"

The boy quickly looked away, face flushing red. The man swiftly jumped down beside the boy and stood towering over him. "I'm not sure what your master has in mind with this game boy. For now, I'm content to play along as it suits my purpose well enough, and of course the coin has been useful."

He grabbed the boy by the throat, lifted him off the ground and brought his face level with his own. "I don't however think for one minute he's got my best interests at heart and I'm not a man to cross. Make sure he understands that." He released the boy with a push that sent him sprawling onto his back and followed it up with a swift kick to the stomach. As the boy lay retching on the path the man opened the basket, took out the fish, and vanished with it into the undergrowth.

5

A KILLING AT LEIGHTON

Sir Roger Mudstone entered the small one-room cottage to discover his servant Travis fast asleep on his back by the fire. He was tempted to give him a swift kick in the ribs, instead he slapped him in the face with the dripping brown trout he carried. Travis spluttered into life and pulled the slimy fish from his face. He jumped to his feet when he saw his master.

"I only lay down for a moment Sir Roger, just a quick rest, nothing more."

Sir Roger gave him a withering look. "You never cease to amaze me Travis with your slovenly and lazy behaviour. Why I've let you live this long is another mystery. Now get that fish cooked, and be quick about it. I'm hungry."

Travis knew better than to ask where Sir Roger had got the fish and was soon preparing it. He removed the head, slit it up the belly, gutted it, then fried it in a skillet over the fire. Sir Roger sat down on a stool next to the fire and removed his expensive Cordoba leather boots.

He rubbed his feet and said, "There's work to do tomorrow Travis. While you've been slacking here in this hovel, I've met with the youth again, the one sent by our mysterious benefactor."

"You've no idea who he is master?" asked Travis.

Sir Roger watching the fish sizzle in the pan shook his head. "Not yet Travis, but I have my suspicions. The boy from his clothes is surely from the cathedral school. Sent by whom is the question. For now, I'm content to play along. Here, give me that pan…"

He snatched the skillet from Travis's hands and rolled the fish in the pan. "Look you've burnt the thing. You're bloody useless, I knew I should have left you to rot in that French dungeon."

Sir Roger brooded over the pan for a few minutes as the fish cooked. Eventually he took a small knife from his belt and ate the fish straight from the pan. He didn't offer Travis any. The other man looked enviously at the creamy texture and succulent white flesh of the trout.

Sir Roger gestured at the door, "Get out there and take care of the horse, I rode the beast hard today."

Travis got wearily to his feet. "Yes master."

Sir Roger had left the horse tied up behind the tumbled down hovel they had been sheltering in these last few weeks. It was miles from anywhere and lay behind a sand dune at the top of a beach. Nearby the river Dray emptied into the English Channel via a wide, muddy estuary.

As Travis fed the horse he looked out over the great expanse of mud and sand and thought it would be hard to find a more desolate spot. Sir Roger's explanation of how he came to know of the place was that he had killed the cottage's previous occupier. Travis didn't doubt him for a moment, as he'd removed the charred bones from the interior himself. While Sir Roger had been off doing God knows what, he'd been patching up the badly burnt roof with old drift wood and reeds.

He went back to the door and stood just inside the threshold. Sir Roger was sprawled fast asleep, wrapped in his riding cloak by the fire. The empty skillet lay beside him. For a moment Travis contemplated walking over, picking up the skillet and bashing his master's brains out. It would be easy and immensely satisfying. He could almost hear the sound Sir Roger's head would make, like the breaking of an egg. He'd bury him in the sand dune at the back of the cottage, then taking his master's heavy purse and the horses, make a life for himself someplace far away. No one could blame him, and he'd happily face his maker with a clear conscience.

Over the time they'd known each other, Travis had come to believe Sir Roger was truly evil. He couldn't think of a single person who'd miss his master and a quite a few places where they'd organise a celebratory feast at the very least. But he knew he was too weak-willed. The time for such bold action had come and gone. He'd made his choice, and he was surely now bound to his master all the way to the very gates of hell and beyond.

Sir Roger stirred in his sleep, his hand coming to rest on the hilt of a short dagger that hung on his belt. Travis smiled sadly to himself, his master had a sixth sense for danger, he truly was the devil incarnate. Their recent survival after an attack by pirates, and subsequent escape from imprisonment in France, had only proved that once again.

～

Travis and Sir Roger crouched behind a stone wall that surrounded the churchyard in Leighton. Riding from the cottage they'd headed inland and around the head of the marshy estuary. Where the river became narrower they'd forded it at a shallow spot. They'd tied up the horses in a small coppice half a mile away from the village. The fields here were open and divided up into strips. As they crouched in the bushes Travis could see figures scattered throughout the fields tending the crops.

Sir Roger was carrying a coil of rope in one hand and his dagger in the other. "You'd better keep up Travis. Just follow me," he waved the dagger menacingly at Travis, "and if you're seen I'll bloody stick you with this myself, understand?"

Travis nodded numbly, appalled at the madness. Sir Roger set off like a hare with Travis close behind. They alternately crouched and sprinted as they followed the dips and hollows in the fields. By some miracle they kept out of sight and reached a wall surrounding the churchyard. From the height of the sun Travis judged it must be approaching noon. He couldn't understand why they didn't just come after dark. Sir Roger might have carried a king's pardon with him at one time, but Travis knew that in this, their home county, it'd would do no good. If anyone recognised them they'd be hunted down and executed as outlaws. He expected no mercy.

Sir Roger, eyes just above the top of the rough stonework, said, "This isn't going to be straightforward Travis. We'll need to improvise. I think something special is in order for this one. That's why we've brought the rope."

Travis eased his head upwards until he could see across the grass to the church. Amazingly there was a line of six or seven villagers stood against the wall awaiting their consultation with the anchorite.

"Look at that," hissed Sir Roger, "You'd think she was the king dispensing charity. What could she possibly tell them that isn't just gibberish?"

Travis whispered, "Anchorites have visions master."

Sir Roger snorted with derision. "Don't we all Travis. Well, perhaps not you, unless it's the odd dream of a cabbage or humping a donkey. Mine are of wine, women and wealth."

"To see things that are to come. Surely it's a gift from God?"

"Don't be a fool Travis. It's simple deception practiced on turnip brains like you. They seem to be two a penny these days. Some old hag starts babbling away to herself and everyone is suddenly proclaiming them a bloody seer. Never killed one yet who predicted their own demise with any certainty, and I've killed a fair few in my time I can tell you."

Travis shivered at the thought. He said, "Is this really necessary master? There'll be a hue and cry for sure, perhaps we can come back later."

Sir Roger's hand shot out and grabbed Travis by the throat crushing his windpipe. He said, "Just leave the thinking to me Travis. As I recall, you're not very good at it. Besides, our benefactor was most specific in his message, and just at the moment I don't want to disappoint him."

Travis wheezed back, "We'll burn master for what we've done already."

Sir Roger gave his servant a withering look. "You've seen me do much worse Travis and you'll see it again, that's if I let you live much longer. Now stop your whining and get over there. I don't care what you ask her, just get a good look inside the anchorite's cell and tell me what you see."

As Travis reached the head of the queue and peered in through the opening, a translucent cloth dropped down inside, blocking his view. A woman's voice said, "I need to eat now. Either wait or come back later."

"No, I must talk with you. It's urgent," said a desperate Travis.

The voice, this time sounding irritated, snapped, "Wait or come back later. I cannot offer advice on an empty stomach, even a humble anchorite must eat."

Travis thrust his arm through the opening and tried to move the cloth aside. A leathery hand grabbed his arm and twisted his wrist. He cried out in pain.

"Patience is a virtue. Now leave me alone, I need solitude to eat," said the voice before releasing his arm. He swiftly withdrew it and with a resentful glance backwards he slipped away and made his way to where Sir Roger waited.

"What the hell was all that about?"

"I'm sorry master, I couldn't see anything, she's blocked the opening with a cloth, eating she says."

Sir Roger cuffed his servant over the head in irritation. "Eating? For God's sake Travis, can I not trust you to complete even the simplest of tasks?"

"Perhaps we can wait for her to finish her meal master?"

Sir Rogers stared at Travis in fury, his eyes filling with the madness that seemed to overcome him all too frequently these days. He hissed, "Wait Travis? Do you think this is some kind of childish prank we're about? By God, I'm going to bloody finish the old bitch off right now."

He clamped an arm around Travis's wrist and pulled him to his feet. Sir Roger vaulted over the wall, dragging Travis with him, and set off towards the church.

Sir Roger gently pushed the heavy oak door open. They slipped inside and Travis pulled it closed behind them. The interior of the church was plain with whitewashed walls. At one end were crudely painted scenes from the bible, good versus evil. About half way along the west wall was a doorway hung with an old leather hide. There was the distinct sound of moaning and groaning coming from the other side. Sir Roger grinned. It sounded for all the world like someone was getting humped. He walked over and hauled aside the hide. His suspicion was confirmed by the sight of a hairy arsed old priest, identified by his scruffy tonsure, lying on top of a semi naked, stick like figure of a woman. They lay on a straw pallet on the floor. The priest turned around and said, "What the hell do you want? Can't you see I'm busy in here?"

Sir Roger grinned evilly. "Forgive me from interrupting God's holy work father. I must say it surprises me it encompasses humping anchorites in your own church. Perhaps I've been wrong about the attractions of the clerical life?"

The priest now red faced and angry said, "Look I don't know who you are but bugger off. I don't appreciate an audience. Some kind of pervert are you?"

Travis peeping around the doorway winced. The priest clearly had a death wish. Sir Roger taking a step forward hissed, "What did you say to me priest?"

The priest got up off the woman and pulled a grubby blanket around his crinkly old body. Still red faced he peered at Sir Roger in the dim light and said, "What is it you want here? If you've come to consult the anchorite, now is not the time."

Sir Roger snarled, "What do I want? Why, from a grubby little priest like you, I think it'll have to be your life."

Without waiting for an answer Sir Roger pulled the short dagger from under his cloak and with one thrust stabbed the priest straight through the heart. There was a spurt of blood as he pulled the blade back out. With a dying gasp the priest toppled backwards onto the women, who responded with a muffled scream. Sir Roger stepped forward and with one hand rolled the priest's body off her.

Sir Roger thought the woman looked vaguely familiar. With the tip of his dagger at her throat he said, "Do I know you old hag?"

She gazed up at him for a moment, then broke into a smile that exposed a mouth full of blackened teeth. "Course you do deary and your old dad knew me even better. You're Roger Mudstone."

Sir Roger looked again and suddenly said, "Good God, Isabel Becc. I thought you dead long ago woman. What age are you now, you must be what, seventy, eighty?"

She ran a black, worm like tongue, over her dry lips. Sir Roger was momentarily repulsed and his dagger wavered at her throat.

"You should know a lady never reveals her age. I'm as spritely as ever I was. I'm an anchorite now, given over to the church, you'll not be thinking of harming me?"

Sir Roger seriously doubted his father's old mistress was as flexible as she had once been. She looked like a wizened old walnut. The ravages of time and circumstance had turned the once voluptuous woman of his teenage dreams into the wreck before him. He said, "Well, the thing is Isabel, you don't seem to be taking your vows very seriously. I think perhaps you should be punished. I see you're still spending time on your back. Old habits die hard, eh?"

Isabel cackled nervously. "Oh, you are a one aren't you Sir Roger. You always were a bit of a joker. Not surprised your father was so disappointed in you."

Sir Roger's shrugged. "I've been striving to become as evil a bastard as he ever was."

She cackled again. "Now I come to think of it, I'd heard you've developed a terrible reputation. The bishop of Draychester has put a price on your head, has he not?"

Sir Roger's face clouded. "He'll come to regret that, we've yet to settle accounts for his ill treatment of me. Now I think we've conversed for far too long. It's time for you to die. Perhaps you've seen your fate already, you being a seer? No? Well, for old time's sake, I'll make it quick."

She started to scream but Sir Roger's hand over her mouth soon silenced her and his dagger completed the task. When the blood-soaked body had finally stopped twitching, he turned to a horrified Travis and said. "Don't just stand there. Help me with the rope."

6

HUNG LIKE A HOG

Scrivener burst into the bishop's private chambers. The bishop sat on a stool by the fire, a goblet of wine in one hand and a fist full of papers in the other. He looked up in surprise at his grim faced friend. "What is it Scrivener?"

"A messenger from the manor of Leighton my lord. Another anchorite had been found dead."

The bishop slowly put down his wine goblet on the floor and ran a hand over his face.

"God's teeth. A coincidence perhaps?" he asked hopefully.

"Hardly my lord. The messenger says it's murder and he reports that the local priest is dead too."

The bishop got to his feet and paced back and forward in front of the fire. "Damn it Scrivener, this won't do, won't do at all. There's been no progress with the first killing?"

"None my lord. I've no reason to doubt the method of her death. Bernard's a good man, Will's learning fast and young Osbert is pedantic to a fault in recording the details. As to the why of it, I am at a loss, although now with this second death I begin to wonder."

The bishop stopped his pacing and asked, "The deaths, how do they benefit anyone?"

Scrivener shrugged. "I'm not sure my lord, on the face of it they don't. I've leave to send the three of our men again?"

"At once."

Down by the riverside, tucked against the city wall, lay a public cookhouse. It was much frequented by travellers as it lay just next to one of the bridges that led into the city. Depending on the season there could be found fried or boiled foods and dishes, fish large and small, meat of dubious quality and provenance for the poor, and finer cuts for the wealthy. For those with a fancy for delicacies, goose, guinea-hen or woodcock were available if you knew who to ask. On a Friday, and whenever his duties allowed, Will would come here in the morning and buy a penny's worth of breakfast. As it lay just outside the walls, the cookhouse wasn't subject to the nightly curfew and whatever hour of the day or night it was always open. Those arriving at the city walls did not have to go without a meal for too long, nor those departing leave on empty stomachs.

Directly across the river from the cookhouse, and easily reached by the bridge, was a field that had been roughly levelled at some time in the past. Every Friday (unless it was some holy day requiring more solemnity) crowds, including Will, were drawn to the horse sales. Whether to buy or just to watch, it attracted a good many of the city's nobles as well as those of a lower status. Will was a good judge of horse-flesh and he took great delight to see the palfreys trotting gently around, the blood pumping in their veins, their coats glistening with sweat. It wasn't just palfreys for sale, there were all types of horses. Some more suitable for squires, rougher yet quicker in their movements. More numerous were the packhorses, with robust and powerful legs. Then occasionally an expensive war horse, tall and graceful, with quivering ears and high neck. Prospective buyers watched on as all were put through their paces. First their trot, followed by the gallop.

Will watched with interest from the edge of the field, a meat pie, still warm from the cookhouse, clutched in one hand. Two lads loudly shouted a warning to clear some space as a race was to be held. Three other boys prepared themselves to take part as riders. Even the horses, in their own way, psyched themselves up for the contest, their limbs trembling, impatient of any delay. The starting signal was given, and they leaped forward. The riders, eager for glory and hoping for victory, tried to outdo one another in using spurs, switches or cries of encouragement to urge the horses to go faster. The whole spectacle fascinated Will, so much so that he jumped as a hand clapped him on the shoulder. He turned around to see a grinning Bernard, and a sour-faced Osbert.

"Thought we'd find you here," said Bernard, "you're becoming a creature of habit."

Osbert looking around with distaste at the sweating horses and riders, "Gambling no doubt."

Will raised a finger and shook it in mock admonishment. "Don't judge everybody by your own standards Osbert."

Osbert tuned red and stomped off back towards the bridge.

Bernard chuckled.

"I take it you've not come for a morning's entertainment then?" asked Will.

"Unfortunately not lad, the good bishop has more work for us it seems."

Will groaned. "Why am I not surprised?"

~

Two men were talking at the door of the church at Leighton as the bishop's men arrived on horseback. They disappeared inside before the bishop's men dismounted.

"God's teeth, what's he doing here?" said Bernard angrily as he got down from his horse.

"Who?" asked Will.

Osbert beat Bernard to it and blurted out, "One of those men is the king's coroner for Draychester, Hugh Coneye."

Bernard scowled. "He's a bloody disgrace is what he is. A brainless cretin and as dishonest as the summer's day is long."

"I take it you're not on friendly terms then?" said Will.

Bernard snorted at Will's attempt at sarcasm. "Come on, lets see what all the fuss is about."

He led them through the door into the dimly lit interior. All three of them came to an abrupt halt at the macabre sight that greeted them. The coroner and the other man had come to a similar halt. It was the coroner who stirred first, turned and caught Bernard's gaze. Grunting a greeting, he looked back to the bodies. Running a hand over his greying beard, he remarked, "Nasty one, not seen the like for many a year. Not in these parts anyway. Reminds me of my time away at the wars with the king's army. The Scots were savages."

Bernard, for the moment ignoring the horror before them, pointed an accusing finger at the coroner. "What are you doing here Hugh? This is church business as well you know. Your jurisdiction doesn't run here."

"Very true of course, that's if they were murdered in the church." He placed a hand on the younger man's shoulder. "Anyway, Sir Eustace is an old friend of mine. It's his manor, and he's asked me to lend a hand. I hear a rumour it's not the first such case involving an anchorite in recent days?"

"And where did you hear this rumour?" asked Bernard.

The coroner smirked. "Oh here and there, here and there, you know how people gossip. I'm surprised Bishop Gifford isn't keeping more of an eye on things. Some would say it's a dereliction of duty."

Bernard took a step forward and poked the other man with a finger to the chest. "I'd be careful what you go around saying. Some people might take it the wrong way."

The coroner took a hasty step backwards. "No need for that, I'm only making conversation."

Will walked across to the west side of the building, pulled back the leather cover and stuck his head into the cell. There was a blood soaked straw pallet on the floor. He said, "The amount of blood in here I'd say it's fairly clear the killing took place in the church. Look, the blood trail leads directly out of the cell to the bodies."

All eyes turned back to the two figures hanging in front of the altar. Isabel Becc, the anchorite, hung semi naked upside down by a rope tied around her ankles. The priest, also naked, hung beside her, the right way up, tied by the wrists.

With his eyes, Will traced the two ropes up to an iron hook set in one of the roof beams high above. The other ends were tied off around one of the wooden posts that supported the roof. A thin trail of blood had dribbled down the victim's fronts, in Isabel's case over her face, and then onto the glazed tiles beneath. More blood was smeared on the floor tiles leading back to the entrance to the anchorite's cell.

Osbert whispered, "Who'd do such a thing? To kill them and string them up like this in such a holy place. It's blasphemy, the work of the devil."

The coroner nodded and said matter-of-factly, "Reminds me of two freshly slaughtered hogs, what with the blood and such."

Osbert turned a sickly grey, put a hand over his mouth to stop himself gagging and made for the church door as quickly as he could.

Will said, "Was that necessary?"

The coroner shrugged. "In my line of work you get used to it, although this is a juicy one I'll freely admit."

Sir Eustace, lord of the manor of Leighton, with an ill-conceived attempt at black humour, gestured at the woman's body. "Well, truth be told, in death she's a bigger attraction than ever she was in life."

"She was the anchorite long?" asked Bernard.

Sir Eustace nodded. "Years. Bishop Thorndyke arranged it with Father Robert and myself. She came with an endowment for her upkeep, not sure from whom it's that long ago."

"Father Robert?"

Sir Eustace gestured at the man hanging in front of them.

"That's him, our priest. A sorry excuse for one, but still our priest. And the woman, Isabel, was our anchorite. Very popular she was, loosely held vows you understand, but she did her best. The villagers valued her wisdom, before becoming an anchorite she was 'worldly' if you know what I mean. Anyway, I must say I was very satisfied with the arrangements. Perhaps you'd pass as much on to Bishop Gifford. A speedy decision on any replacements would be appreciated."

"Replacements," said Will open mouthed. "The bodies are barely cold for pity's sake. Surely our efforts should be concentrated on finding the killers?"

Sir Eustace shrugged. "Of course, of course. I've men out scouring the countryside for the killer, be assured. I meant no offence, but a good anchorite is hard to find, a priest less so. It's better to start the process early, is it not?"

Bernard looked at him with unconcealed distaste. "This arrangement you had with old Thorny, I take it the endowment didn't all go to keeping Isabel here in luxury?"

Sir Eustace, somewhat taken aback by the direction of Bernard's questioning said, "Come, come, my friends, we are all men of the world here. The anchorite required little, and asked for little in fact, by way of any comforts. A very pious and humble woman, at least some of the time. The church benefited by her presence here, the villagers took spiritual comfort in her advice."

Bernard said curtly. "I'm not your friend. And I'm probably right in thinking the only real benefit was to yourself and the priest. You no doubt took your cut of the endowment, as did old Bishop Thorndyke?"

"We had an arrangement, the bishop suggested the entire thing."

"I bet he did, the old weasel. You can take it from me that the arrangement is over. You're a bloody disgrace. When Gifford hears of this you'll be lucky if you can ever show your face in Draychester again."

Sir Eustace turned a bright red. He spluttered, "Are you threatening me?"

The coroner smiled at the unfolding argument. He was enjoying his day out immensely and he'd make sure the tale would be all around Draychester by nightfall. He said maliciously, "Strange Bishop Gifford hasn't cracked down on this sort of thing, perhaps his coffers at Draychester benefit too much? Still, it looks like divine retribution is taking its course now."

Bernard step forward menacingly and the coroner moved hastily backwards. Will, in an effort to calm things down, said, "I don't think a single man could have hoisted them aloft. There were two involved."

Bernard glowered at the coroner, then turned to Will. "It's true, too heavy for one man to haul a weight like that. We'd better cut them down. Can't have the poor sods hanging there much longer. It's not right."

≈

It was heading towards evening when the three bishop's official's left Leighton. As they made their way along the darkening lanes towards the city Will expressed his frustration. "Two people were murdered during the middle of the day and no one saw or heard a bloody thing."

Bernard grunted his agreement. "Brutal as well, no ordinary murder. Hauling them aloft, that was a message. You can't do something like that on a whim, you've got to be hardened to it."

Will said, "Lots of men were with the king's army in Wales and Scotland. I dare say there are many with the killing experience scattered across the shire."

Bernard nodded. "Consider the Greek fire used to incinerate the old woman at Snertherhide. Where else would you acquire such a thing or the knowledge of what it could do except on campaign?"

In the gloom behind them Osbert declared, "It's the devils work is what it is."

Bernard said, "I don't doubt that boy, but I think we're looking for more earthly culprits."

7

THE RAT

The man known as 'The Rat' crept through the nighttime streets of Draychester with the practiced ease of a lifelong thief. He'd lived in the city his entire life, never venturing further than twenty miles from the city walls. After dark the streets were a dangerous place, not that they weren't dangerous in the daytime, but it was a different kind of danger at night. There were places even he, an accomplished nightwalker, didn't dare venture when the light faded. If you lived long enough, then you had learned which side of the streets to keep to and which alleys to avoid. He knew the cathedral precinct behind its stout stone walls and sturdy wooden gates was relatively safe.

It was a moonlit night, and he kept to the shadows as he made his way along the path beside the precinct wall. It led him away from the marketplace gate, which he knew would be securely barred at this hour. It was muddy underfoot, and he moved along carefully until he came to an opening set high in the wall. This was where the scraps from the bishop's kitchens, which at this spot was up against the other side of the wall, were thrown out down a long stone chute. There was a small pile of what looked like rotting offal mixed with fish heads strewn on the ground, perhaps the remains of the night's meal at the palace. A few of his name-sake rodents were feeding happily and seemed reluctant to move on even when he aimed a kick at them.

He nimbly climbed up the wall, knowing each and every hand hole well. With some effort he squeezed through the gap, and on his belly, crawled up the steeply inclined chute. The smell in the confined space was appalling, but he'd long since learned to ignore both it and the splattering of rotten food that inevitably got on his clothing. At the top of the chute was a wooden hatch covering that opened into the corridor that led to the kitchen. He paused briefly behind it and listened intently. There was no sound from the other side. With legs braced either side of the chute, he used both hands and carefully pushed the hatch open and hauled himself out into the dark, stone-flagged corridor. It connected the kitchen to the storerooms and was also used to access the hatch to dispose of waste and slops.

It was warm and stuffy; the heat was coming from the kitchen to the left. The spit boys would be curled up asleep next to the cooking fires, perhaps others slept there too. The spit boys rarely left their place of work, endlessly tending the fire and the cooking meat in stifling heat. He turned right and crept down the corridor. There was another door before the storerooms were reached. It gave access via a short flight of steps out into the cathedral precinct itself. As usual it was unlocked. Easing it open, he slipped through and with barely a sound closed it behind him and made his way to the top of the steps. He paused in the dark doorway and gazed out across the moonlit green that separated the bishop's palace from the great cathedral itself.

In his younger days, when he'd been learning his trade,

he'd made this journey many times. He would take provisions from the storerooms, or search the many rooms of the bishop's clerks for the odd coin or other valuable. Sometimes he'd crept around the great cathedral itself, you never knew what you'd come across.

Now that the bishop's secretary, Scrivener, passed him a fair amount of his dirty work, he'd thought it wise to confine his nocturnal roving to the city itself. Tonight, for some reason he couldn't quite put his finger on, he'd been drawn back to his old haunts.

The Rat had long ago befriended the cook, both of them were addicted to playing knucklebones. The cook was always short of coin and they'd come to an arrangement. This meant that he would find a horn lantern together with a leather bag, for anything he found of interest, hung on a peg in the wall near the top of the steps. The cook, with a little prompting the night before consisting of a few coins, would see to it they were waiting for him. He would also provide an ember in a little pot and leave it within the bag so that the candle could be lit. As usual, the bag and lantern hung where they were supposed to be.

Soon enough the Rat found himself at the very top of the stairs that led into the cathedral library. It would be foolish to steal a book of course, it'd be impossible to sell without questions being asked, but there were plenty of other things to take. There was a scriptorium here, and the scribes' desks offered some rich pickings, smaller valuables that could easily be taken and sold. Even with the moonlight, the big windows in the library provided barely enough light to move around without colliding with desks. Before he'd got the chance to use the lantern, he heard the soft tread of someone else climbing the stairs behind him. He froze, then a thief's instinct kicked in and he darted to the right and stood stock still in the dark corner, hardly daring to breathe but also ready for instant flight.

A darkly dressed figure emerged onto the top step, the cloak it wore stretched down to the floor. It stood virtually beside him at the top of the stairs, paused for a moment to draw a shallow breath, farted noisily, then turned to the left and glided towards the far end of the room.

He remembered the pungent stink all too well, it was peculiar to this man alone. His mouth dropped open in surprise. It had to be him, the man who had put the fear of God into him all those years ago, the man Scrivener had asked him about months before. Even the way he seemed to move, without apparent effort, confirmed the Rat's worst fears. The hairs on the back of his neck rose, and he felt the urgent need to be somewhere else, anywhere in fact but here.

At the end of the long space of the library he knew there was a strongroom. He'd often been tempted to take a look in there himself. The figure stopped in front of the door. On the Rat's last nighttime visit the lock had looked ludicrously insecure, but some thefts would be more easily noticed than others. He'd judged anything taken from the cathedral's coffers would result in some sort of divine retribution and so was best left well alone.

There were some scraping noises, presumably the lock being opened, and he heard the door of the strongroom pulled back. A moment later there was a blossoming of golden light as the figure lit a horn lantern. There was enough light for the Rat to see the profile of the man's face. He knew it by sight, he was good with faces. The man was one of judges who sat on the bishop's court. He couldn't remember ever hearing him speak in public. A vague name surfaced from his memory, Ralph, Ralph of Shrewsbury. From the shadows he watched as the man opened one of the chests and took some papers out.

Now was the time to move. He darted out from the corner and over to the top of the stairs. He briefly saw Ralph look up, but he felt confident it was too dark for his own face to be visible in the gloom. Then he was away down the stairs, moving as fast as he dared, the smell of fart lingering in his nostrils.

The Rat fled around the dark stone-flagged corridors of the cloisters. He didn't think he'd be pursued. From the little he knew, Ralph of Shrewsbury was an old man. That didn't mean he wasn't dangerous. Should he take the information straight to Scrivener? He'd be surprised if the bishop's secretary didn't know about his nocturnal wanderings in the city, and probably tolerated them because of the other services he provided. His appearance at night, within the precinct and unannounced outside Scrivener's very door, might be pushing his luck. What was certain was he needed to tell him about Ralph of Shrewsbury and soon if only for the Rat's own safety.

Keeping to the shadows, the Rat navigated around the outside of the green that separated the cathedral from the bishop's palace. Reaching the stairs that led down to the kitchen corridor, he slung the bag and horn lantern back on their peg and ran down to the bottom. Turning right, he made his way past the rubbish chute and into the main kitchen. The room was dimly lit from the embers of the fire. On the left of the great fireplace was curled a sleeping boy. Under one of the tables lay another, asleep on a thin straw mat. He slipped past into the corridor beyond that led to the undercroft below the great hall.

The cook slept in a little chamber in the undercroft. The Rat had helped carry him back there once, drunk as a lord, from a feast in the great hall. The door was barred from the inside and the Rat could hear a deep snoring from within. He put his shoulder against the wood and leant his weight to it. It creaked but didn't move. In desperation he lightly began tapping on the door and hissed, "Simon wake up! Simon!"

After a time, the snoring came to an abrupt stop, there was a shuffling. A voice said, "Who the devil is it?"

"It's me, the Rat, I need to speak to you."

"Are you out of your mind? What do you want?"

"Open the door, I'll make it worth your while, I swear it"

"Keep your voice down for God's sake. I left the lantern and bag as usual, what else do you need of me?"

"Open up and I'll tell you."

The door opened a crack and the cook stared out dubiously. "You've a nerve," he whispered. "God's teeth, I suppose you'd better come in. What the hell is it that can't wait?"

The cook moved back, and the Rat slipped around the door into the chamber. The cook looked at him nervously. The Rat leant with his back against the door. He said, "I've never cheated you over the years, have I? I've always played fair with our little arrangement?"

The cook nodded reluctantly. "That doesn't mean I want to be dragged in to whatever you're up to this time."

"I swear to you it'll be worth your while. You know Scrivener, the bishop's secretary, he sends me on errands sometimes? "

"Aye of course I know that, and they'll be errands I think I probably don't want to know about?"

"You'd be right my friend. All I need is for you to pass a message to him. I'd almost thought to go to his door tonight, it's that urgent, but I fear even I would be pushing my luck at this hour."

"And what message would that be?"

"All you need tell him is that the Rat says, 'Ralph of Shrewsbury'."

"Ralph of Shrewsbury, is that all? What interest have you in old Ralph?"

"Believe me, you don't need or want to know my friend. That's all you need say to Scrivener, he'll take the meaning of it."

"And when do you want me to convey this message?"

"First thing in the morning, as early as you can. You have reason to be up and about before most. I swear to you that you will be rewarded. Say nothing to anyone else, only Scrivener."

"I don't know. I'm not sure I want to get involved in such things. I'm just a simple cook, that's what I do."

"My friend I swear to you this is important, there'll be plenty of coin for us both."

The cook looked at the Rat and sighed. "All right, I'll do it. This better be important otherwise I am going to look a bloody fool."

"Thank you my friend, you won't regret it."

With that, the Rat slipped back around the cook's door, and was away into the darkness of the undercroft.

A FULL TUB

The bishop bathed at least once a week. There was a little room just off the kitchen, convenient for hot water, in which was located a wooden tub. He paid an attendant, Old Wilfred by name, two loaves daily and a stipend of a pound a year and he took care of filling the tub. Some would no doubt disapprove, he didn't much care. It was coin he thought well worth spending, particularly when it eased aches and pains long suffered since his soldiering days.

This being a bath day, the bishop climbed out of bed in anticipation of a soothing soak. Sitting on the edge of his feather mattress, he ran a hand over his stubble, yawned and then stretched painfully. He decided he'd instruct Wilfred to boil up some herbs. Some camomile, breweswort, perhaps mallow and brown fennel and add them to the bath water.

Suddenly there was a frantic hammering on the door.

"My lord, you must come quickly," cried a voice.

Old instincts kicked in and he jumped to his feet, not before grabbing his dagger from where it rested under the bed. He flung the door open and stood ready to face any foe.

Wilfred, his geriatric bath attendant, stood whimpering in the corridor between two of the palace guards. The bishop suddenly realised he was naked. He grinned apologetically, flung the door closed, hastily pulled a cloak around himself and reopened the door.

"What on earth is the matter man?"

Wilfred babbled, "My lord, there's a man dead in your bathtub."

"Have you finally taken leave of your senses?"

One of the guards said, "It's true my lord, you'd better come and see for yourself."

"Anyone we know?"

The man shrugged. "He's face down in your tub my lord, even so I think I recognise him. Seen him with Scrivener once or twice. He doesn't live within the precinct."

Gifford sighed heavily. His bath would evidently have to wait unless he wanted to share it with an unwelcome guest. "Has anyone summoned Scrivener?"

The guard shook his head. "No my lord."

"Well if he hasn't already heard all this racket, you'd better fetch him."

"Yes my lord."

The body lay face down in the bishop's wooden bath tub, the legs and feet hanging over the edge. The bishop and Scrivener grabbed the back of the man's clothing and between them hauled him out. The body flopped onto its back, lifeless eyes looking up at them.

"You know him?" asked the bishop.

Scrivener sighed heavily and nodded. "A thief and a rogue, but not a bad man in his own way. You may have heard me speak of him my lord, most knew him as the Rat."

"Ah, I recognise him now. He was coming to see you?"

"Possibly, although it's been some weeks since I last had need of his services."

Scrivener could see no outward sign of injury. He crouched down besides the body. There was a small hole in the man's tunic just above the heart. He pulled the garment upwards, revealing the bare skin. There was a bloody wound in the chest not much wider than a man's finger.

The bishop said, "Nasty, but quick I would imagine?"

Scrivener grunted his agreement. "A very thin blade was used, straight into the heart. Either a lucky thrust or someone with a lot of experience. He was probably dead in an instant. I'd be surprised if he made a sound."

"The killer has some nerve Scrivener. To do such a thing here, within the precinct and under my own roof."

Scrivener rose from the body and sat down on the edge of the wooden tub. He looked down at the Rat and pondered.

"Nerve? Well, perhaps my lord, or perhaps simple necessity. Did our dead friend see or hear something he shouldn't? People kill for all sorts of reasons, but this was no drunken stabbing. The Rat was no stranger to this place. I turned a blind eye to his petty pilfering as he was useful to us in so many other ways. "

"How the devil did he get in, presuming he did so last night?"

"The kitchen rubbish chute, he told me once. I think it amused him to let me know one of his secrets."

"I'm sure there are many more he won't be telling anyone about now. You think this is the work of the one we spoke about?"

"Likely I think. We need to find this man, and fast. I fear his madness is only just starting to build my lord."

"We've seen worse, you and I old friend. I trust you to get to the bottom of this and when you do, I'll hang the bugger myself if needs be."

Scrivener smiled at him. "Just be careful my lord. This one's both cunning and dangerous."

The bishop grinned and pulled the dagger from under his cloak. "Oh, I'll be careful all right. My carefulness is always accompanied by steel."

Simon the cook was up early as always. The bishop's household ultimately ran on the meals produced by his kitchen. Everything had to run on schedule but he knew as soon as he arrived at his domain that something was seriously amiss. The kitchen was in complete uproar, filled with a babbling crowd of household servants, guards and cathedral clergy. He squeezed between the throng and was immediately confronted with the sight of two servants carrying out the limp body of his old friend the Rat. They passed within two feet of him and the Rat's lifeless gaze chilled him to the core. His stomach lurched as did his bowels and he felt the desperate urge to evacuate both. He barged madly through the throng, attracting curious glances, and made his way out into the inner courtyard of the palace. Half walking, half running, he made it out of sight before vomiting noisily onto the cobbles beside the wall of the great hall. His stomach gurgled ominously, and he leant on the rough stonework of the wall, his stubby legs shaking beneath him.

"Get a grip Simon," he moaned to himself. The events of

the previous night were running through his mind. The dead man's last request and the burden of the message weighed heavily on him. What was he to do? Did he dare tell Scrivener and risk the wrath of whoever had killed the Rat? He decided he would do the only thing he could think of, which was to take to his bed.

"Is it just me or is this pottage off Scrivener? It's like something I'd be served on campaign."

"It's the cook."

"The cook? To be fair I've always found him quite capable."

"No my lord, I meant he's taken to his bed, sick since this morning."

The bishop threw his spoon down on the table. "This won't do at all. An army marches on it stomach and so does our household. What's the matter with him? It's not contagious is it?"

"Says he has the 'runs' my lord. One of his underlings is cooking today. I'll wander down there presently and see if I can't find us something else."

"You can't go wrong with a bit of bread and cheese," hinted the bishop hopefully.

"Word of the anchorite's death at Leighton is all over the city my lord. Bernard said the coroner was there when they arrived."

"So I've heard. The man is a bloody meddler Scrivener. He sees an opportunity to cause us trouble. I've already received worrying murmurings from some of the more wealthy donors in the city. The story of the other anchorite is known as well. Next they'll be questing our abilities to manage things. We can't afford for this to take a turn for the worse old friend."

"Your predecessor has left us something of a poisoned chalice regarding the anchorites. I've decided I need to go through the archive and unpick just what a mess he's left us. It does however present us with an opportunity to set a trap for our enemy within the precinct."

"Indeed? You'd better tell me more."

9

TO SET A TRAP

S ir Roger had left at first light. He'd roused Travis with a kick and had him saddle one of the horses. He'd rode off without saying where he was going or when he'd be back.

Travis was hungry, he hadn't had a proper meal for weeks and didn't expect one anytime soon. Sir Roger didn't approve of any unnecessary expenditure which included proving funds for Travis to eat. Over his years serving the Mudstone family, Travis had learned to be nothing but adaptable. Soon after his master's departure he had walked the five miles to the nearest signs of civilisation. He was careful to keep out of sight. In a tumbledown shack, used in the spring by the local shepherds, he found a small pile of half rotten turnips. He picked through them until he found a few that might be edible and filled an old sack. He hated everything about turnips, he'd eaten enough to last a lifetime and was sure these would taste as foul as they looked. Still, he was hungry, and you never turned down a turnip when there was little else. He trudged back to the hideaway at the beach, the round trip taking the entire morning, and found a horse tied up outside. Sir Roger had returned.

Travis opened the door to the cottage tentatively, expecting his master to be in a foul mood at his absence. Sir Roger sat before the fire. He looked up at Travis and pointed at the sack in his hand.

"You better not have been wandering about the country-side attracting attention Travis."

"I've seen no one master. I went looking for some food."

"And what did you find?"

"Turnips master."

"Turnips," said Sir Roger said with contempt, "For God's sake Travis, have you no higher ambitions than a turnip?"

"I was hungry master."

Sir Roger shook his head in disgust. "While you've been skulking about the countryside looking for turnips, I've been to Draychester."

Travis looked at him with horror. "But the bishop has put a price on our heads master, why such a risk?"

"I think you'll find most of the price is on my head, you're of little consequence. Anyway, I didn't just ride in on my horse you fool. I hid it at Codlingham just outside the walls, tuppence and no questions asked. It's market day, easy to slip into the city from there."

"But why master?"

"Why? To try and find who our mysterious benefactor is. There's no shortage of the lower sort willing to part with information for a penny or two. It seems that young idiot of a boy is the acolyte of one of the canons at the cathedral. I don't know which one yet but I'm going to make it my business to find out."

"Did no one recognise you master?"

Sir Roger rubbed a finger over the scar on his cheek and

he turned hard dead eyes towards Travis. "I stayed well hidden. A hooded cloak and a dark alehouse hides a multitude of sins Travis."

Travis shivered. Sir Roger turned his gaze back to the fire. "You know what else I heard Travis? Whispers about the death of the anchorites. How the bishop of Draychester isn't doing enough to protect them and misspending the money for their upkeep. No doubt whispers spread and encouraged by our benefactor. I think it's about time we took charge of this game ourselves and stepped it up a pace."

Travis didn't like the sound of where his master's thoughts were heading. He shuffled over towards the cooking pot by the fire and emptied his sack of half rotten turnips by the side of it. Sir Roger said, "Have you heard of Dame Dorothy of Draychester Travis?"

Travis nodded. "Of course master, she's famous, a holy and pious woman of great virtue and the cathedral's own anchorite this twenty years past. She attracts almost as many pilgrims as the cathedral itself."

"I've heard as much myself," murmured Sir Roger, a wicked smirk on his lips.

A horrific thought popped into Travis' head. "Master you wouldn't? It's madness."

"Just cook your stinking turnips Travis and leave the thinking to me."

"So why hasn't old Thorny's tomb been finished? It's been what, five, six years since his death?" asked Will gazing at the ornate tomb base set into the north aisle of the nave within the cathedral.

Above the flat base that was yet to bear the effigy of the bishop was a canopy of three arches embellished with tracery. The stone surrounds and back were painted a garish green and red and in the three panels below the arches were three virgins with crowns on their heads. Will peered at the writing beneath each, "Charitie", "Mercie", "Pitee". He snorted, from all he knew of Bishop Thorndyke it was highly inappropriate.

Osbert said, "The bishop died suddenly, although he had of course planned his tomb some years before. As you know the circumstances of his death were somewhat delicate."

Will nodded knowingly, "You mean they found him dead in bed with a well-known city whore."

Osbert winced, "We try not to speak of it within the precinct."

Will shrugged. "It's common knowledge. From what I've heard, they were crushed by a falling chimney during a storm. Came straight through the roof of the bishop's chambers. Squashed them flat."

Osbert winced again, "And I'm sure he's repenting for his sins in another place."

Will laughed. "I'll bet he is. Still, all the more reason to finish the tomb and forget about his indiscretions."

Osbert gave a nod. "True. There was however some question over the funding. He wasn't well liked by the canons. However, the tomb now nears completion. The effigy of the bishop is the last piece to be put in place."

"It's arrived?"

"All the way from Nottinghamshire. A wagon came a day or two ago carrying it within a big wooden box packed with straw. It's with the masons."

"You've seen it?"

"Not yet."

"Then what are we waiting for?"

The effigy of Bishop Thorndyke lay in repose on one of the stone mason's workbenches. He wore a bishop's mitre on his head, which lay on a pillow. A bishop's staff rested by his side tucked under his arm. Thorndyke's hands were on his chest, raised together, palm to palm in prayer. The whole thing was painted in bright colours. The flesh of the hands pink, the face looking slightly flushed, the eyes closed and with a somewhat pained expression on his lips. His feet rested on another golden cushion.

Will tapped the figure with a finger. "It's bloody life-like, it looks like he's just taking a nap. He's going to be a bit uncomfortable in that outfit for all eternity, but still, I'm impressed. What's it made out of?"

The master mason sniffed slightly dismissively. "Alabaster, very soft stone, easy to work. The carving is nice I'll grant you that. Them Nottinghamshire boys knows their business. Wouldn't last a decade outside of course, the rain would eat it away, not like our work, that'll still be there when we're all dust."

Will turned to Osbert, "You'd be a young lad when the bishop died? Does it resemble him?"

Osbert peered at the figure's face. He said puzzled, "I remember him of course, the face does look familiar but it's not like Thorndyke."

The mason chuckled. "He was bishop before my time here. Someone said he looked like Hugh, one of the city gatekeepers. We sent a drawing to Nottinghamshire. I think they have a few roughly carved models and just work up the face and body."

Osbert was aghast. "Not Hugh who lodges with that widow on Westgate street? He looks nothing like Bishop Thorndyke."

The mason grinned and wagged his finger at them and said, "Ah, I see you know the man. You're saying it's not a good likeness then?'

Osbert shook his head in disgust. "Not of Thorndyke. It's disrespectful at the very least."

Will laughed. "I doubt anyone will object. Nobody liked old Thorny much anyway."

The mason nodded at the effigy and said, "Aye well, I don't think the current bishop is planning any ceremony. My instructions are to bung this one on top of Thorndyke's tomb as soon as possible."

A voice from behind them said, "Finally. I've been looking for you two everywhere." Bernard stood at the entrance to the workshop. "Scrivener wants us to meet him in the cathedral library."

They found the bishop's secretary sat at the desk in the strongroom at the back of the cathedral library. He began by describing the bishop's and his own suspicions that there was a traitor within the precinct.

Will said, "And this traitor, he's behind the killing of the anchorites?"

Scrivener answered. "It would seem to me that would be a logical conclusion."

Will was puzzled. "But why, how does anyone gain from their murders?"

This time Osbert answered for his uncle, "Someone who wants to embarrass the bishop and his household. Sow doubt on his competency to manage the affairs of the church. I've already heard whispers in the city."

Scrivener smiled grimly and nodded at this nephew. "Exactly Osbert. A lot of powerful people have an interest in the anchorites, both those who made grants to maintain them and seemingly those who have been appropriating the same funds for themselves."

"Old Thorny's legacy to us. He'll be laughing at us from whatever pit he's burning in," said Bernard.

Osbert crossed himself.

Will said, "And the killing of the man in the precinct the other night?"

Scrivener paused a moment and then said, "He was known as the Rat. A man I used over the years to do work and go places we sometimes cannot."

Bernard nodded, "I knew him, liked him even. A dirty, thieving scoundrel of course, but not without honour."

Scrivener continued, "I believe the Rat met his end by the traitor's hand. Perhaps he saw something he shouldn't. Unfortunately we can't ask him. His body was placed in the bishop's bathtub either as a warning or a taunt, perhaps both."

"Why are we here Uncle?" asked Osbert gesturing around the strongroom.

Scrivener said, "I believe someone is using what is in here against us." He pointed at an iron-bound chest on the floor. "Nobody has been through the archives in years. To the best of my knowledge the contents have never been indexed. No one has ever had the inclination or the organisational skills. That's no offence to our esteemed archivists, but look at them," Scrivener gestured at the door through which the other occupants of the library could be seen.

The youngest amongst them was a tiny, frail, white-haired ancient, with failing eyesight who had his face pressed to a document. As he mumbled away to himself, his runny nose left a damp trail across the page. Two of his colleagues lay snoring, slumped over their desks.

Scrivener opened the chest and pulled out a sheaf of papers. "There must be two hundred years worth of grants and bequests in there and they're all mixed together. Not all relate to anchorites of course, but it'd take a month to sort through them."

Will said, "So our traitor is just taking the first he comes across?"

Scrivener nodded, "It's only an assumption. The two anchorites who have been murdered were mentioned in the first handful of papers. I've no reason to suspect he doesn't replace things as he found them and I've been careful to do the same. He must come at night. Even our geriatric brethren out there in the library might become suspicious during the day."

Osbert said, "And the next anchorites mentioned, you know who they are?"

Scrivener grinned, "It doesn't really matter. I've prepared my own documents and placed them in the pile after those already targeted. I then removed as many other papers that mentioned anchorites as I could find. If he returns, he can hardly fail to come across a tempting target."

Will nodded in understanding, "Ah, clever, a baited trap."

"Exactly so. A two-fold plan, to identify our traitor here in the cathedral and secondly those who do his bidding outside the precinct."

Bernard smiled grimly and said to Scrivener, "Point us to the right place old friend and I guarantee justice will be done one way or another."

Scrivener said, "I don't doubt it."

Will asked, "When do we see if the trap is sprung?"

Scrivener replied, "Well, we've no idea what sort of schedule the traitor is working to. We have to presume he could visit the library at any time. You start watch tonight."

Osbert said nervously, "Watch?"

"Yes, to watch but not to apprehend, at least not yet. We need to know who he is of course, but we want him to identify those who act for him outside the precinct."

Bernard flexed his fingers together until his knuckles cracked. "Give me a half hour with him and he'll tell all."

"I appreciate the thought old friend but I fear we need to be more subtle. This one has many secrets to give up."

Bernard grunted, "If you say so, but I find you can't usually go wrong with a good thrashing. At least let me loose on those who have murdered the anchorites."

"Now that I can promise you."

The three bishop's officials left Scrivener to his papers and made their way through the cloisters and into the cathedral itself. Dodging the throngs of pilgrims heading the other direction, they left by the main entrance. As they stood in front of the great oak doors Bernard said, "As we're on the bishop's business tonight I suggest we have a drink first."

Osbert gave him a sour look. "Do you not think it better we be clear headed for the task?"

Bernard chuckled and ruffled the lad's hair affectionately, much to Osbert's annoyance. The big man threw an enormous arm around the lad's shoulders, the weight making Osbert sag at the knees. "Osbert is there no spark of joy in that soul of yours? Cheer up for once. A drink and our interesting company will do you good. It's going to be a long night. Will, where do you suggest?"

Will shrugged. "How about the Bell? It's not far, the ale is good and the pies are better."

"I know it, a good choice. Lead the way."

Sat in the Bell with a jug of ale before him and his back to the fire, Bernard sighed contentedly. He looked at Osbert across the table and pointed at his belt, "What are those things you're carrying on your belt all the time now lad?"

Osbert, a little self consciously, removed the cap from the thin leather tube he carried via a leather strap attached to his belt. It was full of quills and a knife to cut them. There were various offcuts of parchment stuffed in between.

Will sat beside him nodded in understanding "Ah your work tools. And the little stoppered horn?"

"My ink of course."

Will chuckled. "Ah, of course. So you've started to always carry the tools of your trade around Osbert?"

Osbert nodded solemnly. "One can never tell when I may be called on to record events for posterity"

Bernard grinned and lifted a cup to his lips. "I'm not sure us having a drink on the good bishop's time qualifies as a noteworthy event my friend."

"All expenses will need to be accounted for; my uncle will expect it," said Osbert darkly. "You paid two pennies for that jug of ale."

"Trust you boy. Even here I can't escape your uncle's penny pinching eyes."

Will laughed and then with more seriousness said, "This business with the anchorites is the talk of the city. I don't understand the motive behind the attacks."

Osbert said darkly, "I hear some of the merchant guilds have voiced their concerns. Many of them made grants to support anchorites in the past."

Bernard nodded and swilled the ale around in his cup. "Whoever is behind it, the city willingly takes advantage of the situation. In a place such as Draychester there is always a battle between the power of the guilds and mayor and that of the bishop."

Osbert said, "You think it's some plot by them?"

Bernard snorted. "Hardly, they squabble and jostle for power as much amongst themselves than anyone else. No, someone else stirs trouble that they take advantage of."

"Then perhaps tonight we will discover this troublemaker," said Will.

Bernard downed the remaining ale in his cup and said, "Perhaps. Anyway, let's have a few more then we'd best return before the curfew bell and our own precinct gate closes. I want to take a look at where we can keep watch before it goes dark."

"There's no other way into the library Osbert?" asked Will.

"Perhaps for someone who practises the dark arts," he said grimly, "the rest of us have to make use of the stairs. One way in and one way out."

They stood before the door at the bottom of the flight of stone steps that led up to the library. Will pushed open the door and looked up. "This would be the place to keep watch then or at the top perhaps? We can hardly stand in plain sight though."

Bernard said, "You forget, we'll have the cover of darkness."

Osbert nodded in acknowledgement but said, "Even so, we'll need to be concealed."

Will said, "We could watch from one of the cloister studies. Any intruder bound for the library will have to pass us via the study itself. If they come from the other direction then we can see across the cloister to the door at the bottom of the stairs."

Bernard grunted his agreement. "I'll find us some dark cloaks. It's going to be a long night, perhaps the first of many."

"I can hardly wait," said Osbert.

It was a partially clear and moonlit night, and the open central courtyard around which the cloisters ran allowed some light to filter into the gloomy study. Osbert, hunched down under a black cloak in one corner, shivered.

"I'm cold. How much longer are we to wait?"

"If we knew that we wouldn't be sat here shivering," hissed Will from another corner.

Bernard, a dark shape tucked in by the side of the doorway, said softly, "Just stay awake and keep your wits about you. And remember, if anyone comes through here, not a word, let them pass. Once they are in the library there's only one way out."

As Will stared out across the courtyard to the opposite cloisters time seemed to stand still. Occasionally a cloud fleetingly obscured the moonlight, sending shadows racing across the cloisters. At one point there was the flicker of movement as a dark shape slipped out in the central quadrangle. Too small for a man, it was Petroc the cathedral mouser, performing his feline duties, or at least out for a stroll. Will smiled to himself. The cathedral precinct always seemed overrun with rats and mice, so it was more likely he was looking for an amorous liaison than anything else. The cat was halfway across the open space when he suddenly froze, then whipped his head round to look behind. Will looked up from the cat towards the far cloister. This time the two black shapes he saw striding along were unmistakably human, although not identifiable because of their hooded attire and the gloom.

"Look, two of them. Do you see?" he whispered to his companions.

Bernard shifted stiffly from his position, the cool night air having sapped the warmth from his limbs. He squinted and caught sight of the swiftly moving figures.

"God's teeth, I see them. Come on, let's head to the stairs and for God's sake keep out of sight and stay quiet."

With Bernard in the lead, they hurried along the cloister, keeping to the walls as much as possible. Bernard came to an abrupt halt, and they almost ran into the back of him. "Stand still and don't move a muscle," he whispered.

They pressed themselves against the wall. The door to the library stairs was just visible at the far end of the corridor. Two hooded figures swept around the far corner towards them. The one in front was slightly hunched, the one behind smaller. Frustratingly, they both had the hoods up on their cloaks covering their heads. They came to a halt before the door and the lead figure took something from under his cloak. There was the slight click of the lock being turned. The dark figure eased the door open and swiftly disappeared through it, his companion following on behind.

"We have them!" hissed Bernard.

"Careful, don't go throwing your fists about just yet, let's see what they're up to. Remember Scrivener said identify them, not clobber them," whispered Will.

"It could all be perfectly innocent," said Osbert.

Bernard grunted. "Don't be an idiot. They're up to no good, it's obvious."

Will slowly reached the door, the others close behind. "I'm going to creep up to the top of the stairs and take a look."

He gently pushed open the door, carefully inched his way through and looked up the dark stairway. There was a glimmer of light at the top.

Bernard sniffing the air whispered, "What's that God-awful stench?"

"Someone's farted," replied Will.

"Smells like rotten eggs," hissed Osbert.

Will, a hand over his nose said, "I'm going up. Stay here, I'll see if I can identify them."

He slowly made his way up the stairs, stopping every few steps to check for any noise from above. As he reached the top he dropped onto his hands and knees and carefully inched his way forward. He pushed his head just far enough forward so he could peer into the gloom of the library. The bulk of the reading desks and the shelves along the back wall were just visible. At the very end of the room was the strongroom, the door was ajar by a few inches and golden candlelight spilled out around it. The faintest murmuring of a conversation reached his ears. He would have to move closer to make out anything more.

A hand suddenly clamped around his ankle, making him jump. Bernard's bulk came to a rest besides him.

"Have a care, you had me jumping out of my skin," Will hissed.

Bernard pressed his face close to Will's ear and whispered excitedly, "Never mind that, do you recognise the traitorous bastards?"

"They're in the strongroom, I've yet to see their faces. If we're lucky, they'll take Scrivener's bait."

Bernard said, "We still need to see them. Let's move across to the far wall under the windows and crawl down towards the strongroom."

"Are you mad? We're sure to make a sound."

"We can't sit here wondering."

Bernard on hands and knees crawled off the top step and out into the library. Will cursed under his breath and followed. The big man shuffled across the space, dodging around desks and reached the back wall. Will struggled to keep up, the hard floor of the library painfully uncomfortable under his knees. Carefully they made their way along the back wall until they reached the far corner. The strongroom door was but a few feet away, but they were hidden in the gloom as they sat with their backs against the wall.

The sound of a boy's voice could be heard complaining. "Why must we use this man master? He grows more curious each time you send me to meet him."

An older voice laughed softly. "I'm sure he does. He'll try to cross us soon enough, it's in his nature to do so. He serves our purpose for now and when that changes, well, let's just say he has no friends and many enemies in Draychester."

"We'll betray him?" asked the younger voice with enthusiasm.

"When he's of no more use. I see you're learning quickly boy."

"His actions are that of a madman master."

"Exactly, he spreads terror and discord with ease, a skill very few others can match. I've selected another anchorite for his attentions. Now sit there boy and disturb me no more while I write the instructions that you're to deliver tomorrow."

Will's backside was going numb sat on the hard floor of the library. It was also cold but they dared not move from their spot. After what seemed an eternity the door of the strongroom opened and the smaller of the hooded figures slipped out and headed towards the stairs.

"That's his messenger gone, now lets confront this traitorous snake," whispered Bernard. He slowly heaved his bulk up from the floor. Will struggled up and before he was fully on his feet Bernard had strode to the door and flung it wide open. The sound of the door groaning on its hinges and the wood smashing into the wall behind was deafening, and the change in light blinding.

There was a muffled cry from the room and then a candle lantern came hurtling out and smashed against Bernard's head, plunging the scene back into darkness. Bernard undeterred barrelled into the room hoping to overcome the occupant by sheer momentum. There was an ear-splitting crash as the small desk was crushed and a splintering from one of the chests as Bernard fell down heavily upon it.

Will stumbled into the doorway and felt something brush past him, leaving a pungent whiff behind. Bernard let forth a stream of curses as he tried to untangle himself from the broken furniture.

"After him for Christ's sake," he bellowed.

Will shouted, "I can't see a bloody thing. Where has he gone?"

"The stairs."

They stumbled towards the stairs, Bernard crashing through the desks and turning a good many into firewood in the process. Will reached the top of the stairs first and plunged downwards at a run, bouncing off the walls as he went. Unable to stop himself, he tumbled through the door at the bottom. He fell on something soft and warm that let out a startled cry. Grappling with the struggling figure, he eventually pinned its arms to the floor.

"Got you!" he panted.

Bernard came crashing through the door and landed next to them. There was a muffled cry from Will's prisoner. He relaxed his grip slightly and dragged the others head up. In the gloom a bloody nosed Osbert gazed back at them tearfully.

"God's teeth," groaned Bernard.

10

TO FOOL A KILLER

The bishop and Scrivener surveyed the wrecked interior of the library strongroom. The door hung off its hinges, the small desk was upside down against the back wall, and one of the document chests was a splintered mess of broken wood and parchment. The bishop turned to his three officials who stood in a rough line just outside the doorway.

"So between the three of you, you didn't manage to see the traitor's face at all?"

Bernard red faced mumbled, "It was dark my lord. The man threw the horn lantern directly at my head."

"In the confusion and darkness he slipped passed us my lord," said Will.

The bishop closed his eyes and ran a hand over his weary face. Opening one lid he focused on Osbert.

"And you, Osbert, you didn't catch sight of his face?"

Osbert, head downcast, replied, "I'm sorry my lord, I heard the commotion. I had already let the smaller figure pass. Then the door on the stairs flew open and the other man fled. In a moment he was gone. They both wore hoods."

The bishop sighed heavily, "Scrivener, tell me he did at least take the bait?"

The bishop's secretary gestured at the broken chest. "As you see the chest in question is destroyed, but apparently he consulted the documents and then wrote a note to be taken to his conspirators outside the precinct."

"Well, that's something at least."

Will said, "We heard them both, one a much older man, the other I took to be just a lad."

"He farted," said Osbert.

The bishop blinked and said, "Who?"

"It's true, the older one did fart, it stank something rotten. Old man's fart it was," volunteered Bernard.

The bishop turned to Scrivener, "It's not exactly a lot to go on is it? A fart?"

"On the contrary my lord, the Rat said the man he met in the cathedral years ago had a peculiarly pungent fart. I laughed at him. In hindsight perhaps I should have taken more note."

The bishop shook his head in disgust, "What do you suggest, we get each member of the cathedral chapter to break wind for us? It's not a task I'm in a hurry to oversee."

Scrivener smiled indulgently at the bishop's attempt at sarcasm. He could tell his master was getting frustrated. "We need to focus on the practical my lord. Will, you heard them speak. This lad is to carry the traitors message?"

Will nodded, "From what we overheard of their conversation, he's delivering it this morning."

Scrivener grinned and rubbed his hands together, "Well then, we proceed as planned. Which one of you is to play the anchorite?"

～

As Bernard gazed at the desolate scene before them he grudgingly approved of Scrivener's selection. Wnychworm was one of those places that had been semi deserted after the great pestilence. From what Bernard could see, no one had much bothered with the place since. The early morning mist rising from the damp fields surrounding the village added a sinister appearance.

The countryside was flat here, and the village stood beside the floodplain of the River Dray. The fields looked fertile, he supposed they must be farmed by the surrounding villages. As for this place, it had lost its population some fifty years before and like many others never recovered its reason for existence.

They three of them led their horses down the single derelict village street towards the church. Osbert inevitably expressed his misgivings. "This plan is a work of madness. There are only three of us. What if there's a whole band of them? We're doomed."

Bernard with malicious glee replied, "Oh I wouldn't worry, as you're playing the anchorite you'll be walled up nice and safe."

Osbert, grey faced, glared at him. "It's a death trap is what it is. We're expendable, as always."

Will joining in said, "Don't moan Osbert, we can hardly have Bernard playing the anchorite now can we? He's built like a barn door. No offence my friend."

"None taken," said Bernard more cheerfully than he actually felt.

The church looked a little shabby, but was the only building in the village that still had a decent roof on it. Osbert looked at the building fearfully, "Why in God's name has Scrivener sent us here? Surely, he could have selected a better place than this to catch the perpetrators of these heinous crimes?"

Will looked around. "Not so. The place is derelict except for the church. We can be sure the only strangers who come looking for our anchorite today will be up to no good. And look, there's an anchorite cell built against the wall."

Bernard led them to the door. "We'd better take a look inside and prepare. There's no telling when our murderers might turn up. We may not know if the messenger has delivered the note yet, but if it was my task, I'd not tarry on any errand given to me by that traitorous sod we encountered last night."

The church door was of heavy oak, bound with bands of iron, but it opened easily enough. The church smelt damp and musty, little used. There were dirty rushes strewn on the floor. Half way down the building on the right-hand side there was a rough opening, beside which stood a stack of stone blocks. "At least it looks like they took the trouble to remove the last occupant of the cell," said Bernard, attempting a joke.

They stood in front of the opening and peered in. It was a simple whitewashed stone cell with a small square opening to the outside. There was a dirty straw sleeping pallet on one side and an old three-legged stool on the other.

"I am not going in there. I look nothing like an anchorite," said Osbert in a hoarse whisper.

Will sighed. "Look, be reasonable Osbert, we have to make this semi-believable to draw them in. You'll be in no danger, I swear it. If we pile the stones up behind you, at a glance it'll look like you're walled up good and proper."

"That didn't help the old woman they burned to death at

Snetherhide. They pushed something through the outside opening."

Bernard clapped him on the shoulder in reassurance. "It won't come to that my friend. I'll put a bolt through anyone's head who even attempts it. I promise. Now come on, we may not have much time. Make sure you have that cloak wrapped about you with the hood up."

Will said, "You have your dagger, some water and food?"

"Yes, I have them," said a sullen Osbert.

Bernard said, "Right then, in you go. Better make the best of it lad."

Osbert shuffled inside and sat down on the stool and watched as the other two swiftly stacked the blocks up in the doorway until they were at neck height. They left the last few feet open.

Will wiped the sweat from his brow and said, "It looks all right. Of course if you lean on it, it might collapse."

Bernard shrugged. "Never mind that. There's no way they are going to get this far if I have anything to do with it."

Will went up to the wall and peered in through the hole they'd left. "Don't worry, we'll only be across the street. We'll keep watch from one of the old buildings. They can't approach the church without us seeing them. Just act like an anchorite, mumble a bit near the outside opening, that kind of thing."

Osbert didn't say a word, he just stared back grim faced.

Bernard took his crossbow and gently rested it on the stonework of the window opening. Directly across the weed-grown street was the church, they could just see the opening in the wall where the anchorite's cell was located.

Will, bundled in his cloak against the cold morning air, stood in the corner of the derelict room staring out of the broken shutters. "You think this is going to work? We disturbed the traitor last night, perhaps he's had time to stop the messenger leaving on his errand."

Bernard shook his head. "Why would he? He doesn't know this is all staged. We disturbed him in his lair, but he's no reason to suppose we know where the next anchorite is to be struck down. He's still free to let others act outside the precinct, so why stop now?"

"True I suppose. So what sort of men do you think these are who come to kill our poor anchorite?"

"Judging by their previous handiwork, I'd wager there's a mercenary with them. I've only previous seen the like in the wars, the king made use of many such of their kind. Tempt a man with enough coin and most will lose any morals they ever had."

"But surely there are easier ways to kill some defenceless old women? Why resort to such cruel methods?"

Bernard pulled his cloak around his shoulders and ran a hand over his grey stubble. "You're still young, you don't understand how some men get a taste for killing and take pleasure in cruelty for cruelty's sake."

Will shivered, and not just due to the cold. "It's some sort of madness you think?"

"For some perhaps, as for others, I just think some men are born evil, spawn of the devil."

Will suddenly laughed, breaking the gloomy spell that had come over them. "God's teeth you're beginning to sound like Osbert."

"God help me but I believe I am," said Bernard joining in the laughter.

Sir Roger had received the boy's message with some scepticism. He'd looked at the crumpled note carefully.

"You're sure this is the right place boy?"

"My master doesn't make mistakes," said the boy with a scowl.

Sir Roger screwed the note up in his gloved hand and flicked it at the boy. It bounced off his head. "Perhaps he's a fool then?"

The boy flinched and then shrugged. "He gives me the note, I deliver it, I don't question him."

Travis retrieved the note from the floor and threw it in the fire. He was worried that Sir Roger had led the boy back to their hideaway which didn't bode well for the youngster's future.

Sir Roger warmed his hands before the fire. "Ah, I see, so you're just his lackey, a bit like Travis is mine, isn't that right Travis?"

"Yes master," said Travis wearily.

Sir Roger grinned maliciously. "See how well trained he is boy. If I were you, I'd be showing more initiative else you'll end up just like him, or worse; dead."

The boy scowled again. "Do you have a message for me to take to him or not? It's a long walk back."

Sir Roger grabbed the boy by the throat, and with one gloved hand lifted him off his feet. He hung there choking. Sir Roger pushed his face close.

"Oh you're not going back lad. I know this place in your master's message. There's scarce man nor beast in five miles of it. It's been practically deserted since the great pestilence. Am I right Travis?"

Travis hesitated then said, "It's true master, deserted since my grandfather's days."

Sir Roger nodded. "See, even Travis knows the truth of it. Perhaps a hermit seeking solitude would reside there, but an anchorite at a deserted church, it strikes me as odd, like a trap in fact. I always have a feeling about these things. Now tell me who your master is."

The boy went blue from lack of air and his eyes bulged out of their sockets. Travis said softly, "Please master, he'll not be able to tell us anything if he's dead."

Sir Roger eventually relented and slowly released the pressure on the boy's throat. He gave him one last glare and shoved the limp body to the ground and followed up with a boot to the stomach.

"No matter, he'll tell me soon enough. I've decided we'll go and pay a visit to this supposed anchorite even if it is a trap, and the boy is coming with us."

"Is that wise master?" asked Travis.

Sir Roger brutally shoved him backwards into the rough stone wall of the cottage. He pointed a finger at him. "Don't tempt me Travis, you know better than to question my plans. Now tie him up and get him onto your horse. You can walk."

Sir Roger congratulated himself for even remembering the miserable wreck that was Wnychworm. He'd not set foot in the place for years. The only thing that had changed was the even more dilapidated state of the main street.

On Travis's horse sat the sullen boy, his hand's tied behind his back, with Travis himself leading the animal on foot. Sir Roger rode his own horse behind. He said, "You know Travis, I remember my brothers and I burnt down the house of one of the remaining inhabitants here. It must be thirty years ago now."

"Ah, the happy days of one's youth master?" mumbled a foot weary Travis forgetting himself for once. Fortunately, Sir Roger missed the implied sarcasm.

"Know what I remember most Travis?"

"No master."

"I'll tell you then. The smell of the smoke Travis, after the fire got going and they'd stopped screaming, the smoke smelt like burnt pork. Gave me quite an appetite afterwards. Funny what you remember, eh?"

"Yes master."

"Not far to the church now. You know what to do?"

Travis halted and turned to the boy on the horse. He reached up and pulled the hood of the boy's cloak over the youth's head. He put his own hood up. "I'm to lead us to the front of the church, look for an opening for the anchorite's cell in the church wall and stop there."

"That's all you need to do. If you bugger this up Travis, I'll have your hide, do you understand me?"

Travis understood only too well and that he and the boy would be sitting ducks in any trap that'd been planned for them.

"Right, I'm leaving my horse tied up here. I need to see if there are any watchers in the ruins. It'll have to be close to the church, somewhere they can keep watch without being seen. Off you go then, and try for God's sake not to get yourself killed, it'd take me years to train someone up to be as incompetent."

Travis set off again down the overgrown street. He was weary, not just physically but mentally. It occurred to Travis that he was completely indifferent to his fate. He honestly didn't know how much longer he could go on, Sir Roger was getting more insane by the day. Perhaps an arrow in the back would not be such a bad thing.

Osbert, inside the anchorite cell, stood at the small opening to the outside world. He was cold and miserable and not a little frightened. The view through the small window was directly onto the street in front of the cell. He could hear the approach of a horse but it was not yet in view. The hairs rose on the back of his neck. He had a bad feeling about this, even more so than usual. The back of his throat was as dry as a bone. He took a drink from the water flask, drew the cloak closer around his shoulders and pulled the hood down to cover his face. He gave an experimental shout in a high-pitched tone. Not loud enough he thought. At the top of his lungs he bawled, "God bless you weary pilgrims, I am but a humble anchorite."

There was the startled neigh of a horse as it reared in shock and threw its rider to the ground directly in front of the window.

Osbert stared out at the struggling black-cloaked figure on the ground. As far as he could tell it had its hands tied behind its back and the string of curses and angry cries were unbefitting of a pilgrim.

"Have you come to seek counsel from a woman wise in spiritual matters?" he crowed.

"You silly old crone," cried the figure on the floor, "I almost broke my neck."

Osbert backed away from the opening, keeping his head down. Another, vaguely familiar, voice whispered from outside, "If you value you life old woman and you can escape from your cell do so now. Our master means to do you harm."

Osbert backed up as far from the outside window as was possible. This was exactly the type of thing he didn't want to hear. In a high-pitched voice he said, "I'm tired, perhaps I can offer you counsel another time."

It was then he heard a sound from the inside of the church itself. Keeping an eye on the outside window, fearing all the time they'd throw something in to burn him alive, he shuffled to the blocked-up doorway. With his back against the rough stonework, he called softly. "Is that you Will, Bernard?"

There was a soft scraping sound directly behind him. He turned slowly and standing on his tiptoes he looked out over the opening. A face that had once haunted his very nightmares, complete with a hideous M shaped welt, leered back. Osbert let out a strangled shriek and stumbled backwards.

The face said, "Well I'll suck a great whores teat! You little festering worm of a bishop's man. I've waited a long time for this."

Osbert could only squeak, "Roger Mudstone!"

Sir Roger roared, "As God is my witness, I'm going to tear you limb from limb with my bare hands. You and those other lickspittles of the bishop cost me a fortune, deprived me of my estates and made me look a fool. Do you think I'd ever forget that boy?"

With that he heaved at the wall and dislodged one of the top blocks. It fell inwards into the cell with a horrendous crash. Osbert jumped back, completely petrified. Another heave and another block crashed down.

Sir Roger was positively frothing at the mouth as he tore at the stone blocks. A red mist had descended and his sole focus was on getting to Osbert. "God's teeth I've been dreaming of getting my hands on one of the bishop's worms and here you are. I'm going to make you suffer boy, so much so that you'll wish you'd never been born."

Osbert huddled in the far corner and prayed for deliverance, or at the very least the intervention of Bernard and Will.

Will heard the horse before he saw it. He eased his head forward through the remains of the broken shutters. He said, "Theres a man on horseback and another on foot leading them, both are hooded."

Bernard smiled grimly, "Well thank Christ for that. I'm getting too old for standing here for hours." As they came into his view he tracked them with the crossbow.

Will stared at the figures who were now directly opposite them across the street. He whispered, "They seem an unlikely pair of assassins. The one on the horse looks to have his hands tied behind his back."

Bernard peered hard, "I'll be damned. I think you're right. Perhaps it's a trick?"

They heard a high pitched quivery voice call out from the anchorite cell.

Will sniggered. "Putting him in there was probably a mistake, he makes a piss poor anchorite."

Bernard grinned and then had to stifle a laugh when the horse reared up at the noise and sent its rider sprawling on the ground.

Will said, "What now?"

"Come, take out your dagger, its time we confronted them. They look harmless but then looks can be deceiving."

They made their way out of the back of the derelict cottage and carefully eased around the side. The figure on the ground was rolling around and cursing as he tried to get to his feet, hands still bound behind his back.

The other man tried to help him up and in doing so his hood came down. The bishop's men both recognised him in an instant.

Will, stunned, couldn't help but blurt out the man's name, "Travis!"

Travis hearing his name looked across the street at them, his jaw dropped as he recognised the bishop's men. Before anything else could be said, a terrified wail came from the opening in the wall accompanied by the crashing of stonework and the bellowing of an enraged man.

Bernard handed the crossbow to Will, drew his sword and strode across the street. He held the tip of the sword at Travis's throat and said, "Mudstone, is he with you?"

Travis stood mutely and simply nodded. Will said, "Where is he Travis? Is that him in the church?"

Travis nodded once more. Will dared a quick glance through the anchorite cell's opening. He could hear Osbert whimpering just below the window. Across the dim interior he could see Sir Roger was tearing into the bricked-up wall like a madman. Will quickly ducked back out of sight.

"We'd better get in the church and do something before Mudstone breaks in there and kills Osbert, he's deranged."

Bernard pushed Travis against the wall and hissed, "Stay here, run again and I swear I'll kill you. I once owed you my life, that's the only reason you're still breathing, understand?"

Travis nodded and slumped down, his back against the church wall as though drained of all energy. Bernard picked up the boy, hands still tied behind him, and slung him against the wall next to Travis. Will thought he recognised him from the cathedral precinct but there was no time for further questions, they needed to save Osbert.

As they approached the church door Bernard said, "Just try to get Osbert out of there alive. Leave Mudstone to me. Now give me the crossbow."

Will handed it to him. The big man held the crossbow in his left hand and a sword in the right. Will drew his own sword and dagger.

Bernard said, "You ready?"

Will took a deep breath and nodded. Bernard shoved the church door open with his shoulder and strode in. He stopped and bellowed, "Mudstone!"

Sir Roger, busy demolishing the stones blocking the anchorite's cell, turned and Bernard immediately fired the crossbow. The bolt shot across the distance between them at shoulder height and smashed into the stonework to Sir Roger's left. He didn't even flinch. "Well, well, if it isn't the chief cur himself and his ginger lap dog. By God, I'm going to enjoy gutting you both. You, big man, I'm going to cut your ears off first and then make the lad eat them."

Bernard shrugged. "As usual, you overestimate yourself. You'll end your miserable life at the end of a rope. I'll probably have to cut your bollocks off first, that's if you've got any." He narrowed the distance between them.

Sir Roger grew crimson with rage. He drew his sword and advanced. "Better you yield now bishop's man. Not that you'll die any the easier, it'll just save me some effort."

Bernard grinned and then lunged at him, their swords coming together with a clash. Bernard backed up a step, encouraging the other to follow. Sir Roger tried a quick slash. Bernard was too quick and jerked back as the blade brushed the stubble on his chin.

"You try my patience, you turd," Sir Roger hissed and advanced again.

Bernard gave way, a smile on his lips. He circled backwards, leading Sir Roger who suddenly tried a hack at the big man's legs; Bernard belying his bulk, hopped easily away. "Losing your touch Mudstone?"

He came at Bernard hard this time. The church echoed with the sound of steel clanging on steel.

As the two fighting men edged up the length of the church, Will made his way across to the anchorite's cell. Sir Roger had demolished the wall down to waist height. Osbert was cowering against the back of the cell.

"Osbert," hissed Will, "Quick, get up, I'll help you out."

"He'll kill us all. He's the devil himself."

Will held out a hand over the wall. "He'll bloody well kill you for sure if you stay in there. Come on, out of there now."

Osbert reluctantly came forward and peered out.

"Watch out!" he cried, ducking back. Will looked around and found Bernard almost on top of him as Sir Roger's furious onslaught forced the big man back down the church. Bernard, blocking each blow, said through gritted teeth, "Stand clear lad."

The tip of Sir Roger's slashing sword caught the rough stonework of the half-demolished wall sending sparks cascading into the anchorite's cell. With a whimper Osbert scuttled away into the dark interior. Will dodged around the fighting men and tried to thrust his dagger towards Sir Roger's left ear in an effort to distract him from his murderous onslaught. He was rewarded with a glancing blow from Sir Roger's free hand. It sent him spinning away with what was sure to be a black eye if he survived the day. He crashed down onto the cold floor, painfully twisting his leg as he did so.

Bernard was starting to struggle and Sir Roger's blade suddenly hacked a tear into the leather on his shoulder. Sir Roger grinned wildly and lunged forward, smashing the hilt of his sword into Bernard's nose. The big man stumbled backwards, one hand clutched to his face, the blood running freely. Sir Roger laughed and pressed forward. Quick as a flash Bernard flicked the blood from his hand into Sir Roger's eyes and slashed at him savagely. His blade left a score across the other man's stomach. Sir Roger backed off, wincing in pain. "You stinking turd," he spat.

Bernard grinned back and then drove forward hard and fast. Sir Roger, now on the defensive, blocked. Bernard jerked his sword upward toward the other's head. Sir Roger took half a step back, avoiding the blade. He braced himself and then slammed his sword down in a savage arc. Bernard managed to knock it aside, but the impact forced him down onto one knee. Sir Roger quickly moved close to deliver what would surely be the killer blow. As he brought his blade down again, Bernard suddenly jabbed his own blade upwards and caught the other man in the elbow. Mudstone grunted in pain and backed away, a trail of blood pouring from his arm.

"Damn you bishop's man. You're a whoreson. I'll take you to hell with me if I have to."

Bernard struggled to his feet, panting. "And I'll gladly put you there." Summoning his remaining strength, the big man stepped forward and launched a flurry of blows. Sir Roger staggered backwards under the onslaught, barely deflecting the blows with his injured sword arm. Bernard slammed his sword at Sir Roger's head, the injured man staggered, and then fell backwards onto his back dropping his weapon in the process.

Bernard lurched over to him. He grasped his sword two handed and began a swing that would split Sir Roger in half.

"Wait!" shouted Will from where he lay stunned. "He's to hang, for all he's done Bernard, he needs to hang like the common criminal he is."

Sir Roger laughed wildly as Bernard loomed over him, his sword paused half way in the swing. "Kill me. You know you want to. You lack the self control, you're just a stinking turd like the rest of them. Just a ploughman in all but name. Go on, do it."

Osbert's terrified white face looked over the remains of the cell wall. He croaked, "He wants to die. Do it and save us all. No one could reproach you, he has the devil in him."

Will and Bernard simultaneously said, "Shut up Osbert!"

"Bernard?" said Will anxiously.

"Give me a moment lad, I'm thinking."

Sir Roger laughed coldly. "As I thought, you haven't got the guts, you're a coward."

Quick as a flash Bernard brought the pommel of the sword down on Sir Roger's sneering face, breaking his nose with an audible crunch. The back of his head smacked into the floor and he was unconscious.

"And you can shut up as well," murmured Bernard before sinking to the floor himself, utterly exhausted. "Go fetch something to tie him up with lad, I'm all but done in."

11

THE COURT IN SESSION

Jocelyn Gifford, Bishop of Draychester, was in a foul mood. He sat slumped in a padded chair in his private chambers. Scrivener sat opposite at a small writing desk. The bishop's stomach rumbled. He was used to enjoying a hearty breakfast, a thing that had become an increasingly rare thing within the bishop's palace.

"I take it that the cook is still not at his duties?"

"I am endeavouring to rectify the situation my lord. It's become apparent the cook's apprentice lacks some of his master's finer skills."

"That's putting it diplomatically, I ate better when we were on campaign against the Scots. The lad is obviously out of his depth, and he seems incapable of controlling the kitchen staff. Have you been in there lately? It's bloody chaos."

"The cook has taken to his bed my lord, and won't open the door to his chamber."

"Well break the bloody door down if you have to. Unless he's actually dead I want him back on duty. I can't think what's got into the man, he's always been so reliable. My stomach thinks my throat's been cut."

"I'll see how he is this evening my lord. I might borrow someone from one of the taverns in the city. We own several after all. Or we can send for something from one of the cookhouses."

The bishop, somewhat mollified, gave a humph in response.

Scrivener sighed and turned back to his paperwork. "You haven't forgotten that we start the court session this morning my lord?"

"I remember well enough," the bishop said gruffly. He reflected that perhaps it would have been better to postpone the Consistory Court hearing he was about to preside over. Scrivener had persuaded him it was better to at least give the outward appearance of business as usual. He shifted uneasily in his chair. "It seems we could be making better use of our time Scrivener, we have a traitor to catch."

Scrivener nodded. "If it were only just the traitor himself we had to deal with my lord I'd agree."

He picked up a paper from the desk and offered it to the bishop for his perusal. "What you see there my lord is also the result of his meddling."

The bishop looked at the lengthy list of prisoners awaiting the court's judgement. "Damn it Scrivener, we'll be sitting for days to get through this lot. And all of these fall under our jurisdiction do they? Does the sheriff's own court not sit at all anymore?"

"It seems to me that the sheriff, in collusion no doubt with the coroner, has purposely been forcing these cases our way rather than handling them himself."

With some venom the bishop replied, "The sheriff is a half-wit who has bought his position. The coroner on the other hand is a devious little toad who delights in making mischief."

Scrivener smiled. "The coroner and sheriff take advantage of the situation aided by the rumours circulating the city. The death of the anchorites and the murder here within the precinct make us look weak."

The bishop nodded. "They embolden both coroner and sheriff and also those others in the city who hold us in no favour."

"Exactly so my lord, and not just here. Eventually, as you well know, gossip will get back to the king."

"Then I suggest we judge ever damn one of those cases on your list if it takes us the entire week. No one makes a fool of me Scrivener unless its myself that's doing it."

"I was afraid you might say that my lord."

By late morning they had barely got through a handful of cases. The bishop was throughly bored and his fellow judges appeared to be asleep. To his left the bald-headed Vicar General of the diocese, Robert Fitz-Herbert, was audibly snoring. As usual, he was richly dressed in a long woollen cloak which he had wrapped around himself as though it were a blanket. On his head he wore a fur lined felt hat pulled low over his eyes.

On the far side of Fitz-Herbert the Commissary General, Walter Bubwith also appeared comatose. Only the small hunched figure sat to the bishop's right appeared alert. Ralph of Shrewsbury sat in his seat, wrapped in his black cloak, silent and brooding as always. The bishop paid him little attention; he had grown well used to his odd appearance, in fact he appreciated the effect it had on some of the prisoners who appeared before the court. To Ralph's left would usually sit the considerable figure of Theobald Beaufort, Dean of the cathedral. Today that chair was empty as his substantial bulk was on business elsewhere.

On the infrequent days the court sat, there would usually be a small crowd of interested onlookers gathered at the margins of the hall. Normally the bishop would know most of them by sight, except perhaps the relatives of those on trial. The numbers were few compared to those drawn to the attractions offered by the sheriff's court in the city itself. As the morning had progressed, it was obvious this was not a normal day. The bishop thought he recognised the coroner's face in among the growing throng.

"Am I mistaken or did I just see that whoreson the coroner at the door?" whispered the bishop to Scrivener. "What's he doing over here? Has the sheriff not enough to keep the man occupied?"

"He seems to have come to gloat my lord, and brought others with him."

"He can gloat all he wants; we'll try every bloody case if it takes all day."

Just before noon a bedraggled figure, hands chained behind his back, was hauled up the steps from the undercroft of the hall and pushed forward to stand before them. The bishop thought there was something vaguely familiar about the man.

"Don't I know you?" The bishop asked the prisoner. The man raised his head briefly and looked the bishop in the eye before dropping his tonsured head again.

The bishop, resting his chin in one hand, studied him with interest. "Now don't tell me, I rarely forget a face. Let me see, I think you're that priest from Farandon? Is that why you're here and not in the sheriffs court, eh? Claiming benefit of clergy no doubt. I believe we've had words before, you can't hold your ale if I remember rightly."

There was no response from the prisoner and Scrivener began to read from his papers. "Matter relating to the death of John de Maldone, on Saturday, the eve of the exaltation of the Holy Cross. Information given to the coroner and sheriff that John de Maldone of the parish of Farandon lay dead, other than his rightful death, in the street in front of the church in the said parish. Thereupon the…"

The bishop, smiling triumphantly, interrupted, "What did I tell you, I never forget a face, so you are that priest from Farandon."

The man made no response. Scrivener gave an impatient cough. The bishop waved a hand in apology. "Sorry Scrivener, carry on, let's hear the sordid details."

"The sheriff and coroner proceeded thither and diligently enquired after the manner of his death. Having…"

The bishop interrupted again, this time with an ironic laugh, "Diligently my arse, not those two. Probably stopped off at a whorehouse on the way there."

The court erupted with laughter and the coroner watching from the crowd turned a bright red much to the bishop's pleasure.

Scrivener gave his master a glare, "My lord, please."

"Sorry, proceed."

"Having summoned the good men of the ward in question, they heard the facts. The jurors upon their oath say that their parish priest, Nicolas Crabbe, and the aforesaid John de Maldone had been drinking all day in the brewhouse of Alice de Walton in the same street where the church doth lie."

"I knew it, too much ale again, eh Crabbe?" said the bishop.

Scrivener drew breath but didn't stop, "Before the curfew Nicolas Crabbe did induce the said John de Maldone to leave the brewhouse with him and climb the steps of the church tower to catch pigeons, numerous of which dwell therein."

There was a stirring from Fitz-Herbert, who opened an eye and said, "Bloody pest they are in Draychester. Crap all over the cathedral. Costs us a fortune."

The bishop nodded to humour him. Fitz-Herbert continued, "Bloody good for nothing in their insolence and idleness. Evil minds the lot of them, busying themselves rather in doing harm than good."

"Is it pigeons you speak of?" asked the bishop somewhat bewildered.

The crowd laughed and Fitz-Herbert eye half open, frowned in frustration and said, "Pigeons? Of course not man. Children man, children. Can't stand em. Throw and shoot stones, arrows and different kinds of missiles at the pigeons nesting in the walls. Playing ball inside and outside the cathedral, breaking and damaging the glass windows. Appalling, the youth of today..."

He closed his eye and promptly fell asleep again.

Scrivener raised an eyebrow. "A useful insight into the case before us I'm sure."

The bishop ignoring Fitz-Herbert's bizarre outburst said, "Lets get to the meat of it. How did this Maldone fellow meet his maker?"

Scrivener looked back to his papers and began to read aloud again. "The two were seen in the tower from the street below. Drunk beyond measure they could be seen to quarrel and Nicolas Crabbe did take up a piece of wood and strike John de Maldone upon the head causing him to fall from the tower into the street below. His brains were spilled from his skull of which injury he did expire"

There were some "ooh's," and "aah's" from the crowd which the bishop smiled at indulgently. He said, "A nasty way to go I'd wager. Still, if you can't hold your ale then don't go to the brewhouse. What say you gentlemen?"

"Hang him," said a sleepy Fitz-Herbert.

Bubworth opened one eye and said, "A good flogging wouldn't go amiss, then find him a parish on the Welsh border, let him rot there."

Ralph just gave an enigmatic smile and a twitch. The bishop wasn't surprised, he couldn't actually recall him ever speaking. The bishop nodded his acknowledgement of his fellow judges' verdicts. "A not too surprising spread of opinion there I must say. So Nicholas Crabbe, sometime priest of Farandon, what say you for yourself?"

The man looked up and croaked, "I throw myself upon your mercy my lord."

"Hmm is that all? That may not be your best response. Tell me, this John de Maldone, you knew him well did you, considering you killed him over a pigeon?"

Crabbe hung his head in shame. "One of my parishioners, a good man when sober. He leaves a wife and seven children. I blame myself, it's the drink my lord, he called me a whoremonger priest."

"Really. A wife and seven children you say. Then I've a good mind to make you bloody well marry her."

Crabbe gazed up at the bishop in confusion. "I'm sorry my lord, I don't understand?"

The bishop pointed a finger at him. "You heard me, I've decided, you're to take the widow as your wife."

There was a ripple of laughter and approval from the crowd around the outside of the hall. All apart from the

coroner who scowled and with a backward glance departed the hall.

Crabbe protested. "But my lord, I'm a priest!"

The bishop shrugged. "And also a murderer. I can always have you hanged if you prefer?"

Bubworth stirred again and offered up another nugget of wisdom. "Some of the wives I've known, many a man would prefer the noose instead." He then gave a guilty look and promptly fell asleep again.

The crowd howled with laughter. When the noise had died down the bishop said, "Well it's a bit late to come over all pious now Crabbe. Anyway, being a priest has never stopped many taking a wife, holy orders or not."

In desperation Crabbe replied, "She's not a pretty woman my lord, touched with the pox some years past and she's of an age of my own grandmother and with a fearsome temper."

This time the laughter was even louder. The bishop, smirking, held his hand up for quiet. "Well then, that's all to the better, you can take that as part of your punishment. Seems very fair to me. And Crabbe, stay out of the brewhouse. In fact, if you're seen in there again I will have you hanged. That's my judgement. Now get him out of here."

Scrivener stifled a laugh and said, "A somewhat irregular ruling my lord?"

"I've been sat on my arse all morning, I'm uncomfortable and I'm hungry so I'm not of a mind to follow precedent. See it is done."

"As you wish my lord. I'll ensure the matter is taken care of."

"Good, let's move on. Next."

Sometime in the mid afternoon, the kitchen, in the cook's absence, provided some bread and cheese and a

flagon of ale. The bishop demanded something more substantial, and they dispatched one of the kitchen lads to the marketplace for hot pies. He returned with a dozen containing a meat filling that didn't bear close inspection, but the bishop and his colleagues were too hungry to care.

The coroner had evidently passed across any case that even hinted of a clerical connection. And so it went on throughout the long afternoon.

John Monmouth, stabbed in the side with a thwitel by Thomas of Worcester, the chaplain. Verdict, Thomas to hang.

John de Wycumbe, found dead in the fishery below the church of the friars to the south of the city, having drowned. Verdict, the friars ordered to provide a fish every Friday for a year to the widow.

Thomas Small, arrested for a burglary at Snodmire church, died in prison with a wound to the left eye given to him by an iron fork. Verdict. The Iron fork confiscated from the priest at Snodmire and a two shilling fine.

Adam de Haigh knocked off a bridge by a passing cart, belonging to the abbey at Drayreach. The said Adam drowned in the river below by misadventure. Verdict, the abbey to pay for the upkeep of said bridge for a year.

As afternoon turned into evening the crowd gradually thinned. With the closing of the precinct gates, only those that dwelled within remained to watch. The bishop was determined to get through the list. Eventually it was Scrivener who brought the proceeding to a halt. There was still a good quarter of his list of prisoners left. He could tell his master was tired, although he was too stubborn to admit it.

"We've been through all the serious cases my lord and those that remain can be dealt with next time. No-one can

say we haven't done our duty today, certainly not the coroner or sheriff."

"That damn weasel the coroner. I swear if they ever pull this trick again I'll have his hide."

The bishop ran a hand over his tired face. He looked around and realised the hall was nearly empty now. The court's other judges had long since vanished. Bubworth had made the excuse that he needed to pass water. He did not return. Not long after, Fitz-Herbert, who was well past his sixtieth year, complained of fatigue and shuffled off, presumably to resume his slumbers in a more comfortable location. Ralph of Shrewsbury must have disappeared at some point but the bishop couldn't swear to have seen him leave, the man was an enigma.

12

THE COOK

The cook hadn't stepped out of his chamber for nearly three days, not since the morning the Rat's body had been discovered. The door was barred, and to all enquiries he'd shouted that he had a severe case of the flux.

He'd finally had to admit to himself that he couldn't keep this up, and the terror of seeing the body of his friend had somewhat abated. Neither he, nor the chamber smelled too sweet, and he'd drunk all the water and meagre rations. There were hardly any rushlights left and the chamber, without a window, would have no light if he stayed much longer. For most of the time he'd slept. It'd been a fitful slumber, as he'd half expected Ralph of Shrewsbury to come knocking at any moment.

As he lay on his straw mattress, he concluded that perhaps Ralph didn't after all know the Rat had confided in him. In which case, passing on the murdered man's message to Scrivener would surely now be madness. It wouldn't bring the Rat back from the dead and it wasn't really any of his business, he was just a cook. He resolved to forget the entire thing and get back to work in the kitchens. He would

however stay out of Ralph's way whenever possible, which would hardly be difficult as the man slipped about the place like a ghost most of the time. God alone knew what chaos now reigned in the kitchens. If he wasn't there to supervise things swiftly got out of hand. The bishop was no doubt already grumbling. Perhaps he should make some plan to cook the favourite dish of his master to appease him. He'd learned it from a cook in London, a dish made with pounded meat. The ingredients were pork and chicken, some eggs, bread, and a jug of ale. Perhaps he'd add a pinch of cinnamon. He realised he had no idea of what the hour of day was, having lost track of time shut up in the chamber. Listening hard, he heard none of the usual hustle and bustle of the daytime life of the palace. Maybe the hour was late, no matter, it was time to get back to work.

He opened his door tentatively and carefully put his head out and looked left and right. The passageway was cool and dark and he saw no one. It was night. He stepped out of the room and closed the door softly behind him. With stiff limbs from so long abed, he made his way to the privy that lay far down the passageway. He took a deep and satisfying piss in the gloom, then padded all the way back past his own chamber and along into the kitchens.

The first thing he noticed was that the kitchen lads were missing from their usual position tucked next to the huge chimney breast. No doubt off making mischief instead of tending to their duties. The glow from the fire was dim, just a few embers remaining. It'd be out by morning and a bugger to get going again. They'd know about it when he caught up with them.

He lit two tallow candles and the gloom retreated a little. There were pots and pans piled up everywhere. He cursed under his breath. There would be hell to pay on the morrow; things should work better than this in his absence. He cleared a space at one of the wooden preparation tables and then walked over to check the little locked cupboard where the spices were kept. The key hung around his own neck, the spices were too expensive to be left unsecured in the kitchen.

The key turned easily in the well-oiled lock and he opened the door. Inside were a set of shelves holding spices in small leather bags. He sighed in relief, everything was where it should be. Reaching for the most precious of all, the bag containing the cinnamon, he suddenly gasped as he became aware of an excruciating pain in his back. A hard, boney hand came from behind and clamped itself over his nose and mouth. Another hand reached over him and grasped the cinnamon bag. He struggled, but the pain in his back was overwhelming in its intensity. With two fingers the hand forced open the top of the bag. The other hand released his mouth and nose. He gasped and spluttered, even more so when the open end of the bag was crammed into his mouth and the dusty powder forced into it. The hands released him and he collapsed, a thin-bladed knife embedded in his back and cinnamon cascading from his open mouth.

Ralph of Shrewsbury smiled as the cook feebly struggled and spasmed on the floor before becoming still. The old man poked the cook with his boot just to make sure he was lifeless, then left as swiftly as he'd arrived, leaving only a pungent whiff behind him.

~

It was still two hours before dawn when one of the kitchen spit boys, who'd taken to sleeping in the great hall, made a detour via the kitchen on the way to take a piss. He stumbled over the body of the cook, took one look and knew his master was dead. Stumbling from the kitchen, he ran along the passageway, up the stairs, and out into the inner courtyard. He gave a cry of alarm that fetched not only one of the bishop's guards running from the gatehouse but raised half the inhabitants of the precinct from their slumbers. The guard took one look at the cook's body sprawled in the kitchen, barely resisted the urge to spew his guts, and decided he'd better wake Scrivener whatever the hour. He would let the secretary tell the bishop himself, the guard didn't want to be on the receiving end of what would surely be the bishop's wrath.

The bishop looked up from the cook's body. Scrivener could see the rage in his master's eyes. He tried to contain the anger with black humour as was his nature. "Do you know how hard it is to find a good cook? We'll be eating from the city's cookshops for the next six months."

Scrivener gave a weak smile in reply.

His master patted the dead man's shoulder sadly. "He was a talented cook, I'll give him that much. I'll not have this Scrivener, not under my own roof. The murderer, vile scum as he is, mocks us with this." He brushed some cinnamon from the dead man's mouth and looked at the powdered spice on his fingers.

Scrivener nodded. "A thin blade to the back, much like the Rat's death. I agree the fiend mocks us with the cinnamon, it was unnecessary, he thinks himself clever than us all."

"And so far that's proved true. The Rat I could understand, with the nature of his business, but the cook, what reason could there be to murder him?"

"The more I think on it, the Rat and the cook had an unlikely friendship. Someone helped the Rat on his night time escapades within the palace. I've seen them drinking and gambling together on more than one occasion."

"You think that's why the cook took to his bed, with the Rat murdered not twenty yards from his own chamber?"

"He feared for his life, rightly so it seems. Perhaps the Rat told him something, at least the killer may have thought so."

The bishop brought his fist smashing down onto the worktop. "This has to stop Scrivener, do you hear me? I won't have it. We'll find this murderous son of a whore if I have to demolish the palace and cathedral stone by bloody stone to do it."

"Yes my lord."

W ith the last of Bernard's strength they had tied up the unconscious Sir Roger, and then between them dragged him to the back wall of the anchorite's cell. Travis, all the spirit seemingly drained out of him, had meekly followed his master into the cell and slumped down beside him. The sullen boy was pushed in after them.

Bernard, injured, and by now utterly exhausted, started swaying on his feet. With Osbert's help, Will somehow managed to get the injured man towards the front of the church. Bernard sat down against the wall next to the doorway, his breath ragged. "I'm sorry lads, I'm done. Must be getting old."

They made the big man comfortable, covering him with his riding cloak adding Will's on top for good measure. He soon fell into an exhausted slumber. Will's own left leg had gone black and blue and felt hot and swollen. He thought it badly sprained rather than broken, but he could hardly bear to put any weight on it. His head ached from the glancing blow he'd received from Sir Roger.

Will stood propped against the stonework of the church doorway. He winced in pain as he tried unsuccessfully to put weight on his left leg. "We can't take them back with us Osbert, not in the state we're in. Bernard can barely stand and I can't walk with this leg, let alone get on a horse. You need to ride at once for Draychester. Go straight to your uncle and the bishop. Tell him to send the biggest and meanest of the guards. I wouldn't be surprised if the bishop comes himself when he finds out Mudstone is here."

Osbert peered fearfully from the door of the church. The light was fading fast. "It'll be dark soon. How am I to find my way?"

"There'll be a moon, you'll do just fine. Listen to me, the only thing to fear is right here, and he's tied up in the anchorite's cell with the others. Do as I say, stop for no one until you get to Draychester. Now go." With that he pushed the lad out from the doorway and gently shut the door behind him.

Osbert stood before the doorway for a moment and a shiver ran up his spine. He drew in a breath, pulled his cloak close around his neck, crossed himself and went to fetch his horse.

As Osbert left the deserted ruins of Wynchworm the twilight faded into moonlit darkness. The moon lessened the inky blackness of the night, but wasn't so bright as to dull the glow of the stars above. Osbert was never comfortable in the countryside and the night brought out the worst of his fears. He would always prefer the confines of the cathedral precinct and the comfort of the protecting walls of the city. Out here, along the muddy track of the road and the wide open fields, he felt small and vulnerable. Will had been right about one thing though, the further away from Mudstone he got, the safer he felt.

Osbert struggled to remember the way they had come. Looking upwards he saw a thin layer of cloud had rolled in, behind which the moon now hung smoky and yellow. Passing a pond on his right, the moonlight reflecting off the water, he thought he remembered it from earlier. Perhaps it was the same spot they had passed just after turning off the king's highway onto the track to Wynchworm. And sure enough, as he pressed on, the track came out on the side of a much wider road. Osbert stopped and peered left then right in the gloom, unsure of which way to turn. To the right the road had a slight gradient. His travelling companions often laughed at his poor sense of direction, but tonight Osbert trusted his memory of the morning's ride. With his knees he nudged his horse right and with a snort the animal started to move. The way was smoother here, the road better maintained, and he urged his mount into a faster trot. Soon enough the glint of the river Dray came into sight on his right. Osbert sighed in relief. The water was flowing towards him and he was headed north, back towards Draychester.

"Pssst. Boy, I can hear you snivelling away over there. Get yourself across here if you want to save your life." Sir Roger had awoken, battered and bruised with hands tied behind his back. He could feel the dried blood of his wounds caking his chest. Around his ankles was a rope binding his legs tightly together. He lay with his back against the wall of the anchorite cell. The only light was that of the moon coming through the small window on the outside wall of the cell. Travis, similarly tied, sat next to him, head slumped forward. The boy, only loosely tied by the hands, crouched in a far corner watching them, his eyes unseen but dull and hard. He whispered, "Leave me be, there's nothing you can do now. We'll all hang when we get back to Draychester."

Sir Roger whispered, "With that attitude you're probably right. Let's hope they hang you first then I don't have to hear too much more of your snivelling."

The boy hissed, "Shut up. I'd have never been here if it wasn't for you."

"Ah, I see you've still some spirit left in you after all. Ever felt a noose around your neck boy, choking the life out of you?"

The boy shivered in the gloom. Sir Roger, with broken teeth, grinned back. He'd not been too attractive before, now he was downright intimidating. "I thought not. I've cheated the hangman more than once boy and I can do it again. Isn't that true Travis?"

After a moment Travis, head still slumped on his chest, whispered, "He's not lying boy. The devil always looks after his own."

"Come on boy, get over here and untie me," urged Sir Roger.

The boy peered across at him. Finally, making a decision, he struggled and after a time freed his hands. Then, hesitantly, he crawled across the space between them. Sir Roger inched himself around so that his back faced the boy, who then picked at the knotted rope binding Sir Roger's hands.

"Hurry boy, we haven't got all night."

Much to Sir Roger's impatience, it took ten minutes to

free his hands. The rope around his ankles was dealt with a good deal faster. He struggled painfully to his feet and swayed a little for a moment, trying to summon up the strength to go on. The boy shuffled over to Travis and tugged on the ropes around his ankles.

"Leave him," whispered Sir Roger harshly. "We've not the time and he's always been next to useless. Now you boy, you at least show some promise."

Travis, hardly bothering to raise his head from his chest, said dully, "Where will you go?"

Sir Roger peered down at the slumped figure of his faithful servant and said, "To find the boy's master and, one way or another, settle some old scores." He turned away, then hesitated and looked back down at Travis. "You've always been a worm Travis, the boy has proved himself more of a man than you've ever been. I should really kill you but you're not worth the effort."

14

THE VISION

D ame Dorthy's visions came at the most inconvenient times. Although her anchorite cell was probably the most luxuriously furnished in the diocese, she was still in an enclosed space, comprising two stone-built chambers attached to the great cathedral in Draychester. The bucket she squatted over was copper bound and had a wooden cover that could be closed when not in use to mask any smell. As the familiar feeling came over her, she screwed her eyes tight shut and a wall of rippling colours assaulted her. In the background she could hear the pigeon cooing softly. She swayed precariously over the bucket and her shaking hands resting on the rim sent the contents sloshing out over her feet. She cursed loudly in a most unholy like manner and held on tight as the vision resolved in front of her.

She saw flashes of a building which looked like the bishop's palace here in Draychester. One moment it was as she remembered it, the next it was just the barest of ruined stone walls viewed from a distance on a sunlit day with strangely dressed figures walking around the stonework with evident interest. In the background she recognised the familiar bulk of the cathedral. The scene dissolved again and this time she saw a man's face with dead looking eyes and a strange scar burnt into his cheek. She pictured him looking through one of the openings from the cathedral into her own cell. He thrust his hand through and tossed something onto the cell floor that smashed and spread a wall of flame across the rushes towards her. She gasped in terror, but before she could react further, the scene dissolved into something else. This time she saw a dark hooded figure crouched over a table scattered with documents. The location was again familiar to her, the cathedral's library. The figure raised its head up and looked her straight in the eye. She knew the face, Ralph of Shrewsbury, a wisp of a smile played on his lips and he raised a bony finger and pointed directly at her, it wasn't a friendly gesture. The scene drained away and was replaced with a vision of an angry crowd of people surging in agitation around and through the gates of the cathedral precinct. A thin line of the bishop's guards attempted to hold them back. The bishop's men pushed and shoved as the crowd surged backwards and forwards.

The vision changed yet again, this time to a view as though she were a bird flying high over the streets of a great city. She recognised little except the bulk of the cathedral, in the surrounding streets she could see strange carts moving, of various colours and shapes, there appeared to be no horses to pull them. On either side of the streets walked a multitude of strangely dressed people. Finally, the view faded to black, and the visions were over, for now.

As usual, none of it made much sense. She'd long ago stopped trying to find any meaning whilst a vision was in progress. It was only later she would try to remember what she'd seen. The whole thing was utterly exhausting. She called to her attendant, who was usually hovering just outside one of the windows between the cell and the main body of the cathedral.

"Maud, I need to rest. Close the shutter, let me sleep a while."

Maud thrust her head through the opening and asked breathlessly. "Have you had another of your visions my lady?"

"Maud, please, my head is pounding."

"What did you see my lady? Tell me, did you see me my lady? My future perhaps?"

Dorothy snapped back, "Yes Maud, I saw it all. You marry an ugly fat merchant, he's thirty years your senior and looks like a hog, smells like one too. You'll pop out another squalling brat every year for twenty years until he drops dead and so do you."

"There no need to be like that, I was only asking," screamed Maud and slammed the wooden shutter closed making Dorothy wince. The girl had been her attendant for only a few weeks. They never seemed to last more than a month or two. Dorothy couldn't understand why, she tried to keep a civil tongue in her head but the visions were both a gift and a curse. Her head would always pound for hours after one of her episodes and she needed to rest. When she'd had a few hours to recover she'd send as usual for Benedict de Ward, one of the cathedral canons. He was always willing to write down as much as she could remember of the vision and offer an interpretation. The pigeon would help too of course, these days he was her most faithful companion.

Scrivener came across de Ward sat on a bench in the great hall. The canon was a curious-looking fellow. Small and skinny, his clothes hung off him as though he'd recently survived a famine. In his mid-thirties he was balding and seemed to have lost several teeth at some point which gave him a pronounced lisp.

Scrivener took a seat opposite and said, "I believe the venerable Dame Dorothy has had another of her visions?"

De Ward said enthusiastically, "Indeed, I have only just heard myself. As soon as she's recovered I will record what she has to say. It's the first vision this year, I was thinking that perhaps the gift had left her."

"Yes, you must both be relieved, yourself and the Pigeon of Perception as I believe it's now known. Dorothy herself seems to suffer for her visions."

De Ward wasn't sure if Scrivener was mocking him or not. Just the thought made him bristle with indignation. He had no illusions it was he, and he alone, who had made Dame Dorothy famous.

"You may mock me Scrivener, as others have done before you. The fact is, the old maid had been prattling on for years, with no one taking a blind bit of notice I might add, before I took charge of things."

Scrivener smiled indulgently. "Far be it from me to mock de Ward. I'm genuinely intrigued. My understanding is old Bishop Thorndyke originally suggested your involvement?"

De Ward looked at Scrivener shrewdly. As far as he knew Scrivener and Bishop Gifford had seemed content to let the current arrangements continue. They'd certainly never discussed it with him in detail before. He decided to be candid. "As you know, Bishop Thorndyke was somewhat unorthodox. Dame Dorothy was one of his projects…"

"Ah, is that what he called it? I have the distinct impression that Dorothy was perhaps one of the old bishop's many mistresses. A noted beauty in her now distant youth?"

De Ward flushed, "I really wouldn't know about that."

Scrivener nodded. "Perhaps not. Still, as an anchorite she lived a far from austere life in her cell, even before your involvement."

"I'm not sure what you're implying?"

"No need to be so defensive de Ward. I'm aware of Thorndyke's dubious schemes to fill the coffers. I'm sure Dorothy has played her part, wittingly or not."

"You think Dame Dorothy a fraud then?"

"Come, come, de Ward, did I say that? I'm only curious. So, tell me about the pigeon."

De Ward, somewhat reluctantly said, "It was at Saint Margaret's fair, four summers ago now. There were men playing thimble-rig. You know the thing, three thimbles and a pea. The pea is placed under a thimble and they are mixed up. You wager on which thimble the pea is under."

Scrivener nodded. "I know the game, or should I say scam. Sleight of hand separates the witless from their coins."

De Ward shrugged, "I thought as much myself. The unusual thing was the pigeon."

"The Pigeon of Perception?"

"The same bird yes, although it was just a pigeon to me then. One of the players, a stooge probably, took a pigeon from under his cloak. He had it chose a thimble by pecking at it. It was remarkably successful."

"I've no doubt it was," scoffed Scrivener. "Drew a crowd did it?"

De Ward nodded. "Indeed, a considerable crowd. A lot of money changed hands."

Scrivener smiled knowingly. "Let me guess, you acquired this pigeon?"

De Ward squirmed in his seat uncomfortably and said, "I confess I did. You must understand the bird was most convincing."

"Perhaps not as much once you'd acquired it though? I won't embarrass you by asking how much you paid."

"It was foolish, I admit it. I was angry of course, I nearly throttled the bird, but then it occurred to me it could be put to use in another way."

Scrivener grinned. "Ah, I think I see where this leads. So the legend of the Pigeon of Perception was born?"

De Ward nodded proudly. "Bishop Thorndyke was most supportive of my idea."

"I bet he was, the devious old goat. So you record Dorothy's visions, perhaps impart some interpretation, and the pigeon picks which ones will come true?"

"Yes, I write each one down on a piece of parchment, lay them on a table and we allow the pigeon to peck at those it thinks will come true. It's made Dame Dorothy famous. The pilgrims are always keen to seek her advice. Even the new king has made a not inconsiderable donation to her upkeep."

"From what I hear the pigeon is nearly as famous as she is," said Scrivener.

"Yes, its attracted quite a following. I might add the cathedral has benefited enormously. Some pilgrims are attracted as much by Dame Dorothy and the bird as our famous shrines. The bird itself has turned out to be remarkably perceptive."

Scrivener regarded de Ward thoughtfully. "I'd very much like to see this pigeon in action. When will the bird be doing what it does?"

De Ward licked his lips nervously. "Perhaps an hour or two after vespers. Usually when I've recorded Dame Dorothy's visions I take the pigeon to the chapter house where it's quiet. The papers are laid out, and it chooses."

Osbert, hanging on for grim life, let the horse gallop the last few miles towards the city. He was a poor rider at the best of times, but the animal seemed to know the way well enough with little guidance. It was a blessing as in the gloom he had only the vaguest sense of his location.

It was only as the horse clattered across the bridge that led towards the south gate that he finally tried to exert some control over the sweating beast. He felt sure that they would gallop fun tilt into the huge oaken doors of the gate. It was still hours before the bell would sound for the end of the curfew in the city. The gates would remain barred until then. The horse came to a sliding halt feet from the iron-studded woodwork. Osbert dropped from the saddle, almost as exhausted as the horse itself. He knew it was useless to hammer on the gate. A single rider, not much more than a lad at that, would likely receive a torrent of abuse. He needed to get someone from the city watch to take him seriously. If he walked along the base of the wall he would eventually come to a higher section that indicated the start of the castle walls. No doubt there would be a sentry awake up on the sheriff's section of the walls, but he'd feel better if he could catch the eye of someone on the city watch.

He trudged along, leading the exhausted horse by the reins. He thought he saw some movement above.

He called, "Hey, you up there."

There was no response, so he shouted louder.

He definitely saw some signs of movement this time. A white face peered down at him from between the castellations.

"Be quiet fool," hissed the voice, "you'll have to wait for morning if you want in, just like everyone else."

"I need you to summon the sergeant of the watch, and then get the gatekeeper at the bridge gate to open up at once."

"Are you mad boy? Who the hell do you think you are to demand anything?"

Osbert bristled. "I'm an official of the bishop, my uncle is the bishop's secretary. This is a matter of life and death. You'll do as I bid or you'll find yourself chained up in the undercroft of the bishop's palace."

"You'd better draw closer to the wall then boy, I can hardly hear you."

Osbert drew his horse forward and received the contents of the guard's piss pot on his head.

He could hear the man above laughing. Between his guffaws the guard gasped, "Been tupping some young filly out in the sticks have you boy? You'd better learn to come home a bit earlier."

Osbert shook the filth from his cloak as best he could. Now furious, he scrabbled about on the ground until he found a stone and hurled it up at the battlements. He was rewarded with a yelp. He followed it up by shouting, "You ignorant clod. You'll be spending the next month cleaning out the guard room cess pit."

A face peered down at him and shouted angrily, "God's teeth boy, if I have to come down there I'll thrash you to within an inch of your life."

Suddenly an older voice from above said, "What the hell are you bawling about Alfred?"

"Some little bastard down there just threw a stone at me."

Another face appeared and peered down. Osbert looked back and recognised the sergeant of the watch.

He shouted up, "Sergeant, thank God. It's me, Osbert, the bishop's official, Bernard and Will need help, they're injured. You must summon the bishop and my uncle at once."

The sergeant peered into the gloom and finally nodded. "I recognise you, Scrivener's sister's boy isn't it? What the hell are you doing down there? The curfew bell is hours past. You'd better come to the gate boy."

"He's just thrown a bloody stone at me Sarge," whined the other man. Then gave a sharp yelp of pain. "What the hell was that for?"

Osbert heard the sergeant's voice say, "That's just to remind you what a stupid, lazy arsed idiot you are. Now get your backside down to the gate."

Although the hour was late Scrivener had persuaded his master to accompany him. He didn't quite know why he wanted the bishop to hear the old woman's strange prophesies, but he felt it important.

They walked together from the bishop's palace, across the cathedral green and into the great cathedral itself. As they passed the shrine of Saint Swithun, lit with a multitude of candles, the bishop came to a halt. Around the base of the shrine, interspace between the candles were heaped small wax images, left by pilgrims. They were formed into shapes representing recently injured or healed parts of the body. The bishop picked one up and examined it curiously.

"What would you say this is Scrivener?"

"Looks like a leg my lord, or perhaps an arm? It's hard to tell."

The bishop gently replaced it on the shrine, sighed and said, "And do you think the saint takes any notice of the pilgrim's offerings Scrivener? Or do we just encourage them so we can collect and sell the wax?"

Scrivener shrugged. "The income is useful my lord, and the offerings give the afflicted hope and a means for the healed to give thanks."

The bishop shook his head sadly and said, "I sometimes wonder where it will all end my friend, this pigeon business included."

They entered the great chamber of the chapter house and found it empty apart from de Ward. He appeared startled to see the bishop with Scrivener.

"My lord, I wasn't expecting you," he said nervously.

They came and stood beside him. Bishop Gifford gave a thin-lipped smile and folded his arms. "Scrivener persuaded me to come view you and this damn pigeon. So de Ward, I'm hoping to be enlightened."

The chapter house was a large circular room with a central stone column. It was located off the eastern cloister of the cathedral. Around the inside wall was a continuous run of benches where the dean and chapter would sit to discuss cathedral business. A table was built around the central column. On this de Ward had carefully laid out his papers. He'd lit enough candles to cast a golden glow over the proceedings. Scrivener reached out a hand to pick up one of the documents. De Ward swiftly said, "Please, don't touch the papers yet, not before the bird has chosen."

"Ah the bird," said the bishop, "so where is the famous Pigeon of Perception?"

De Ward gently reached under his cloak and withdrew the bird from some inner pouch. It lay nestled between his hands cooing gently and eyed Scrivener and the bishop curiously.

The bishop bent forward and eyed it back. "I suppose it's a fine-looking bird, mind you it'd look as good served at dinner tomorrow night."

De Ward quickly drew his hands back and cradled the pigeon to his cheek. He said outraged, "My lord! This is no ordinary pigeon, you can't suggest we send it for the table?"

The bishop held a hand up. "Rest easy my friend, my comment was said in jest. I wouldn't dream of eating the bloody bird. Anyway, if it's that good it'll know my intentions before I do and fly off."

Scrivener stifled a chuckle and said, "Perhaps you'd better let the bird do its work de Ward."

De Ward gently placed the bird on the table and it strutted slowly along the edge of the circular wooden top. It made a complete circuit without stopping.

"My understanding is the bird pecks at certain of the papers, yet it's stopped at none," said the bishop.

"It always walks around the column three times my lord, on the fourth it will make its choice."

The bishop nodded sagely. "Well, I'm glad to see it's not impulsive. At least it weighs the options up first, eh?"

Scrivener grinned at his friend, who raised his eyebrows back at him. De Ward chose not to reply and watched pensively until the pigeon circled the column for the third time.

"Now is the choosing," he whispered, and the candles seemed to respond to a sudden draft by flickering dramatically. Indeed, the bird now seemed to have changed its approach. It stopped at the first paper and cast a beady eye at it, then hesitated and moved on. It repeated the process at the next paper, but this time it cooed, bent down and gently pecked the surface. It walked on and de Ward swiftly responded by removing the paper into his hand.

"Ah," breathed the bishop, "we have our first prophesy I believe."

"When do you know it's finished?" asked Scrivener curiously.

"When it stops walking of course," whispered de Ward as though it was the most obvious thing in the world.

When the pigeon was done de Ward had three papers in his hand.

"What about the other papers?" asked the bishop.

"They never seem to come true my lord. I know not what they mean." He waved the papers in his hand. "As for these my lord, the bird is surely guided by God himself for they will come true soon enough."

The bishop eyed him sceptically, then held out his hand for the papers. "Then you'd better let me look at what our feathered friend has selected. I think its about time this little enterprise of yours came under closer scrutiny. What do you think Scrivener?"

"Indeed my lord. Perhaps we should all retire to your chambers and take some wine. De Ward you'll join us."

De Ward reluctantly handed over the papers to the bishop, placed the pigeon back under his cloak and followed them out of the chapter house.

Scrivener poured goblets of wine for each of them. De Ward sipped his with some relish, unused to the best Gascony which graced the bishop's table. The bishop sat on a stool beside the fire and picked up de Ward's papers. "Well then, let's see what Dorothy and the pigeon have predicted."

De Ward placed his wine on the table and took the famous bird from under his cloak. Once again it nestled in his hands softly cooing. He said, "I shall have to take it back to Dame Dorothy's cell soon. She gets agitated if the pigeon is absent for too long."

"I believe the woman has a fearsome temper?" said Scrivener.

De Ward grimaced. "She can be difficult it's true. Still, she has such a gift."

Suddenly the door burst open and the huge bulk of one of the palace guards stood panting in the doorway. He rested his hands on his knees and bent over, struggling for breath.

The bishop threw de Ward's papers onto the table and jumped up. "What the hell is the matter John?"

He gasped, "I ran all the way back from the gate my lord, I'm fair winded..."

The man stood struggling for breath. The bishop impatiently said, "Spit it out man, there's obviously something amiss?"

"It's young Osbert, Scrivener's nephew, down at the gate."

"I bloody well know who he is, now get to the point."

The man took a few more breaths and said, "Him, Bernard and Will, my lord, they've had a run in with Roger Mudstone. Bernard and Will are injured. He says the big man is hurt bad."

The colour drained from the bishop's face. He said, "Mudstone, Christ's bones. Someone fetch me my sword."

15

A RESCUE

Ralph of Shrewsbury sat in his favourite chair and gazed down on the inner courtyard of the bishop's palace far below. It was only first light and the air was chill. The shutters were wide open and he was wrapped deep in his dark black cloak. If he'd been visible to any below he would have looked much like a crow watching for carrion.

He had occupied the chambers, up here in the very corner of the bishop's palace, for longer than most other residents of the precinct had been alive. The only visitors, apart from the carefully chosen who served him, were generally of the unwilling kind. Access was via steep stairs and narrow passageways unknown to most. From the activity down below, he had already surmised that something out of the ordinary was occurring.

Men and horses were arriving from all directions. He recognised some as the sheriff's men and even more of the bishop's own household guards. There were shouts and muffled curses as equipment was fetched and horses were brought from the palace stables to be saddled.

There was the sound of the door opening behind Ralph

but he didn't turn his gaze away from the courtyard. He saw
the bishop's own grey mare being led out. The man himself
soon emerged, striding down the steps leading from the
great hall, followed by Scrivener and his nephew Osbert.
Ralph noted the bishop mounted his horse with practiced
ease. He looked more the old warrior than a cleric. There
were brief barked orders and the heavily armed party clattered out of the courtyard.

A hooded figure appeared at the side of Ralph's chair.
Without a word he held out a hand and was passed a folded
note. He broke wind noisily in anticipation of the note's
contents, the noxious fumes making the figure at his side
gasp for breath. He unfolded the note carefully and read
with interest.

A chuckle escaped his lips. He said softly, "I've underes-
timated Scrivener and the bishop. They set a trap, a crude
deception in some ways, but I believe I've allowed myself to
be somewhat deceived. How refreshing."

"Refreshing?" whispered the figure.

"It's a rare enough pleasure these days to be challenged.
It's been a long time." Ralph suddenly shuddered with the
thrill of possible discovery. He farted again, this time letting
rip. The figure by his side brought the long sleeve of the
cowl over its face and coughed. Ralph continued, more to
himself than his nasally challenged companion, "Mudstone
and the boy are expendable of course. They will be sacri-
ficed if needs be. Still, to snatch them away from the bishop's grasp would be more pleasing. You'll need to be quick,
do you hear me?"

The figure coughed and said, "But they are already
captured."

Ralph chuckled again. "The bishop's men who hold him
are apparently injured. I'm confident that a man like Sir

Roger, if he yet lives, will not stay captive for long. Of that
you may be sure. If the boy is with him, then so much the
better. "

The figure reluctantly said, "Then where shall I look?"

Ralph shrugged. "I have information that Mudstone has
been hiding in that old beachcomber's hovel down near the
river mouth. If he manages to escape he'll go there first. Find
them."

"And if I succeed, shall I bring them to Draychester?"

"Close by I think. What better place for them to hide,
almost in plain sight? You know the place to take them?"

"Yes."

"Have some restraint. I hear Mudstone can be very
trying. I know your temper and I don't want him dead just
yet."

As he crept slowly out of the anchorite's cell and into the
main body of the church Sir Roger hesitated. The boy was
leading the way. He sensed that Sir Roger wasn't following
and came to a halt.

"Please, we must go," he whispered.

"Wait," Sir Roger hissed back. It was almost pitch black.
Although Sir Roger couldn't see them, he could hear the
bishop's men snoring up at the main door. He turned his
head towards them, hatred radiating from him. His over-
riding instinct was to kill them both. He had no blade but he
was sure he could improvise. Still, he didn't think he was
capable of any sort of fight if it came to it. His head was
pounding and he could hardly move his arm. The pain in
his elbow was intense. Reaching a hand up to his face, Sir
Roger verified that he did indeed have a broken nose, not to

mention missing teeth. Reluctantly, he shuffled forward
again. The boy guided them towards the back of the church
and the small door that Sir Roger had entered through
hours before.

Emerging into the crisp night air had the instant effect of
clearing Sir Roger's head but set his broken teeth throbbing.
He leaned for a moment against the stonework of the
church to rest, despising himself for the weakness. He
grabbed the boy by the shoulder and whispered, "Go find
the horses and for God's sake be quiet about it. Don't even
think about disappearing, there's no place on this earth I
won't find you."

As the boy vanished around the corner of the building,
Sir Roger stumbled forward into the bushes at the edge of
the graveyard. At least he could get himself out of sight
while he waited. There was no telling when their escape
would be discovered. His arm felt hot and sticky, the blood
had oozed from the wound again. He cursed at the injustice
of it all. By all rights the bishop's men should be dead,
instead here he was, running away like a hound chastised by
its master. He looked up at the hazy moonlit sky and
muttered, "By all the saints' blood I'll have my revenge on
them all."

The cart rattled and rolled as it made its way down the
narrow lanes. Each rut in the road inflicted a bone jarring
jolt to the cart's occupants. The carter wincing said, "God's
teeth, I wouldn't normally bring a cart the way even if I was
on a promise with a whore. As far as I know there's nothing
down here but the beach. Have you got something down on
the sand that wants hauling back?"

The small hunched figure who sat next to him mumbled, "Something like that."

The carter turned and tried to see his companion's face but it was hidden deep within the hood of a black cowl. He pulled on the reins and slowed the cart. "Not much of a talker are you? You dress like a Benedictine but the more I think about it you're the damnedest monk I ever came across. What are you getting me involved in here?"

The cart came to a halt. The monk sighed deeply and turned to the carter. "Did I ask you to think? No. I just asked you to drive the cart. A simple enough request."

The carter reached out a hand as though to pull back the figure's hood. "You're no monk. Who are you?"

A hand emerged from one of the deep sleeves of the monk's cowl, it was clasping a thin-bladed dagger which was suddenly thrust into the side of the carter. As well as being excruciatingly painful it penetrated deep into a kidney. The carter gurgled once and slumped over.

The monk said, "And now look, I've had to kill you," and then gently pushed the dying man off the side of the cart.

The body landed with a splash in one of the muddy ditches by the side of the road and was all but covered by the dirty water. The monk grunted in satisfaction, took up the reins and urged the horse pulling the cart onwards. Within a few minutes the rutted track ended and they emerged onto the sand at the top of the beach. The monk brought the cart to a halt, looked around and saw the hoof prints made by a horse heading towards a sand dune. The monk grunted again, presuming the cottage would be concealed behind it somewhere. One thing the monk wouldn't be doing was walking in on Sir Roger Mudstone unannounced. The knight's reputation made that a suicidal gamble not worth taking.

Climbing down from the cart, the monk saw there were some pebbles rounded by the sea. They had been left behind by the worst of the winter storms at the top of the beach. The monk collected a few in each hand and walked towards the sand dune

Sure enough, there was a tumbled down cottage tucked in behind the dune. A quick glance confirmed there was a horse tied up at one side. There were no other obvious signs of life. The monk didn't approach any further but carefully transferred all but one stone into a left hand, and with the right hand hurled the remaining stone at the door of the cottage.

The stone ricocheted off the door with a boom. The hooded figure transferred another stone between hands and threw again. The door was suddenly flung open and a wild-eyed and blood stained Sir Roger Mudstone waving a sword attempted to charge out. He cursed as his battered body let him down and he came to a juddering stop on the sand only a few feet from the door.

"Who the devil are you? Come any closer monk and I swear I'll run you through."

From around the doorway peered the boy. He said, "Hold Sir Roger. I believe my master has sent somebody. I recognise her."

Sir Roger was confused, "You talk nonsense as usual boy, what do you mean her? Now, show yourself or by all the saints, you'll regret it."

The monk lowered the hood to reveal a dark-haired, plain faced young woman who looked back at Sir Roger with eyes like two hard flints.

She said, "I have a cart and two more cowls you can wear for disguise. I suggest if you want to live you'll follow me back to the cart. We can be at Draychester in an hour or two.

The bishop's men are no doubt already combing the countryside for you."

Sir Roger hissed back, "Draychester, are you mad? The day I take orders from a woman is the day I die and I still don't know your master's motives."

The woman shrugged. "Suit yourself." She turned around and started to walk back the way she'd come. The boy left the doorway, gave Sir Roger a wide berth and hurried after the receding back of the woman. Sir Roger shouted a string of obscenities at him but after a moment reluctantly decided to stumble after them.

The boy sat up front on the cart next to the woman. Both wore the black cowls of the Benedictines with the hoods covering their heads. Sir Roger lay in the back of the cart, similarly dressed. His head throbbed as did his injured arm and he felt feverish and weary. "Woman is this your rescue plan or is it your masters?" he asked.

The women bristled inside her hood. "I can be quite resourceful on my own. I have no need of a man to tell me how to carry out my orders."

Sir Roger snorted. "So it is your plan then. You think the bishop's men won't see through these disguises? It won't just be them either. They'll have raised the hue and cry across half the county. Every village idiot and his brother will be looking for us."

"Perhaps you'd rather get down from the cart and look to your own salvation then? From what I've seen, you've made a piss-poor job of things so far."

The boy gasped at her audacity. By now he knew Sir Roger's temperament all too well. Sir Roger crawled up the bed of the cart towards them. "By God woman, do you know who I am? Insult me again and I swear I'll thrash you to an inch of your life."

The woman slowed the cart and brought it to a stop. She turned around and looked down at him with utter contempt. "I don't think you're in any fit state to be making threats Mudstone. Do you? Now shut up or get off and die. The choice is yours."

Sir Roger said nothing more but his eyes radiated hate. She turned back to the road, but she could feel the simmering anger from behind. There was a madness in those eyes that chilled even her to the bone. If he got the chance he'd probably try to kill her, of that she had no doubt.

Sir Roger was constantly scanning the fields and path ahead as the cart bumped along the rutted road. They passed a few figures working in the fields and the occasional villager passed them on the road. Sir Roger kept his face hidden deep within his cowl as they passed by. The cart attracted nothing more than a cursory interest as far as he could tell. After a mile or too the woman directed the horse to the right down a narrow and muddy track running through over-hanging trees. The boy said, "You've turned off the way to Draychester."

The woman said sharply, "Of course boy. Did you think we'd be riding up to the very gates of Draychester in this cart?"

"I don't know what to think. I do know this isn't the way to Draychester," he said sullenly.

Sir Roger propped himself up in the back and looked about. "The boy's right woman. Where are you taking us?"

She sighed impatiently. "You're questioning me again? Do you think I am some simpering woman who knows nothing?"

Sir Roger tried to keep his anger under control. "If you're driving me to my death, I'd very much like to know."

After a moment the woman reluctantly said, "We head to the river. There's a barge moored there, it's carrying stone up to Draychester for the building works at the new guild hall. My master has an arrangement with the bargemen to bring things into the city, things we'd rather no-one else know about."

Sir Roger thought for a moment and grudgingly said, "It's not a bad plan."

"Thank you," she said sarcastically.

Sir Roger eased back down and without a hint of irony said, "You've got a big chip on your shoulder woman. You should be careful who you upset."

The woman ignored the comment and said, "When we get down to the river let me do the talking. This isn't the first time I've dealt with the bargemen."

There was a barge moored at the riverside, just as the woman had said. It was maybe thirty feet in length and ten feet wide and sat low in the muddy water of the Dray. There was some decking at either end where a man could stand with a long pole to navigate the river. In the middle were three open compartments loaded with rough-cut stone. A plank led from the barge to the riverside bank. Two men sat on the grass next to the plank eating bread and drinking from a wineskin passed between them. They turned curiously as the cart creaked to a stop at the end of the track.

The woman lowered the hood of her cowl and got down from the cart. One man, his mouth still half stuffed with bread spluttered, "Oh it's you. Wondered who'd be bringing a cart down here. Lucky you caught us, we're almost ready to get moving again."

The other man, thin, with a shrew like face, took a long swig from the wineskin and then wiped his mouth on his sleeve. He belched deeply and regarded them with bloodshot eyes. "If you're here you'll be wanting us to take something up river again."

The woman jerked her thumb back at the boy and Sir Roger. "Take them to Draychester. You'll keep them concealed as best you can."

The man gave another guttural belch and said, "You must be joking. Do you see anywhere to conceal two men? What they done?"

"You don't need to know and I'll pay you well for the trouble."

The woman brought out a leather bag from under her cloak and weighed it in her hand. The coins could be heard clinking from within. The man with the bread fixed greedy eyes on the bag. "Suppose we could move some stone around. They can sit on top of it and keep their heads down. No one pays us much notice anyway."

The belcher shrugged. "Suppose we could. The one in the back looks done in to me. Sure he won't die on us?"

The woman said, "Believe me, he's hardier than he looks. The boy can help him. They're to stay onboard the barge until it's dark. Then I'll come and fetch them. Get them there safely and you'll have more coin from me tonight. Enough so you can get drunk for a week if you like."

Belcher held out a hand for the money bag. The women dropped it into his palm. Sir Roger slowly shuffled down the back of the cart on his backside and gingerly lowered himself down. He hobbled to the front of the cart and barked at the boy. "Get your arse down here boy. Help me onto the barge."

The boy looked at the woman, who nodded. He reluctantly got down. "Where are you going?" he asked her.

"I'm taking the cart back to the city. It obviously can't be left here."

Sir Roger, from deep within his cowl, glared at the two bargemen. "Are we leaving or are you just going to stand there?"

16

DESPAIR

Will had been awake since first light. Perhaps some sixth sense had made him want to check on their prisoners. He'd managed to hop and stagger along the interior wall of the church to the opening of the anchorite's cell. Peering through the opening and finding only Travis in the cell, still tied up and asleep, he'd let out a cry of despair. Stumbling inside, he fell on Travis in a fury. Grabbing the man's flimsy tunic, he half dragged him up off the ground in a rage.

He shook him hard and shouted, "Where's your master Travis? Tell me now, or by all the saints I swear you'll regret it."

Travis hung from Will's arms like a rag doll. The effort made Will's injured leg throb so badly that he had to let go and Travis flopped back down in a heap.

Travis without looking up croaked, "He left in the night with the boy."

Will said, "I don't understand, why are you still here?"

"He didn't ask me to go with them, nor did he let the boy

untie me. He had a mind to kill me, I could see it in his eyes."

"Are you saying he's abandoned you to your fate?"

"I made my choices a long time ago Will. I wish he'd killed me before they left, I was more than ready for it, and God knows, I deserve it, I'm so weary of it all."

Will crouched down painfully and grabbed Travis by the chin and wrenched his head up. "Travis look at me. If you've a shred of decency left in your body, you'll tell me where he's gone. He can't believe he can get far, not in the state he's in."

Travis eyes were dull and lifeless. "You'll never capture him, you know that, don't you? The devil looks after his own. These last two years, the things I've seen him do, you wouldn't believe. I've let him destroy my soul and I'll burn in hell Will."

Will slapped him hard. "Travis, where has he gone? Think man, or have you completely lost your senses? What did he say before they left?"

Travis shook his head. "To find the boy's master, that's where he said he was going. I believe he also means to kill Dame Dorothy if he has the opportunity."

Try as he might he couldn't get anything else from Travis, it was as though the life had completely drained out of the man. It was lucky that Bernard could barely move, Will shuddered to think what the big man would be capable of given the circumstances. Travis's fate was in the hands of the bishop now, that's if anyone came to find them. He prayed that Osbert had arrived safely at Draychester.

The bishop, with Scrivener and a sizeable party of men,

arrived in Wynchworm an hour after dawn. Will and Bernard sat slumped against the wall of the church just inside of the door. The bishop crouched down in front of the battered pair and listened to their report intently. His face darkening when he learned of Sir Roger's escape. He stood up before they could offer any further explanation and strode outside and began barking orders. Men began to spread out from the church, scouring the derelict buildings of the village for the fugitives. Nothing was discovered and they were soon moving further afield in their quest.

Scrivener, not unkindly, held up a hand to silence any further detailed explanation from the men. "Save it for later my friends. Osbert has told us most of it. From the look of you I believe you did what you could. I for one am glad you're both still alive. For now, let the bishop do what he does best. He was a formidable solider once and he still is. I don't believe Mudstone can get far."

The bishop returned with two of his men. He gestured to the opening to the anchorite's cell where Travis was still confined. He had a murmured conversation and the two men nodded. One of them, built like a bull, flexed his hands, cracking the knuckles with a determination that boded ill for the captured man. The smaller of the two, a mean-looking fellow with sunken eyes and cheeks, took a wooden cudgel from under his cloak and cradled it in his hands. With a last curt order from the bishop, they strode over to the anchorite's cell and vanished through the opening.

Will shuddered and said to Scrivener, "It won't help him but I really don't think Travis knows much."

Scrivener nodded. "Still, it has to be done, you know that Will. Whatever he knows they'll make him give it up, you can be assured of that. As for you two, return to Draychester while I join the bishop. You look terrible by the way, did I say that?"

Will looked over to Bernard and saw he had lapsed into an exhausted sleep against the wall. Will said, "Thanks. I feel as rough as our big friend there looks."

Bernard lay despondent in the back of a cart on the way back to Draychester. Will sat beside him, wincing from the pain in his ankle as the cart jolted along the rough roads.

The big man said, "I should have killed him when I had the chance lad. But I've bested him once, I'll find the whoreson and do it again, only this time I'll finish the job."

Osbert riding wearily beside the cart said, "I for one hope to never set eyes on him again as long as I live."

Bernard peered over at Osbert through bleary eyes. "You did well last night lad. You must have ridden like the wind."

Osbert turned red. It wasn't often Bernard gave out praise. "I would have been faster if they'd taken me seriously at the city gate."

Bernard grinned. "Aye well, knowing them, at that time of day and long after the curfew bell, they probably assumed you'd been out sowing your wild oats."

Osbert spluttered in a mixture of embarrassment and indignity. Bernard and Will laughed and it seemed to break the air of gloom that had hung over them.

Will shook his head. "You know, maybe Travis is right, Mudstone has the luck of the devil or maybe at least the guile. How many times has he cheated his fate?"

Bernard said, "The state I left him in he can't get far and I doubt the lad will be much use. The bishop will scour the countryside for twenty miles around, he wants the man as much as we do."

Will nodded. "I pray you're correct. What I don't understand is how the man in the cathedral library fits, for he surely holds the key to this."

Osbert said, "Perhaps my uncle Scrivener has made progress in discovering his identity, he says the cook has also been murdered."

Will shook his head in amazement. "Why in God's name would someone murder the cook? It's madness."

"My uncle says the cook was a friend of that thief who was murdered and placed in the bishop's bath tub. He thinks they knew the identity of whoever is behind this, and that's why they were killed."

The bishop waited on his horse while two of his guards ransacked the tumbled down cottage for clues. Others went around the back of the building. He felt in his bones this was just the spot Roger Mudstone would choose for a hideout. It was certainly remote enough and well hidden. Someone had been down the track to the beach recently, there were cart tracks and footprints in the sand. He turned to Scrivener who sat impassively on his horse by his side. The bishop gestured to the cottage. "Didn't the old beachcomber who lived here turn up dead?"

Scrivener nodded. "You've a good memory my lord. It was two summers ago. About the time Mudstone came to Draychester to see us about his brother's will."

The bishop ran a hand over the stubble on his chin. "Not a meeting I'm likely to forget. I'm sure this is where they've been hiding."

"What little we got from the man Travis would seem to confirm it my lord."

The two guards emerged from the ill-fitting door of the cottage. "There's been someone here. We found embers of a fire that are still warm."

Another guard came from around the building and shouted, "There's fresh horse shit back here my lord. The beasts have been tied up around the back at some point."

The bishop sighed. "I presume our mysterious traitor is aiding them. By all accounts Mudstone was half dead, he can hardly have escaped unaided with only the boy for help. Those cart tracks and footprints aren't a coincidence. And where would you suppose they'd go Scrivener old friend?"

"Towards Draychester my lord." Scrivener said without hesitation.

The bishop nodded. "So, back to the city we go."

17

THE WAIT

Bernard moodily supped from his cup and said, "It's been what, a week? Where the hell do you suppose the whoreson is hiding?"

They were sat at the back of the Swan, a semi-respectable tavern close to the marketplace. Semi-respectable because you could occasionally buy wine instead of ale if the server thought you had the coin. The back of the Swan offered some partitioned booths where you could drink in private. Bernard sat on a stool, his upper body hunched over the small table cradling his wine between his huge hands.

Will and Osbert sat opposite on a long bench.

"It's more like ten days," Osbert said.

"And if we knew the answer to that question we wouldn't be sat in here," added Will.

They had been endlessly discussing the same question for days. Mudstone and the boy had vanished.

"Have they got anything more out of Travis?" asked Will.

Bernard shook his head. "He's not spoken a word since

they took him from the anchorite's cell in the church and believe me they've worked on him."

Osbert shuddered and crossed himself. "He sold his soul to the devil."

"Where is he now?" asked Will.

Bernard said, "Chained up in the undercroft under the bishop's great hall. He'll hang and maybe suffer worse before that. Stupid bugger. I don't know why he doesn't just tell all he knows, it'll be easier on him in the end. Wouldn't be surprised if he's lost his mind."

Will nodded. "Will they wait to hang him until Mudstone is captured?"

Bernard gave a humourless laugh. "Who knows when that will be. Half the bishop's guard and some of the sheriff's men have been out scouring the countryside every day for the last week. Nothing. The other half have been searching in the city. There's not a trace of them."

"My uncle and the bishop are convinced they came here to Draychester," said Osbert.

From the front of the room there came sounds of a scuffle and raised voices. Bernard raised an enquiring eyebrow.

Will sighed, put his cup down on the table and stuck his head around the wooden partition.

A tall, scrawny looking man, with a rough woollen tunic was trying to force his way through the front door of the tavern. He was evidently drunk given his bleary eyes and the string of slurred obscenities coming out of his mouth between guttural belches. An equally thin lad, who Will recognised as the taverner's son, was trying to push him back out. The struggle seemed to be in a stalemate as neither appeared to have the physical strength to overcome the other.

The other patrons of the tavern sat around looking at the struggle with amusement and offered the lad the odd encouraging word whilst continuing to drink. No one moved to assist him and there was a roar of laughter when the drunken man kneed him in the bollocks.

"What is it?" asked Bernard.

"Just some drunk struggling with the taverner's boy."

There was a collective intake of breath from around the room. Will stuck his head around the partition again.

He sighed and said, "They've got the knives out now."

Bernard stood up and moved out beyond the partition. He folded his arms and leant against the wall to watch. "I like a good knife fight."

From across the room strode the taverner himself. He carried a heavy wooden cudgel. He barked, "John, leave him to me. I've warned him more than once."

The boy, still on the floor cradling his groin in one hand and a knife in the other, crawled away across the floor. The drunk came weaving after him half heartedly brandishing a dagger. The taverner, never breaking stride, walked right up to him and smacked him in the side of the head with the cudgel. The drunken man collapsed to the floor like a sack of grain. A great cheer went up from the watching drinkers.

Will winced, "Christ's bones, that'll hurt when he finally wakes up. If he ever does."

The taverner grabbed hold of the lifeless man by the chin and dragged him towards the back of the tavern.

As he passed Bernard the big man nodded amiably and gestured at the unconscious man. "Afternoon Tom. What's his story then?"

The taverner stopped and nodded a greeting. "Bernard. Just some drunk. Been causing trouble in every alehouse on the street for the last week. I stopped him coming in here a few days ago. Won't take no for an answer, the bloody fool."

Bernard prodded the man with his foot. He was a curious-looking figure with thin legs and strong thick muscled upper arms with the face of a weasel. He wore cheap clothes and worn-out boots.

"Know who he is?" asked Will curiously.

The taverner shrugged, "Henry at the Lamb says he's some sort of river man, Nicholas by name. Been drunk as a lord all week and caused trouble in every alehouse and tavern he's entered."

Will said, "How does a simple river man afford to be drunk for a week?"

"Had a leather bag of coins when I saw him last. The fool was brandishing it about. Surprised no one has cut his throat."

"What are you going to do with him," asked Osbert.

"There's a midden heap at the bottom of the yard out back. I'd thought to leave him sleeping it off on top of it."

Bernard grinned. "Quite a crack to the head you gave him there. You may have addled his brains."

The taverner shrugged again. "No one pulls a blade in here unless it me, and especially not on my own son."

Will said, "I'm still curious. I'd like to know where he got that coin. It's not been honestly earned that much I know."

Bernard rubbed his chin, puzzled. "What are you thinking, some connection with our troubles?"

Osbert said. "The river runs north to Draychester from near that abandoned cottage the Bishop and Scrivener found."

"It does, doesn't it? And he's a strangely wealthy river man," murmured Will.

Bernard clapped a friendly hand on the Tavener's shoulder. "Leave this one to us Tom."

The taverner looked like he wanted to ask more. He glanced between the three of them, thought better of it and shrugged. "He's all yours, just get him out of my sight."

The three of them exited through a back door, Bernard dragging the unconscious river man by the feet. The yard behind the tavern was full of dirty water and filth, and the side of the man's face was soon caked in it.

"Careful," said Will, "You'll drown the poor sod."

The stench was foul. Will supposed the patrons of the Swan frequently relieved themselves out here. Bernard grinned and dragged the man over to the midden pile and propped his head up on it just clear of the surrounding mud. He pushed the man's head over to one side to examine the huge swollen lump left by the taverner's cudgel.

"He's not going to come around anytime soon. Not after a blow like that. Hours I would guess. We'd better search him."

Bernard produced a knife and expertly cut the man's belt and dragged off his tunic. There was a leather bag with a drawstring stuffed into the top of his hose. Bernard gingerly extracted it. He opened it and poured a pile of coins into his hand. He grunted in surprise.

Will said, "He's been drunk for a week and he's still got that much coin left? No doubt there was a lot more to start with."

"I will need to record the exact amount, everything will need to be accounted for," said Osbert, taking the leather tube of quills and the inkhorn from his belt.

"Christ's bones, are you purposely trying to annoy me?" said Bernard. He poured the coins back in the bag and thrust it with force at Osbert. "You'd better be quick, we're all going down to the river."

The three of them made their way down the narrow alleyways that led towards the riverside. The path became steeper and dirtier as they approached the actual water front. At one point a group of apprentices came chasing after a barrel filled with stones, whooping in delight as it thundered past the three bishop's men who were pressed against a wall. Bernard aimed a kick at them and shouted obscenities after their receding backs.

The filth in the street ran down unchecked towards the river and it was difficult to keep their feet dry. Osbert uncharacteristically cursed as he slipped on what look suspiciously like an old turd and nearly fell. Will and Bernard roaring with laughter grabbed him by the arms to keep him upright. Osbert red faced said, "Is it really necessary for us to come down here."

Will wiping tears from his eyes said, "It was you who pointed out the river connection."

"You don't normally take any notice of my suggestions," he grumbled.

"For once I think you may have pointed us in the right direction. What say you Bernard?"

The big man grunted. "A river man with that amount of coin is worth us taking an interest. What other trail have we to follow at the moment?"

They emerged from a passageway between two low squat warehouses. They were on a wide strip of stonework fronted by wooden decking resting on piles driven deep into the side of the riverbank. The wharf was a hive of activity.

Although the Dray was only navigable by shallow bottomed vessels this far from its mouth, the waterfront was continually being expanded. There was trade in wool, grain, timber, iron, salt, wine, cloth, wax, dried fish and a hundred other commodities to feed, clothe and support Draychester's increasing population.

A barge was being unloaded directly onto the wharf and there were barrels and crates scattered all around. A line of men was working to move the goods from the vessels onto the wooden decking. Two carts stood waiting to be loaded. Just out on the river were more barges loaded with stone. At each end of the barge stood a man with a long pole for manoeuvring the vessel.

One of them shouted. "By all the saints, what is taking you so long you whoresons? We've stone to unload before nightfall."

One of the men on the wharf turned and dropped his hose to show his bare hairy behind and bawled, "Kiss my arse. Wait your bloody turn." The rest of his fellow workers roared with laughter as did Will and Bernard.

Osbert watched on with his usual disapproving look.

Will still grinning said, "I do believe we're at the very bottom of the city, in more ways than one."

Bernard approached one of the men unloading and asked, "You know a Nicholas, a riverman, face like a weasel, thin and skinny?"

The man regarded Bernard for a moment, then nodded. He said, "That would be Nicholas the useless, foul-mouthed, drunken trouble maker you're asking after?"

Bernard grinned and nodded back. "Sounds like we're taking about the same man."

"Not seen him in a week, maybe more. You looking for him?"

"Oh I know where he is. I want to know who he works with?"

The man pointed out into the river at the waiting stone barges. "He's one of them, stone barge man, useless buggers all of them."

Will asked, "Will you be long unloading? We need to talk to them."

The man shrugged. "We're taking our time to piss them off."

Bernard grinned again. "Then I guess we'll have to wait."

The three bishop's men leant against the wall of one of the warehouses while the barge was slowly unloaded. The sun was warm in the afternoon sky making Will feel sleepy. He rubbed his eyes, yawned and looked at the stone barges waiting on the river. "I didn't think the bishop was adding to the cathedral at the moment Osbert?"

Osbert shrugged. "It's not for the cathedral. I believe this stone is destined for the new merchant adventurers' hall. The guild has big plans "

"And plenty of coin," added Bernard.

Will said, "So where's all this stone coming from?"

Osbert gestured down river. "Down along the coast somewhere. It's shipped as far up the Dray as they can get it on a cog, then transferred to the barges to bring it to the city. The guild wants their new hall finished this year."

"How do you know all this Osbert?"

"I have a good memory and I overhear a lot of things."

"Remind me not to tell you any secrets," said Bernard.

Will laughed. "Do you have any secrets Bernard?"

"We all have secrets lad," the big man gestured to the water. "And before I get the chance to tell you any, it looks like we can finally ask some questions."

The stone barges were moving towards the now empty

wharf. There was some bad tempered shouting between the barges as they manoeuvred alongside. When they were close enough, the man at each end jumped up onto the wharf holding a rope which they tied off around wooden stumps.

With four bargemen now on the wharf, Bernard called across. "Nicholas the bargeman. He works with you?"

The men regarded Bernard with suspicion and not a little nervousness. Eventually one of them said, "Who's asking?"

"A friend."

One of the others said, "He doesn't have any friends. And if he did, you don't look like any kind of friend he'd have. Friend."

The man hawked and then spat a green glob onto the wharf directly in front of Bernard. Will and Osbert winced and took a step back to allow Bernard the space he was surely going to need. The big man advanced and the bargemen, apart from their cocky spokesman, edged back towards the water.

Bernard shook his head sadly. "You know what I hate the most, it's people with disgusting habits. My old mum taught me spitting was the worst of the lot, she'd give me a clip around the earhole for spitting."

"A dirty whore was she?" asked the man flippantly. Never taking his eyes off Bernard, he reached down and pulled a dagger from the back of his boot.

Barnard took a step forward and gave an evil grin. "You know I think she may have been. Perhaps she knew your dad? We could be related." His hand shot out with lightening speed, knocking the man's dagger from his hand. It arced away and landed in the water with a splash. He grabbed the man in a crushing embrace around the shoulders.

"And as family we really shouldn't be keeping things from each other now should we?" Bernard said, forcing the bargeman to his knees.

"God's teeth you're going to break my legs," moaned the man. His companions made no move to assist, common sense prevailing over any sense of solidarity.

Bernard increased the downward pressure on the man whilst keeping an arm locked around his neck. "So, back to Nicholas. He seems to have a lot of coin. Enough in fact to be drunk for a week. Now why would that be?"

The bargeman said, "We've not seen him for a week, I swear. If you know where he is, why not go ask him?"

Bernard smiled. "You know I might just do that, if he ever wakes up from the crack on the head he's just received in the tavern."

He eased the downward pressure slightly from around the man's shoulders and dragged him by the neck over to one of the wooden stumps. With one hand he heaved on the rope tied around it to create some slack. He shoved the man's head under it and then released his hold. The pull of the barge tightened the rope and pinned the man by the neck against the post. The man's eyes bulged as he choked and he scrabbled with his hands against the thick hemp rope. Bernard squatted down in front of him and said, "So, let's start again. Where did he get all that coin?"

The man croaked, "A woman paid us for a job."

Bernard nodded. "A woman. That's interesting. For what?"

The man fought for breath and spluttered, "Brought two monks up river on the barge. I need air."

Bernard stuck one of his fingers between the rope and

the man's neck. It eased the pressure just enough for the man to draw in a shuddering breath before Bernard withdrew the finger.

"Where did you take them?"

"Here to the wharf. Air, please."

Bernard pulled the rope away from the man's neck again.

"You've had dealings with this woman before?"

The man gulped air. "She always comes to us, I don't know her name. We bring things up river for her, she always pays well."

"And you don't know who she is, you've never been curious?"

"I swear I don't know her name. I saw her once in town, going through the precinct gate." The man started to splutter and turn blue. Bernard grabbed hold of the rope and pulled it fully clear of the man's neck. It had left a bright red mark gouged into his skin.

"How old is she?"

The man gasped for air again, trying to speak, his mouth gaping like a fish on the riverbank. Eventually he said, "She's not a girl, but two score and ten, no more. Plain looking. A servant?"

Bernard shook the rope in a beefy hand. "You tell me."

The man said. "Yes, yes, she looks like a servant."

Bernard nodded and loosened the rope even more. "These two monks, where did they go after leaving the wharf?"

"She came for them, brought a cart down here. One of them looked injured, the other, not much more than a boy, helped him in. I don't know where they went."

Bernard grunted. Still squatting, he turned his head around to look at Osbert and Will who were leaning against the wall watching. "So now we're getting somewhere."

Will said slowly, "Two monks, one injured. Where would you go?"

Osbert replied, "Dressed as monks, to a monastery."

"My thoughts exactly," said Will with a smile.

The abbey of Saint Mary lay only half a mile from the city of Draychester across the river Dray. One of the major roads from the city led across a bridge and directly passed by the abbey's gatehouse. Even at the best of times it made for an uneasy relationship between city and abbey.

Abbot Richard was not happy about the fugitives he'd taken in. Not that he'd had any choice in the matter. The abbey's chief benefactor had seen to that. The abbot knew little of the shadowy figure from the city who provided a generous portion of the abbey's income. His predecessors had established the arrangement years before, something they came to bitterly regret. He only realised the full extent of the poisoned chalice he'd inherited when he became abbot. Mostly their benefactor stayed out of their affairs, but when he made demands, well, they couldn't be refused.

The abbot's ever whining prior, a limp and scrawny waste of a man called Duncan, predictably was outraged at the turn of events. "What were you thinking agreeing to this? If they are discovered here we'll be ruined."

The abbot hissed back, "It wasn't some request Prior, it was an order. You know as well as I Duncan that I simply had no choice in the matter."

The prior wrung his hands in nervous tension, "Brother Abslem was up at the bishop's palace yesterday. Bishop

Gifford is in a fearsome rage, he has men scouring both the city and countryside."

The abbot took a gulp of rich red wine from his ornate goblet, his hands trembling. "Well, he's not going to find them, is he? Not when we have them hidden away here behind our own walls."

"We can't keep Mudstone hidden in your chambers much longer. You know it's impossible to conceal things in a place like this."

The abbot glared at the prior. "What would you have me do Duncan? If you have a better suggestion now is the time to voice it Prior."

The prior whimpered, "It's only a matter of time before the search moves closer to the abbey."

The abbot ran a hand over his tired face. "Perhaps not, perhaps it'll all just blow over. Anyway, they wouldn't dare search the abbey, and certainly not my own chambers, I won't allow it."

"You might not have a choice."

The abbot was getting irritated. How he wished the problem would just disappear. "Can you do nothing but whine Duncan? If you must speak, then for God's sake, think of something constructive to say."

The prior helpfully suggested, "We could ask them to leave. Mudstone is more mobile now."

The abbot barked a bitter laugh. "Do you not know his reputation prior? I dare you to ask him to leave, he'll snap that scrawny neck of yours like a twig. Frankly, I'd rather face the bishop's men."

"This is intolerable. How on earth did we get into this situation?"

The abbot shoved the wine jug across the table. "Greed and pride prior, pure greed and pride. I'm sure we'll be made to regret it. For now drink some wine and pray our benefactor is of sounder mind than our unwelcome guests."

When Sir Roger had first arrived at the abbey he could hardly walk from the beating he'd taken. The abbot, petrified of the consequences of discovery and wishing to conceal his unwelcome guests from the rest of the brothers, had Sir Roger placed in his own bedchamber. The boy was easier to conceal and was hidden in a seldom used room in the guesthouse. Days later, Sir Rogers's body was still black and blue but the cuts had long since been salved and stitched by the infirmarer, Brother William.

The broken stumps of his front teeth were more troublesome. Sir Roger's constant cursing and groaning with the pain had led the abbot to summon Brother William once again. The old man had examined the injured man's mouth and administered a few drops of poppy juice from a small bottle which he mixed with a generous amount of water. The pain relief had been almost immediate, and Sir Roger had slumped into a drug-induced slumber.

The abbot's relief was almost as heartfelt. "Thanks be to God. It's a pity we can't keep him drugged all the time. You know why he is here William? You were a man of the world once, we discussed this before. As few people as possible need to know about this. You understand me?"

The old man regarded his abbot with a shrewd gaze and said, "I shall, as always, keep my counsel but it will be hard to keep his presence here secret for long. It would also be unwise to keep him drugged."

"If anyone asks he's a distant relative, taken ill on a personal visit to me."

The old man shrugged. "As you request my lord."

Hours later, when Sir Roger awoke in pain again, he had forced the abbot to call Brother William to administer more of the juice. He wrenched the bottle away from William and poured some into a cup of water, swirled the mixture around and downed the lot. He placed the bottle under his tunic. As William turned to leave, Sir Roger's arm shot out and grabbed the old man painfully by the wrist. "The poppy juice brother, is it dangerous?"

The brother squinted at the disfigured man, then nodded slowly. "More than a few drops at once and it can be fatal. If you take it for too long a period then you'll need it every day just to function."

As Sir Roger's eyes glazed over he murmured, "Sounds just like a good wine."

The old man nodded again. "Even too much wine can become addictive my son. This is much more powerful, be careful if you wish to wake again."

Sir Roger dripped the poppy juice into his cup of wine and then downed it in one go. He looked up at the abbot, his pupils visibly swelling. His entire appearance unnerved the abbot. From the dead eyes, via the black and blue of the broken nose, the rough beard that failed to cover the hideous angry red scar of the letter branded there, down to the broken stumps of the front teeth. With shaking hands, the abbot gulped from his own goblet of wine.

Sir Roger was sitting on the edge of the abbot's own bed. He ran a tongue over the stumps of his front teeth and winced. "Your benefactor in the city, who is he abbot?"

The abbot said, "You don't know him yourself, even though he protects you by forcing us to hide you?"

Sir Roger hauled himself up onto unsteady feet and leaned towards the abbot. "The boy has told me little, and I didn't get the chance to force it from him. I'll ask you again. Who is this man?"

The abbot said bitterly, "I've never met him though he makes his presence and his wishes known through others."

"Like the woman who brought us here?"

"Yes."

"Tell me, what hold has he over you?"

The abbot looked into Sir Roger's dead eyes and hesitantly replied, "My predecessors were greedy and prideful, they squandered the abbey's funds to a great extent. We have few such wealthy benefactors. Without his help we would have been in disgrace, forced to leave this place."

Sir Roger smirked through his broken teeth. "Ah, now it becomes clear, he controls the purse strings."

"Yes, for many years now."

Sir Roger swept his eyes around the abbot's richly furnished bed chamber. "Still, it doesn't seem like he keeps you too deprived."

The abbot nodded. "He has undoubtedly been very generous. But the abbey doesn't control its own destiny. Only God should have such power."

Sir Roger lay back on the abbot's luxurious bed and laughed until his eyes streamed with tears. The abbot shrank back. Eventually Sir Roger's chuckling turned into a hacking cough. When that too had subsided he croaked, "Tell me, what instructions did the woman give to you?"

"To conceal you here against those who seek you. My understanding is the bishop, amongst others, desires your capture."

"Nothing more?"

"The woman would return at some stage with more instructions for us both. Frankly, the longer you stay, the more worried I become."

Sir Roger gave the abbot a death stare that chilled him to the core. "I need to speak to the boy, bring him to me."

The boy stood next to the abbot's bed where Sir Roger lay sprawled. On Sir Roger's chest was a sliver platter on which lay half a roast chicken. A goblet of wine stood on a small table on the opposite side of the bed just in reach of his hand. Sir Roger's broken teeth meant that he was forced to tear the chicken up into small strips and his greasy fingers had left stains on the abbot's fine linen. The abbot reflected sadly that they were probably ruined and in any case he'd have to have the whole thing stripped and burnt when he got rid of the obnoxious fugitive.

Sir Roger said, "So glad you could join us abbot. This chicken is delicious by the way, my compliments to the cook. The wine is not bad either. Gascony?"

The abbot nodded reluctantly.

"Thought as much, none of the rough stuff for the good brothers I'll wager? Or is this stuff just for you? Don't tell me, it is, isn't it? Nothing wrong with a few vices abbot, I won't tell anyone."

The abbot, red faced, asked, "What more is it you want of me, or of the abbey itself?"

"Don't worry, we'll get to that. I've been having a little chat with the lad here. For one of such tender years he's already remarkably corrupt. A black soul indeed, and he learns fast. With the right guidance, I'm sure he'll go far.

Reminds me of myself at his age. The happy days of one's youth, eh?"

Sir Roger took a long drink of wine from his cup and dropped a few strips of chicken in his mouth. He chewed carefully, wincing a little before swallowing. The abbot looked on somewhat bemused.

Sir Roger wagged a finger at the abbot. "Now from all I've heard the boy's master must be a truly a remarkable man. He's led me on a merry dance and believe me, I'm not a man easily deflected from my purpose."

The abbot held up his hands in an apologetic gesture. "As I've said, I've never met him."

Sir Roger nodded amiably. "So you've said, and I believe you. Between us all it seems the boy, is in fact, the only one who has actually met this mysterious man. He even seems to hold the lad in some regard, perhaps sees him as a protégé."

The abbot, nervous but now filled with an over-whelming curiosity, turned to the boy and blurted, "Who is he boy? You must tell me at once."

The boy looked sullenly back but didn't say a word. Sir Roger grinned through his broken teeth.

"Thought that might pique your interest abbot. It seems his master normally prefers to keep his various schemes at arm's length. As for myself, well I usually like to get up close and personal."

"I'm not sure I understand you?"

"I'm sure you don't. Step a little closer and I'll tell you everything."

As the abbot moved forward Sir Roger whipped the plate from his chest with his left hand. The chicken flew faster than it ever had when alive and crashed into the wall with a greasy splat. The abbot watched it's flight until the

plate crashed into the side of his head and sent him staggering towards the boy who produced a dagger from under
his tunic. The boy grabbed the startled man's cloak, pulled
him close and jabbed him brutally in the guts, twisting the
knife and driving the blade as deep as he could until he felt
it scrape against bone. He pulled the knife out and the
abbott sank to the ground with hardly a sound but with a
spreading red stain soaking through his clothing.

Sir Roger lay back on the bed, arms folded behind his
head. He nodded approvingly. "Nicely done lad. Shame we
wasted the chicken though, I'm still hungry."

The boy looked down at the body and went off to retch
in the corner of the room.

Sir Roger began methodically searching the abbott's chambers. The boy moved to help, but Sir Roger waved him back
towards the wall.

"I've done this a thousand times boy. It'll be quicker if
you just watch. On second thoughts you can get the good
abbot there into his own bed. He's bleeding like a stuck pig.
Strip him and use his clothes to mop that blood up off the
floor, we'll be covered in it soon enough if you don't."

Sir Roger opened a chest that sat in a corner. It was full
of papers. He pulled these out onto the floor, then stood
back. The chest seemed deeper from the outside than it did
when he peered into the now empty interior. He placed a
foot inside and jerked his heel down. The false bottom of
the chest broke, revealing a further space below. He pulled
the splintered wood away and retrieved four leather bags.
He picked one up, opened the drawstring and poured silver
coin out into his hand. Sir Roger turned to the boy and said,

"Mark my words boy, you'll never meet an abbot who doesn't have some coin put away for a rainy day or to pay for the services of a good whore."

The boy wiped the vomit from his lips and met Sir Roger's gaze but said nothing. He reluctantly dragged the body of the abbot by his feet towards the bed. It left a trail of thick red blood across the richly woven rug.

"You don't say much, do you? I like that about you boy. Silence is a much underrated virtue."

They were both startled by the sudden opening of the outer door to the abbot's chamber. The prior stood frozen in the doorway, his mouth hung open in silent shock at the scene.

Sir Roger moved without hesitation as the prior sprang back to life and turned to flee. With well practised ease he grabbed him from behind and clamped a hand over the prior's mouth before he could make a sound. Sir Roger dragged the now struggling man back into the room and closed the door with a swift kick of his boot. "Bloody hell. I was hoping we could do this without too much trouble." He gripped the prior's neck tightly in the crook of his arm and twisted the man's head to one side with a sickening crunch. The prior went limp and Sir Roger released him to fall to the floor.

The lad looked at the fresh body and back to Sir Roger. Sir Roger looked around the room and shrugged. "Shove this one under the bed. He's only a thin little runt, he should fit snugly."

Some sixth sense alerted Brother William that something was wrong. He woke from a restless sleep and lay still on the

hard bed, his arthritic hip and knees were a dull background pain. The joints of his big toes a sharper one as he
flexed them. He remembered that some passing physician, a
guest of the abbot, had once tried to sell him a paste made
of pigeon dung, supposedly spread on the soles of the feet it
would ease the pain. He snorted at the memory.

But it wasn't his aching bones that had pulled him from
sleep. It was something else. The small window in his cell
was still dark. He judged Matins was still some hours away,
and the abbey was quiet. One benefit of being the infirmerer
was that he had his own cell, and no one questioned his
movement around the abbey night or day. There was always
a sick brother to tend or a pilgrim needing his attention in
the guesthouse.

The old man hadn't always been a monk. Unlike many
of his fellow brothers, he'd once had a life in the outside
world. He'd followed the king's armies tending the
wounded, his skills appreciated and sought after. His calling
to God had come to him late in years and now it suited him
well enough, this quiet, contemplative life in the abbey. For
all that, he retained a keen sense of the ways of the world.
He didn't know what games the abbot and the prior were
involved in, nor did he much care. What he was sure of was
that they were far out of their depth. The man he'd been
treating in the abbot's chambers was a sure born killer.
William knew his type from old, he had the look of a mercenary and was arrogant and self assured with it. Outside the
walls of the abbey he knew the man, and the boy who had
arrived with him, were being sought.

The old man hauled himself upright and dressed
quickly. He made his way from his chamber out into the
inner courtyard of the abbey. He paused a moment. There
was a slight breeze, and the sky was dark but not entirely

starless. He hurried over the cobbles towards the abbot's lodge. He lifted the wooden latch and pushed the heavy oak door inwards into the narrow passageway that led into the building. It was darker here, which made him nervous, but Brother William knew the way well. There wasn't a sound to be heard, and as he advanced into the heart of the building he saw nobody, neither lay brother nor monk.

Brother William stood outside the abbot's chamber and without knocking opened the door. There was a dim light from the remains of the fire. Listening intently, he heard nothing at all, not a breath or a snore. The hair on the back of his neck, what little remained of it, stood up. There was nothing untoward visible in the main room. He stepped inside and moved towards the bedchamber. There was a definite shape in the bed.

"My lord," he whispered.

Then louder, "My lord abbot."

Brother William walked over and gently shook the figure. There was no response, he needed some light to be sure of what he suspected. He walked back into the main room, closed the still open door and fumbled about until he found the horn light on the table. Removing the candle, he knelt down in front of the fire and blew on the embers. Managing to conjure a flame, he lit the candle. The room was cast in a flickering golden light. Finding some more candles, he lit them all. Brother William entered the bedchamber again and studied the figure in the bed. The abbot appeared to be lying face down under his covers, an unnatural position for the abbot he was sure. Pulling the coverings back made him draw in a sharp breath at the crimson stain oozing out from beneath the naked man. He was unsteady on his feet now, not just because of the shock. Looking down, Brother William realised his foot rested on

what appeared to be a hand sticking out from under the
bed. With trembling knees he bent down and looked under
the bed. The pale white face of the lifeless prior stared back
at him. He struggled to drag the upper part of the prior's
body from under the bed, revealing the unnatural angle of
his broken neck. From what he could judge neither of them
were long dead.

Brother William knelt there on his arthritic knees next
to the abbot's bed and said, "How dare you bloody die like
this. Had you no thought of your fellow brothers? The
scandal will surely ruin us all. Inconsiderate to the last, both
of you."

He eventually got to his feet and walked back to the
other room and sat in the abbot's chair. The soft padding
cradled his old bones, and he sighed contentedly. He
stretched out his legs and leant back. It had been some years
since he'd sat in such a chair, well before his time at Saint
Mary's Abbey. Looking around the abbot's chambers, he
took in the rich wall hangings, the golden candlesticks and
goblets. Through the door to the bedchamber he could see
the fine coverings on the bed where the abbot himself now
lay dead. Perhaps he'd been too hasty in leaving the outside
world, he realised he did in fact miss such things. Was it
really such a sin to feel that way, to seek some creature
comforts in his old age? He rubbed a hand over his old
nobbly skull and came to a decision.

Moving back to the abbot's bedchamber, he stood over
the naked body of his deceased superior. He hesitated a
moment and then rolled him over. The abbot's dead eyes
stared up at him accusingly. The killer had been brutal.
He'd seen such wounds and worse before. Even so Brother
William's stomach lurched and he reproached himself, this
was no time to be squeamish. He turned his attentions to

the prior, who still lay half under the bed. The prior's light and scrawny frame was easily moved, and William dragged the body fully clear from the bed. It was only slightly more difficult to strip the body. It was now where some strength would be required. Brother William bent down and grabbed the prior under the armpits and dragged him back to the bed. This time with considerable difficulty he manoeuvred the prior up onto the bed beside the abbot. He stepped back and considered the scene. It needed something more. With even more effort, he rolled the prior face down on top of the abbot. He walked back into the other room and looked about. There were two chests in the room. He opened one and found it empty and with a broken bottom. In the other chest he found clothes and a small dagger that he recognised as the abbot's. He picked it up and took it back to the bedchamber and pressed the fingers of the prior around it. Finally he flung the coverings back over them both, then carefully extinguished the candles and left the abbot's chambers to the dead.

Will stood at the end of the abbot's bed and looked at the macabre scene. "A crime of passion you say Brother William? You suspected nothing between them before this?"

Brother William stood at the doorway to the bedchamber and said, "Not until one of the lay brothers found them this morning. We had already convened a chapter meeting when you arrived, it's a very delicate matter. We were of course about to send a message to the bishop."

"It's an unnatural act, that's what it is brother. They were tempted by the devil," said a horrified Osbert.

Bernard leant against the wall in the abbot's bedchamber, his arms folded, said, "Don't be so naive Osbert. I dare say there may be many such in a monastery. Still, I don't believe the truth of what you say happened here brother."

Brother William, grey-faced, said. "I'm not sure I understand you?"

"That's the prior on top is it?" asked Bernard.

Brother William nodded.

Bernard said, "Give me a hand Will, let's roll him off the abbot."

"Really?" asked Will with obvious distaste.

"Don't be squeamish. It'll take but a moment."

Brother William said, "I must protest, it is most unseemly."

Ignoring Brother William, Bernard pulled the dagger from the prior's dead fingers and then with Will's help pushed the now rigid body off the abbot's corpse.

Osbert gagged at the site of the brutal wounds covered in congealed blood that were revealed on the abbot's abdomen. He covered his mouth, pushed past Brother William and fled the room.

Will felt slightly queasy himself, it wasn't a pretty sight. He focused his attention elsewhere. "Have you seen the prior's neck Bernard? It looks like it's broken."

Bernard turned to Brother William. "I seriously doubt the prior stuck your abbot in the guts with a dagger whilst having a lovers' tiff then broke his own neck."

Will said, "Brother, you need to tell us the truth. We didn't come here by chance. We followed a trail, we came looking for Sir Roger Mudstone and a boy. Surely you've heard of the search for them?"

Brother William murmured, "Of course, of course. We

are but a short distance from the city gate. We hear most things, even if some of us are unworldly."

Bernard nodded and looked at the monk shrewdly. "And you brother, you're not unworldly. I sense you came late to the cloisters."

Brother William nodded. He turned and walked back into the day chamber and sat down heavily in the abbot's padded chair.

Bernard and Will followed him out. Will said, "I think I can see what's going on here brother. Cover up one scandal with a lesser one?"

Brother William was silent for a moment, then nodded. "I had the best intentions of my fellow brothers and the abbey in mind. We shall be ruined."

Will said, "Tell us the truth and something may be done. Not all is lost."

Brother William rubbed his tired eyes. "It's true, Mudstone and the boy were here. Mudstone hidden in the abbot's bedchamber, the boy in the guesthouse. The abbot and the prior, fools both of them, they had no choice but to offer shelter. They had their instructions."

"Instructions? From whom?" asked Will.

"A woman brought them on a cart. She carried a message from our mystery benefactor in the city ordering us to shelter them. I know not who he is. He has been our biggest donor for many years. You must understand that the monastery has never been independently wealthy. They had little choice."

Will shook his head. "Little choice? These were outlaws. Killers hunted by the whole shire."

"We're completely dependent on his generosity. I don't know the full details, only the abbot and prior could tell you that, but I believe there were many strings involved."

Bernard loomed over Brother William, "Never mind all that, where did Mudstone and the boy go brother?"

"I don't know. I discovered the abbot and the prior during the night. Mudstone and the boy were gone, my superiors were dead. There's little question who the killers are. I feared the bishop's wrath more than the apparent scandal of the other room."

"So you did a little rearranging of the scene brother?" said Will.

"The lesser of two evils my son. We'll be ruined. Your bishop isn't noted for his liking of monks."

Bernard said, "Mudstone, he has taken coin you think?"

Brother William shrugged. "One chest over there has a false bottom, it's broken. I believe he probably took coin that the abbott had hidden."

Will said, "Osbert, stop throwing your guts up out there and make yourself useful."

A white-faced Osbert appeared at the outer doorway. He wiped his mouth on his sleeve and said, "Wherever that man travels he leaves a trail of destruction behind. I believe he's insane."

Will nodded. "I think you'd better fetch your Uncle Scrivener. Someone will need to sort this mess out here at Saint Mary's. Bernard?"

"Agreed. Go now boy."

Brother William rubbed his weary eyes again. "This man, Scrivener, I've heard of him. The bishop's secretary, a clever man I think?"

"He is that," said Will.

"And the bishop?" asked Brother William.

"Perhaps Scrivener can intervene on your behalf. I'd advise you to tell him everything you know; leave out nothing."

18

THE HUNT

Will and Bernard stood outside the gatehouse of Saint Mary's Abbey and looked back towards the city. The walls were only a half a mile distant. The river, crossed by a bridge, was before them. Will said, "If they left here in the dark they can hardly have gone straight into the city. The gates wouldn't have been open for hours."

Bernard grunted. "True, and Mudstone, without some disguise and with that face of his, will stand out like a sore thumb."

Will nudged some mud from the end of his boot and said, "Dressed like one of the good brothers they only need to keep their hoods up. Easy enough then to go unrecognised."

"I know Mudstone, he won't have been bloody stupid enough to stand outside the gate for hours, not with coin to spend. There's one place that's close by they could wait, the cookshop. Someone there may have seen them."

They trudged back up the muddy road that led back to the bridge over the Dray and the city gate. Crossing the bridge, Will glanced over the low stone wall down into the turbulent water of the river. It reflected his current mood. They turned right just before the gate and followed the city wall which ran high above the river bank until they came to the cookshop.

The barn like building was built up against the city wall itself. A thick plume of smoke rose from the roof and the smell of cooking meat wafted from the open door.

"Just the smell of it is making my stomach rumble," said Bernard.

"Are you never not hungry?" asked Will only half in jest.

Bernard grinned. "Once or twice a year."

The area immediately in front of the door was crowded with customers jostling for position to get served or eating what they'd just bought. It was a mixture of locals, pilgrims either on their way into the city or just leaving, and country people up to buy or sell produce at the market. The two bishop's men pushed their way through the throng towards the door.

There were several angry comments and one young hothead grabbed Bernard's arm as though to haul him back. "Wait your turn, I was here first."

Will winced. Bernard turned on the youth with an evil smile. "Hungry are you boy?"

The youth unnerved, instantly released his grip on Bernard's arm and took a step backwards. Bernard stepped towards the boy and jabbed a finger into his shoulder. "I'm here on the Bishop of Draychester's business. There's a killer on the loose, we're hunting him and you're slowing us down. Perhaps he'll kill you next, how does that sound? Want to die for a hot pie boy?" He jabbed his finger harder this time, and the youth stumbled backwards, regained his footing, took one last fearful look at Bernard and hastily disappeared into the crowd.

"A little harsh," said Will.

Bernard shrugged. "I'm hungry and I'm in a bad mood."

He turned back to the cookshop, elbowed a few more punters out of the way and both of them found themselves at the open door. Behind a crude wooden counter was a scene of frantic activity. Pots were boiling, dishes were being stirred, meat was roasting on spits in front of a fire, pies were baking. A cross-eyed man in a grease-covered tunic stood behind the counter.

"All right there? What you after this fine day? There's a fresh batch of pies just come out of the oven. Can I tempt you?"

It was hard to say which one of them he was talking to as each eye seemed to rove independently of the other.

Bernard said, "Give us two pies. What are they?"

"Meat."

Bernard said, "What kind of meat?"

"Dunno, lamb?"

"You don't know what kind of meat is in your own pies?"

The cross-eyed man shrugged. "Not always, it's difficult to tell sometimes. You want to buy some pies or not?"

"Give us two. Were you working early this morning?"

"Course I was. I hardly ever leave the place. Who's asking?"

Will said, "We're here on the bishop of Draychester's business. Last night, or early this morning, did you serve two monks wearing cowls like they were from the abbey across the river?"

The man sucked air through his teeth. "You don't say. Bishop of Draychester, eh. Don't see His Grace the bishop down here too often. Not sure our cooking is good enough for him, although we make a good pie if I say so myself."

Bernard leant over the counter and grabbed the man's

tunic and pulled him close. He said, "We haven't got all day fool. Did those we've asked about come in here or not?"

The man fought to focus his eyeballs at such close quarters. He spluttered, "Early it was, hardly anyone else about. Two of them, just as you said. A pie each they had, they were last nights as we'd not finished baking fresh you understand. They were still good mind."

Bernard said, "I don't give a rat's arse what pies they bought, what did they look like."

"One was tallish, walked with a bad limp. Never saw his face, he had his hood up, didn't speak at all. Handed the lad some coin from a leather bag to pay me. Now the lad, him I do know."

"I knew it, they were here," said Bernard.

Will said eagerly, "This boy, you know him? Who is he?"

Bernard relaxed his grip on the man's tunic and he slid back onto his feet on the other side of the counter.

"Miserable little bugger, got an attitude on him. Been coming in since he were a nipper. Always thought he was connected with your lot at the cathedral or the bishop's palace."

"Why do you say that?" said Will.

"He used to run errands all the time from up there. I asked him if he'd joined that lot at Saint Mary's, him being dressed as a monk and all. Told me to mind my own business, so I did. Makes no odds to me as long as the customer pays."

"He said nothing more?"

"Nothing. What about those pies?"

Bernard produced two silver pennies and slapped them down on the counter with a flourish. They left with their food and a renewed sense of purpose.

It was market day and the narrow streets were busy and crowded. Bernard came to a stop. They were on Butchers Row. As the name implied this was a street of butchers. Just to emphasise the fact the ditch down one side of the street was half filled with rotting offal.

"Christ's bones. Is there some reason we've stopped here?" asked Will who'd been following his silent and moody friend as he led them further into the city. The big man just grunted and stood there pondering. Will covered his nose and mouth with his sleeve. The smell was appalling.

He tried to lighten the mood. "I think you may have discovered where our pie filling came from. I'm not sure about anything else."

They were getting jostled by the crowd that pushed past them.

"So are you going to tell me where we're going?"

"Susanna. I've been trying to think of the old maid's name. She worked at the bishop's palace for years, long before I came. We'll be lucky if she's still alive, luckier still if she hasn't lost her mind with age."

"I've absolutely no idea what you're talking about."

"Just follow me. I'm sure the house is around here somewhere."

Bernard strode off and Will made to follow when a finger jabbed him painfully in the middle of the back. He turned around angrily, and looked upon someone he'd thought never to see again. His jaw dropped in shock.

The man before him was older but still had the same figure, tall, thin and bony. On his feet were wooden pattens worn over his leather boots. He had on a long dirty blue cloak and wore a felt hat perched on his head, under which a tuft of matted red hair poked out. He looked back at Will with mean, bloodshot eyes and a sneer on his grey, ill looking face. He said, "Too high and mighty to talk to your own uncle are you boy?"

Will looked back with ill-concealed distaste. "I haven't been a boy since the day I knocked you onto your boney arse and left that shite hole you call home. What in God's name are you doing here?"

The man looked around furtively. "I've business in the city and I've been looking for you. Last I knew you were to hang. Now I hear you're working for the bishop himself."

Will looked at him suspiciously. "What is it you want uncle? I'm busy and I can't think of a single thing we've got left to talk about."

His uncle ran a clammy hand over his face and said, "We're family boy, like it or not, I need your help."

Will gave a hollow laugh and poked his finger at his uncle who took a step back. "Family! I can only imagine you jest with me. I haven't clapped eyes on you in five years. Family look out for one another, the only thing I ever got from you was an angry word and a slap around the head."

The other man hissed, "I took you in and clothed and fed you boy, after your fool father got himself killed soldiering and then your mother died. I deserve a little thanks. You stole my best horse and two months takings when you left."

Will reached out and shoved the other man backwards into a wall. Others on the street, sensing trouble, gave the pair a wide berth. "You miserable whoreson. I slept in the outhouse with the dogs most nights. At least the servants got paid once in a while. I worked from dawn to dusk in that stinking tavern for you. You thrashed me every bloody day.

Whatever I took I was owed ten times over. Is that what you're after, coin? It is isn't it?"

His uncle held out a placating hand. "Business has been bad recently Will and my health isn't what it was. I'm ill. The tavern isn't doing well. You've struck lucky here in Draychester boy, getting yourself a nice easy life. I'm not asking for much, you can help me out if you choose."

Will shook his head in disgust then laughed in disbelief at his uncle's audacity. "What'd do I care of you or your bloody tavern. If I'd had any sense, I would have burnt the place down when I left, with you in it."

The man reached out and clutched at Will's arm. "Will I'm begging you. I owe people money, I'll lose the tavern or worse. It'll be yours one day, who else am I going to leave it to? Hear me out, you'll regret it if you don't boy, I promise you that."

Will forced the other man's hand from his arm. He said, "Just leave me alone, I'm building a different life for myself here. If I ever see you again it'll be too soon, and you'll be the one regretting it." Seething with anger, he strode off without a backwards glance.

Bernard stood waiting impatiently just up the street. He asked curiously, "What was that all about?"

Will shook his head. "Nothing, just someone I used to know."

A horse being led suddenly blocked their way. The rider sat the wrong way around, tied to the saddle and with a fool's cap upon his head. He was being led to the pillory. Will glanced at him and thought he recognised another face from his own misspent youth. He looked battered and bruised already and there would be more to come. Will knew him for passing false coins, perhaps it'd caught up with him. A gaggle of angry citizens tagged on behind. Will looked away, a shiver passing down his spine. He murmured, "There but for the grace of God." Then they were gone, and the way was clear once again.

Bernard led him down an alley by the side of one of the shops. They had a challenge navigating the passage without putting their boots in the foul smelling mud.

Will shouted, "You sure this is the way? The muck will be over the top of my boots at this rate."

"Come on."

The alley came out into a small courtyard surrounded by two storied wattle and daub houses. There was a young woman sat on a stool in front of a doorway nursing a baby.

As they walked across the courtyard towards her she shouted, "If you're looking for Bendy Alice she don't see customers at this time of day. Lord knows she needs to get a bit of sleep, even though she does spend most of the day on her back."

Bernard came to a stop before her and grinned. He said, "We're not here looking for a whore. I'm looking for Susanna, an old maid who used to work at the bishop's palace. Does she still live?"

"Well she was still with us this morning love. She's my nan and don't I know it. Sharp tongue on her that one."

Bernard said, "Can we speak to her? I think she might be able to help us. There'll be a few pennies in it for the trouble."

The woman eyed them curiously. "She's not been out of bed these two years past. What is it you want with her?"

"It's her memories I'm interested in. I'm Bernard, and this is Will, we're here on the bishop's business."

She hesitated a moment and then said, "Why not. She'll be pleased of the visitors if nothing else. You'd better come in."

Still cradling the baby, she led them inside. In the front room a few inches' width warp of coloured yarns stretched from a post in the corner out across the floor. A set of thin wooden cards clustered along the warp at arm's length from the loose end. Several balls of coloured yarn were wound onto small wooden shuttles nearby.

Will said with interest, "You're weaving belts and straps?"

She nodded and planted a kiss on the baby's forehead, "In-between nursing this one. They'll end up stitched around the sleeves and neck of some fancy lady's gown."

They followed her into the back room. In the corner, beside the fire, was a simple sleeping pallet on which lay a wizened old woman. Her head was propped up on a pile of folded blankets and her eyes were bright and lively.

"Nan, you've got some visitors."

She looked first at William and then at Bernard and said in a surprisingly strong voice. "I don't know you young man, but I do know you, its Bernard isn't it?"

Bernard grinned, relieved that the woman's memory seemed intact. "It is, and how are you Susanna?"

She grinned back. "As right as I'll ever be. My mind's willing but my body is flagging. My granddaughter's a good girl. She looks after me well enough."

Susanna's granddaughter pointed at two stools and bid the bishop's men to sit. Bernard eased his bulk down, leant forward and stared into the old woman's curious eyes. "You'll remember I work for the bishop and his secretary, Scrivener. This is my friend Will, he's a bishop's man too. Now I know that you worked within the precinct for more years than I've lived."

She nodded slowly. "A lifetime, starting as a young girl. If my legs hadn't given out these past two years, I'd still be there yet. Is this about the trouble up there? I still get to hear all the gossip."

Will nodded. "Yes, we hunt a killer both there and now in the wider city too."

Bernard rubbed his tired eyes. He smiled at the old woman and said, "Can you tell us about a boy, perhaps you remember him. He's still young yet, with a miserable disposition, as though he carries the worries of the world on his shoulders. Seldom has a friendly word for anyone. Perhaps serves some older figure. Lives within the precinct and maybe runs errands."

"That would be Randel," she said without hesitation.

"You seem sure?"

"He's the lad you describe. Known him his entire life. I knew his mother too, poor thing, died giving birth to him. The lads always been strange. Something missing in him, that's a fact. Seems to care for nothing and no one. Hardly surprising."

"Why do you say that?"

"The mother was a servant and the boy's a bastard, although I believe I know the father and an odder one it'd be hard to find. The lad's not had an easy life, but there's something dark in his soul. Found him torturing one of the mousers once. Fine cat it was too, I gave him the hiding of his life and he never once cried out."

"The father, who was he?"

She shook her head. "One of the canons. Hard to believe it was the man the lad's mother named. But she swore to me it was him before she died."

Will said, "The boy's father, he's still alive?"

She laughed. "Some would say not. He already looked

old to me when I was a young woman. Farted like an old man as well. You'll never mistake that smell for another. It's unnatural that he yet lives. He uses the boy to black ends, I do know that. Runs his errands and God knows what else. I don't believe the boy knows it's his own father who corrupts him so."

Bernard breathed, "And the father's name?"

"Why, it's old Ralph, Ralph of Shrewsbury."

Ralph of Shrewsbury sat before the fire in his chamber, high in a corner of the bishop's palace. His bare feet were held out towards the heat. He missed the boy massaging his arthritic toes. He heard the door open and someone came and stood beside his chair. He didn't look around.

"Well?"

The woman said, "I went down to the abbey. It's swarming with the bishop's men. I saw Scrivener there."

After a moment Ralph said, "Mudstone and the boy, dead or captured?"

"Neither. It seems they have killed the abbot and prior and fled."

Ralph chuckled. "I'm surprised it took so long." With a sigh, he lowered his gnarled feet to the floor.

The woman continued, "Mudstone is insane, there's no telling what he might do. The boy may try to lead him to us and reveal our involvement to the bishop."

With a hint of amusement Ralph said, "Do I detect a note of disapproval in your tone?" He broke wind silently but the odour soon drifted up to the woman's nose. She gagged and took a step away from the chair.

"I only fear for your safety and all you have achieved."

A boney hand shot out and grabbed her painfully around the wrist, it dragged her closer. His leathery fingers reached out and stroked the back of her hand. "Perhaps you fear more for your own neck child? Fear is good, it means you're still alive, embrace it."

Revolted, the woman shuddered but made herself stand still. Ralph chuckled again and released her. He said, "Mudstone is a bringer of chaos. Let him do his worst. When his rage has run its course either he'll be dead or we'll eliminate him ourselves. Either way, he serves my purpose."

'And the boy?"

Ralph pondered, then shrugged. "I hope you're not getting sentimental. He's survived thus far. Let him make his own decisions. He'll return to the fold or not, it's his choice. I'm confident he knows where his best interests lie. "

The woman licked her lips nervously. She said, "Mudstone is dangerous. I think perhaps you underestimate him."

Ralph turned slowly in his chair and looked up at her. His eyes were like two black whirlpools. She gasped and stumbled backwards. He said, "I think you'd better go now."

She fled without a backwards glance.

The bishop's men left the house where Susanna lay via a back door that led into a small orchard surrounded by a wooden fence. There were only five or six apple trees but they looked well cared for. Bernard headed for a gate on the far side of the space. Will had difficulty matching the big man's stride. He was talking at Bernard's back. "Find the lad, find Mudstone?"

Bernard grunted and said, "It's all we've got. We need to get back up to the cathedral precinct."

"You seriously think old Ralph of Salisbury is capable of this web? From what I've seen he can hardly keep awake he's that old. I don't think I've ever heard him speak."

Bernard looked back at Will and shrugged. "I barely know the man. He's there and then he's not. Never much thought about him. All I want for now is Mudstone. Come on."

The gate appeared to be stuck. Bernard leant on it and the door sprang open into the street knocking a richly dressed man into the mud.

He sat in the street and looked at his mud and shit splattered finery with an expression of outrage. The crowd in the street streaming past splattered him further. Bernard offered the man a hand.

"You whoreson, look at the state of me," he roared and pulled out a dagger.

Bernard withdrew his hand, "Suit yourself." He forced the man back into the mud with a swift push from his boot to the chest. They left him there fuming in the mud.

Will, running to keep up, said, "You really know how to make friends."

"Should have let me help him get up. Ungrateful sod."

As they made their way through the streets towards the cathedral precinct Will detected an uneasy atmosphere in the air. The cry of the street vendors seemed shriller and more bad tempered than usual. The people in the street more inclined to barge into each other, the beggars more aggressive and demanding than normal. It became overcast. The air was heavy as though a thunderstorm was overdue.

19

A RIOT

Sir Roger and the boy pushed deeper into the crowded streets that were filled with the overwhelming sounds and smells of the city. Sir Roger was getting increasingly agitated; his teeth hurt like hell and his head was pounding. The poppy juice was long since spent and he was in a foul mood. His ears buzzed with the cries of porters and water-bearers, wagons creaking past and bells ringing. From the alleys and lanes came the sounds of pewterers and blacksmiths beating out their wares. The cries of the street traders rang out incessantly, "Hot sheep's feet", "Mackerel", "Ribs of beef and many a pie."

Sir Roger stumbled in the stream of refuse and filth that ran down the middle of the street and nearly fell.

"God's teeth I hate this stinking city," he cried in frustration grabbing the boy to remain upright.

The boy glowered at him and reflected that the city always stank, always had and always would. It was nothing to curse about. It had an odour all of its own, a combination of dung heap, tannery, slaughter-house, ale brewer, vinegar-maker and cook-house.

"I need a drink," said Sir Roger.

The boy shook his head. "Are you mad? We can't be seen in some tavern or alehouse. You'll be recognised. We agreed I'd lead you to my master. These monks cowls are a thin disguise."

Sir Roger turned and pushed the boy into an alleyway. He pinned him against the rough wattle wall with one hand and grabbed him around the throat with the other.

"It's your master again now is it boy? You change allegiances far too often for my liking. Just give me one more reason and I swear to God I'll gut you like a hog in this very alleyway. Understand?"

The boy croaked a reply that Sir Roger took to be a yes. He slowly relaxed his grip. The boy spluttered and wheezed as he drew breath. Sir Roger pushed him back out into the street and with a hand on the boy's back shoving him forward he said, "We're going to find a drink."

They were jostled in the crowded street as they made their way. Sir Roger stamped on feet, using his one good elbow to dig into the ribs of those in his way and shoved others into the mud. In his wake he left a trail of shouted obscenities and threats.

"In here boy," he said bawling in the lad's ear and shoving him through a low doorway into a gloomy interior. The floor was bare earth and dirty rushes. There were low benches and stools set out around the room. In the centre a fire sent smoke up to the rafters.

Sir Roger jabbed his finger in the boy's back and directed him to a corner. The boy sat down sullenly and Sir Roger sat opposite, his back to the wall so he could face the doorway.

A thin-faced woman emerged from some back room.

She wiped greasy hands on an equally greasy apron and approached them. She raised an eyebrow in enquiry.

Sir Roger kept his face well hidden in his hood. He kicked the boy under the table. The lad glared at him but eventually mumbled. "Bring us your best ale."

She gave the lad a suspicious glance. Sir Roger reached under his cloak and took out a leather money bag and removed two pennies and pushed them across the table towards the woman.

She wiped her nose with the back of a hand. As she bent to pick up the coins she gave a furtive glance at Sir Roger, but he lowered his head even further.

"You from Saint Mary's brothers? I hear there's some trouble down there this morning?"

The lad said nothing, even after another kick under the table. Sir Roger eventually gave what he hoped sounded like a non-committal grunt, lowered his voice and said, "Not our concern woman, we're from another place."

"Travelled far have you?"

"Far enough, now fetch us some ale."

The woman left with a scowl, returned with another scowl and slammed two cups down and a jug of ale which spilled onto the table.

"If you're after food you'll have to go elsewhere." With that, she left them to it. Sir Roger snatched up a cup and poured himself a generous measure and downed it in one. He slammed the cup down and hissed at the pain from his broken teeth. "Christ's bones if that's her best ale I'd hate to sample her worst."

The boy looked around nervously, then leant forward and whispered angrily, "Why are we here? I thought you wanted to speak with my master."

Sir Roger poured himself some more ale. He made no

move to fill the boy's cup. "I'm not sure to speak is all I want with him. I've a mind to inflect some serious pain. He's played a dangerous game at my expense. I don't know to what ends. Look at me. It's hardly been to my benefit has it? After everything I worked for I'm sat here dressed as a monk."

The boy shrugged. "He arranged to free you and your servant from France and you were paid for the killing of the anchorites."

Sir Roger smashed a fist down on the table, bouncing the cups and jug. He hissed, "Why boy, why?"

The boy shook his head and said bitterly, "He plots and schemes all the time. He rarely explains himself, at least not to me. All I know is he seeks the bishop's downfall and his removal from Draychester."

"At least in that we have interests in common. Well, it seems he has some bloody explaining to do to me, and when he's done, he'll be lucky if I don't finish him off like you did the poor old abbot of Saint Mary's." Sir Roger fingered the broken stump of one of his teeth and hissed in pain. He sloshed some more ale in the cup and swilled it over the remains of his front teeth. "If all you've told me is true, tell me, how does he get away with living in the cathedral precinct? He's under the very nose of that bastard the bishop and his lackey the secretary."

The boy hesitated and then said, "I believe he's been there so long he's outlived anyone who knew his true nature. Hardly anyone pays him any attention anymore, they see an old man with addled wits. He's so old, it's unnatural that he yet lives."

Sir Roger sneered at the boy. "Unnatural or not, young or old, they all squirm the same on the end of a blade boy. I hope you're not wavering because," his hand shot out and grabbed the boy's in a finger crushing grip, "you are either with me, or I'm afraid, you're dead."

The boy gasped in pain and hastily tried to pull his hand away. Sir Roger glared at him, then released his grip. He grabbed hold of his cup, poured out the rest of the ale and slurped it down. He stood up and pushed past the boy, who reluctantly got to his feet and followed.

The woman who had served them stood in their way as they made to leave. Business was slow and she tried to replace her scowl with something masquerading as a smile. "There's more ale if you want it brothers."

Sir Roger turned to her, keeping his face hidden in the depths of the cowl he said, "Tell me woman, that taste, did you wash your feet in the ale after you brewed it?"

Before the outraged woman could say another word, he barged past her to the door.

The bishop sat in his chambers on a stool before the fire, drinking from a cup of wine and brooding. As he sipped his wine and looked into the flames, he reflected that this really wasn't like him. Across the room one of Scrivener's underlings, Walter by name, sat at a low desk sorting papers for him to review.

"Drawn the short straw this morning have you Walter, having to sit with your miserable old bishop?"

The junior clerk was a little flustered, "Master Scrivener was called away on urgent business at Saint Mary's Abbey this morning my lord. He asked me to assist you."

"Really, Saint Mary's? Pain in the bloody backside monks, nothing but trouble. Can't think what he would want down there with them."

"He didn't say my lord, his nephew came for him and they left together."

The bishop grunted in reply and turned back to the fire. He drank some more wine and said, "I can't seem to shake the gloom that's come over the place these last few weeks Walter."

The clerk couldn't think of anything to say other than, "Yes my lord, these are trying times."

The bishop ran a hand over his face and said, "You know I usually spend at least half the year on the road performing my duties. Look at me, holed up here, waiting for events to happen, it's not like me. Christ's bones Walter, I count myself a friend of the king himself, I sit in parliament, I keep a fine house in London, yet here I am brooding about anchorites, traitors and that whoreson Roger Mudstone."

The clerk rustled some papers and coughed discretely. The bishop sighed in reply. "Yes, yes, I know we have letters to attend to. The administration of this place is a never-ending task. It's bloody boring is what it is Walter and there's no escape."

"Yes my lord. Shall we begin?"

"And lastly my lord, we have some papers that you left on your desk. Scrivener asked if you'd read them yet. He said de Ward had written them."

The bishop turned from the fire, this time with a spark of interest in his eyes. "Ah, the record of the ramblings of Dame Dorothy our resident anchorite I think you mean Walter."

Walter sniffed rather dismissively. "Indeed so my lord."

"Do I detect a hint of disdain Walter? You're not a believer in the Pigeon of Perception I take it?"

The young clerk hesitated and then said, "It's not my place to judge my lord..."

The bishop smiled and said, "But?"

"I do think perhaps de Ward could spend his time more profitably on other matters."

The bishop nodded. "Perhaps he could my young friend, but he's undeniably made Dorothy and the pigeon popular. The pilgrims stream through our front gate daily. And it's filling the cathedral coffers. She's attracting more pilgrims than all our other shrines put together, or maybe it's the bird's fame, it's hard to tell."

"So you wish to read these papers my lord?"

The bishop held out a hand. "Why not, although from what I've heard, Dorothy generally makes little sense."

When he'd finished reading Dame Dorothy's latest visions, the bishop was disturbed. What de Ward had recorded in his spidery pen work was chilling. He almost believed de Ward had made it up to fit recent events. The scene in the cell was eerily reminiscent of the anchorite murders elsewhere. Was Dorothy in danger? He would never discount Mudstone's madness, but surely even he would hesitate to murder such a holy woman. The figure in the library was uncannily like the one Bernard, Will and Osbert had disturbed. Could that really be Ralph of Shrewsbury? It was incredible to think of the decrepit figure he knew as Ralph plotting such schemes. Yet the more he thought about it he realised he knew virtually nothing about the man, he just blended into the background. As for the other vision, it sounded very much like a riot.

"Walter, would you think me foolish to believe there was some truth in Dorothy's visions?"

The young clerk was flustered again. Eventually he gave a none committal, "Dame Dorothy is a woman of great piety and I think God moves in mysterious ways my lord."

The bishop nodded sagely. "Indeed, indeed he does Walter." The bishop got to his feet and took his sword from where it rested against the back wall. He said, "Well then, we're going to need to find one of the masons, some chisels and I dare say a few hammers. Oh, and five or six of my guards. And tell me, do you know where Ralph of Shrewsbury resides within the precinct?"

The clerk looked back at him bewildered. "My lord?"

Will and Bernard tried to force their way into the mass of people crammed into the marketplace but it was impossible. Will tugged on Bernard's arm. The noise in the square was overwhelming. At the top of his voice he bawled, "We're never going to get to the gate through this lot. What in God's name is going on?"

Bernard shook his head and shouted back, "I'm not sure, dangerous though, a riot maybe."

Will pointed back to the street they'd just come up. "Let's go around to the side gate."

They pushed their way out of the crowd and made their way against the flow of people back down the street.

"This way," said Will diving down a side street with Bernard close behind. At the far end of the narrow street they could see the wall of the precinct.

"Are you sure we can get through here?" asked Bernard.

Will pointed. "There to the right, there's a path, it leads around to the side gate."

When they got to the wall Bernard could see a narrow

pathway with the wall on one side and the backs of houses on the other. The bishop's men squeezed down the path, stumbling over the rubbish and splashing through the mud, holding themselves off the precinct wall with one hand and off the houses with the other.

"Have you been down here before lad?" shouted Bernard from up ahead.

Will shouted back, "A few times when I've wanted to get back to our quarters in a hurry. It's quicker than the main gate sometimes."

Bernard stumbled in the mud and filth. "It's also full of shite under foot."

"Everything has its drawbacks."

The big man emerged through the final gap and they found themselves in the street that ran to the side gate of the bishop's palace. The wooden door in the wall was only half open and one of the palace guards was moving to close it.

Will and Bernard shouted to him to stop. He held the gate open for them and they squeezed through. He said, "I'm just closing up."

Will nodded. "We know, it looks like there's a riot in the marketplace."

The guard shrugged. "I knew something was going on, I could hear the noise from here, but that's not why I'm closing up. The bishop's orders came before that started."

"Where is he?" Bernard asked.

The guard pointed at the cathedral. "I saw him go into the cathedral with some guards not long since. Do you know what's going on because I'm damned if I do?"

Will said, "Just keep that gate closed. Let no one in or out. Understand?" The man nodded and barred the gate behind them.

Bernard grabbed Will's arm and hauled him forward. He

said excitedly, "Come on, to the cathedral, that whoreson Mudstone is close, I know it."

The trouble had started almost from the first toll of the market bell. The bell hung next to the market cross in the centre of the square and rang out to signal the commencement of the day's trading.

The market clerk was John of Mowbray, an ill-mannered and temperamental man. In his younger days he'd been strong muscled but he'd run to fat. Now he was built like a stout little barrel with a thick neck and a balding head. His eyes were permanently blood-shot and his eyelids puffy and swollen.

John had exited the precinct gate that morning in a dirty white coat with a blue hood and stomped across the square between the stalls to hammer at the bell angrily. He'd immediately turned and walked to a stall of a fishmonger named William Plimstock. The ill will between the two was well known and had being brewing for months.

John had pushed his head under the awning of the stall and hissed, "I'm watching you today Plimstock. Don't think I don't know what goes in this marketplace."

Plimstock walked from around the back of his stall carrying a fishmongers' shovel. He held it before him menacingly and jabbed it towards the fat market clerk, forcing him away from the stall. He shouted, "And what is it you think you know you old turd? You're hard pressed to see your own bloody feet when you get up in the morning. Come on, spit it out..."

The clerk had an evil smirk on his face. He jabbed his

finger at the angry fishmonger. "I've evidence now man. You won't be able to deny it this time."

Some fishmongers from the other stalls came out from behind their stalls. They congregated around the two men, an angry muttering in the air.

Plimstock swung the shovel before him and just missed the clerk's head. "Mowbray you miserable old fart. I think you've finally lost your senses. You've never a kind word to say about anybody. Now get back behind the precinct gate old man and leave us in peace or I swear I'll plant this shovel in your ugly face."

The clerk looked around at the angry faces and back at the shovel-wielding fishmonger. The clerk's face went red with rage. "You all heard him threaten me, the clerk of the market. I'm warning you for the last time Plimstock." He turned and pushed his way through the surrounding men, followed by a chorus of catcalls and a shower of fish heads aimed at his back.

Over the next hour the square filled with those who had no obvious intention of buying from the purveyors of apples, fish and vegetables who plied their wares on trestle tables beneath the awnings. The stallholders were a mixture of those who lived permanently within the walls and those who came up from the countryside to sell their wares only on market days. City dweller or countrymen, they all knew there was trouble in the air. Some of the more prudent started packing up their stalls in anticipation of trouble.

Just after noon the clerk, now backed up by some of the bishop's guards, emerged through the precinct gate and roughly pushed his way through the throng to Plimstock's stall. Two of the guards grabbed the fishmonger and pulled him struggling towards the market cross in the centre of the square. He slipped as they pulled him and banged his head on the cobbles. They dragged him upright concussed and with blood streaming from a deep gash over his eye. The clerk mounted the steps around the base of the cross and pointing down at the fishmonger bellowed, "I have it on good authority this man has been selling below price. You all know the rules, break them and face the consequences. If you don't like it, find somewhere else to hawk your wares. Remember, I know all your games and scams."

The noise level in the square dropped instantly and a hundred heads turned to watch the drama. One of the nearest stall holders red faced with anger bawled, "And who the hell has been filling your ears with all that bollocks Mowbray? I'm telling you now, Plimstock broke no rules. Where's your evidence? Are you judge and jury as well now? I'll vouch for him myself, as will we all."

The clerk glared angrily at him. "And why would I take the word of a stinking whoreson like you?"

The man turned a deeper shade of red and stepping menacingly towards the clerk said, "You fat scheming weasel faced turd, how'd' you like me to give you a good thrashing?"

The clerk pointed a finger at the man and turned to the guards and said, "Did you hear that? He's threatening me. You can't make threats to a bishop's official. Arrest him."

There was an instant outbreak of angry shouts, threats and insults hurled at him from all sides. The guards were growing nervous and made no immediate move. Between swollen eyelids the market clerk's blood-shot eyes scanned the crowd trying to identify further troublemakers.

One of the guards, alarmed at the ugly turn of events, tried to play peacemaker. He held up a hand and said, "Now there's no need for all this lads. I'm sure it's all a misunderstanding. Let's all just calm down."

The guard was instantly pelted with rotten fruit and old fish heads. The stinking shower also came down on the clerk, splattering across his coat and tunic. He tried to shelter his head with an arm but his bald head was soon running with a mixture of fish guts and decomposing turnip.

Out in the street there was a low, sullen murmuring in the passing throng. The noise made the hairs on Sir Roger's neck stand up. The atmosphere was charged, like the feeling just before a battle, when the lines of opposing forces are drawn up before each other. He clutched his dagger under his monk's cowl and said excitedly, "Something's in the air boy, can you not feel it? It's either going to thunder or there's a riot brewing, maybe both."

As they made their way towards the marketplace the noise turned into the low snarling of many voices, and it grew louder and louder until it became a sullen, muttering roar. They joined the back of the crowd. The boy shouted to Sir Roger, "He's caused this, I know it."

Sir Roger turned to a richly dressed merchant. With his face still hidden he bawled, "What's going on friend?"

The merchant smiled grimly. "Some dispute over prices brother. The clerk of the market has accused one of the stallholders, a fishmonger, of some infringement or other."

"Is that all?"

"Two of the bishop's guards dragged him from his stall and beat him. He stands bleeding there still while they argue with the other stall holders. It's ugly. There's trouble brewing, mark my words, the stallholders won't stand for such rough treatment."

A body of men carrying sticks, clubs, stones and the occasional dagger emerged from an alley and pushed their way into the crowd. Sir Roger knew crowds like this, he lived for the thrill of them and he judged this was building into a fine example. They were jeering, eager and dangerous, a barely contained mob. He purposely jostled one of the men as they passed, causing him to spill some stones cradled in his arms. The man cursed Sir Roger, who in reply made the sign of the cross, before the man hurried after the others into the crowd. Sir Roger bent down and selected a large stone which he cradled in his hand and then concealed under the long sleeves of his monk's cowl. He grabbed the boy's arm in a vice like grip and dragged him protesting into the crowd.

"Please, this is madness. What are you doing?" cried the boy.

Sir Roger looked back at him wild-eyed. "I do believe I'm going to start a riot and pay an unannounced visit on your master."

Sir Roger stood some twenty feet away from the market cross and seized the opportunity presented. With his hood concealing his face he bellowed, "You and the bishop offend God with the treatment of this man. I say strike them down!"

The guard was flustered at Sir Roger's outburst. "Now brother, you're a man of God, let's not get upset, we'll sort this out peaceably."

Mowbray the clerk stood seething and bedraggled on the top step of the market cross. He was retching at the smell of his clothes, now splattered with the dregs of the marketplace waste. He screeched, "You're scum, all of you. Each and every one of you a whoreson."

Sir Roger cradled the stone in his hand. He'd selected well, the weight was comfortable and the size just right to fit in his palm. He judged the distance and threw it with the ease of long practice of such situations. The crowd collectively held their breath as they watched the stone sail high into the air before falling swiftly to hit the clerk, with an audible smack, on the forehead. He swayed momentarily, before spinning round and toppling backwards from the steps without a sound. Then all hell broke loose, which had been Sir Roger's intention from the start.

The crowd suddenly pushed forward into the small line of guards who retreated towards the gates. Two of them tried to rescue the clerk and drag him back, but a mass of kicking feet soon overwhelmed them, followed by stabbing hands and a rain of stones. The clerk himself, semiconscious on the floor, was viciously trampled and stomped on by the enraged crowd who surged over him. Stalls were soon overturned with contents scattered underfoot. Beggars and others sensing the opportunity darted between the brawling figures, pilfering food and goods. Chickens and pigs ran amok between the fighting men. Maids screamed, merchants were relieved of their purses, ladies tripped and apprentices whooped in excitement. In the chaos, old scores were settled and new ones created.

Sir Roger abandoning all pretence of disguise threw off his monk's robes. Using a short sword and dagger he'd been concealing, he brutally hacked his way towards the precinct wall. He shouted to the boy, "Are you coming, or are you just gong to stand there quivering?"

The boy reluctantly followed. Sir Roger reached the wall and found himself directly behind the remaining bishop's guards. He inched along the wall towards the gate. The enormous oak doors had started to close with one of the gatekeeper bawling at the guards to retreat. Sir Roger jammed himself in-between them and punched the gatekeeper in the face, knocking him to the ground. This kept the doors open and blocked the guards from retreating any further. The boy cowered at the side of the gate, unable to keep his eyes off the chaos consuming the marketplace.

"Get out of the way fool," said one guard waving his sword menacingly at Sir Roger.

Sir Roger leered back. "And if I don't, you're going to stab me with that are you?"

"Move now or I won't be responsible."

With one smooth motion, Sir Roger thrust forward and speared the unfortunate man through the stomach. He looked down disbelievingly at the blade in his guts, dropped his own sword and looked back up at Sir Roger with a bewildered look.

"Dimwit," said Sir Roger and withdrew the sword. The guard collapsed in a heap.

The crowd was pushing the guards backwards towards Sir Roger. He ruthlessly took advantage by stabbing one in the back, effortlessly removing the hand of another and grabbed the last by his tunic and slid his sword up under his ribs. The crowd roared its approval. He turned back to the gates and pushed them wide open. The gatekeeper had sensibly crawled out of the way. He stepped aside and stood by the boy as the mob streamed through hellbent on mayhem.

"I love a good riot. So boy, lets go find your master."

∾

As Scrivener and Osbert passed under the stone archway of the city gate a stream of people rushing in the opposite direction met them. The sound of the mob could be heard even from here.

Scrivener cursed. "God's teeth. I knew it."

Osbert said, "What is it Uncle?"

"That lad, is a riot, no doubt aided and abetted by our traitor who has been fanning the flames for weeks."

They pushed onwards towards the main gate of the bishop's palace, but they came to a stop far short of the marketplace. The mood was ugly. There were random acts of violence in progress on every side. Doors were being barred and shop fronts shuttered.

A merchant who Scrivener knew came hurrying by. Scrivener put out a hand to slow him. The merchant gave him a sour look but halted.

"Tell me friend, what does the mob do down there?"

The merchant looked back fearfully towards the marketplace and the bulk of the cathedral behind. "Last I saw they were through the gate and into the cathedral precinct. I decided I valued my neck more than my curiosity and left. That damn monk started it throwing a stone at the market clerk."

"A monk you say?"

"Two of them in black cowls. Now I'm off to secure my house. There's no telling when this will end."

The merchant hurried off up the street.

"Sounds like Mudstone and the boy were involved. Should we go back and get the men we left at Saint Mary's?" said Osbert.

Scrivener shook his head. "A bit late for that lad, and if we try to reach the gate via the marketplace we'll be right in the thick of it. The bishop will need help to control such a mob. Perhaps we can call on our good sheriff to assist."

Osbert looked incredulous. "Do you really think he'll act when the mob serves to discredit the bishop? He would see us all murdered first."

Scrivener smiled slyly at his nephew. "I'm sure he'd much rather stand aside and watch the destruction, but I think it's about time he did his duty for once and help keep the king's peace."

"Why would he help us?"

"Why? Osbert don't be naïve lad, I know enough about his corrupt schemes to send him to the gallows three times over."

"You'd do such a thing?"

"The threat will be enough. Come on, there's no time to lose. We head for the castle."

The two of them made their way from the marketplace and by a series of side streets crossed the city to where the castle with its great keep stood. There was a heated discussion at the main gate before they were reluctantly admitted.

They were led to the sheriff's quarters by one of the sergeants. As they made their way through the narrow passageways of the main keep the sergeant said, "The lads are itching to get out there. You know how it is, they're always up for a good scrap. If it was up to me we'd be down in the marketplace already."

Osbert was outraged. "So the sheriff has given specific orders not to assist?"

The sergeant looked sheepish. He came to a stop and turned to Scrivener for moral assistance. "He hasn't specifically said not to assist, but I can't go against his wishes. I'd be lucky to be put on ditch clearing duties for the next year.

Scrivener you know my hands are tied. As long as the city is not actually on fire he's content to sit by."

Scrivener patted the sergeant on the shoulder. "Don't worry, I think he might change his mind when we've had a chat. Lead on."

The sergeant looked at him dubiously. "Well whatever it is you think you know, I hope it's damn good."

The sheriff, Sir John Luttrell, appeared to be in excellent spirits. He sat in a sumptuous chair in the great hall of the keep, humming some alehouse ballad, with his muddy boots up on the table. With a golden goblet in one hand and cramming sweetmeats into his mouth with the other, he didn't look at all surprised to see the bishop's men. He beckoned them over with a flick of his fingers and a sneer. "Scrivener, just passing were you? Not often we see one of the bishop's men up at the castle."

Scrivener gave a brief bow. "Good afternoon my lord. We were wondering if it had missed your attention that there appears to be a riot taking place in the city?"

The sheriff, with mock innocence, said, "God's teeth, really? Can't say I've noticed. Hang on, I did take a walk up on the wall earlier. Saw a bit of smoke coming from the marketplace, not much else. Mind you, my eyesight's not what it was. Did you hear anything about a riot sergeant?"

The sergeant looked pained. "I believe I did mention there was a disturbance earlier my lord."

The sheriff shrugged. "Well you know I take a nap and a bite to eat at this time in the afternoon. I can't be expected to remember everything."

"Perhaps you'd like me to lead some men down there sir and sort it out," asked the sergeant hopefully.

"Nonsense sergeant, we really shouldn't interfere, I believe the marketplace falls under the bishop's jurisdiction, isn't that right Scrivener?"

"I believe the trouble has spread out from the marketplace into the streets my lord. There also seems to be one element who have made their way into the cathedral precinct itself."

"Surely you must secure the king's peace within the city," spluttered an indignant Osbert.

"Surely I must secure the king's peace," mocked the sheriff in a high pitch imitation. "Who is that Scrivener?" asked the sheriff peering at Osbert with disdain.

"My nephew Osbert my lord."

"Ah, your sister's boy I believe. I've heard about you boy. That explains his naivety. You have my sympathies lad," the sheriff gave a shudder, "your mother is a formidable woman."

Osbert, outraged, was about to launch himself into a tirade when Scrivener stomped down hard on his foot.

"Perhaps I could have a word in your ear my lord?"

The sheriff peered at Scrivener with distrust and then, with greasy fingers, reluctantly gestured him forward. Scrivener approached slowly, gave a disarming smile and bent down to whisper in the sheriff's left ear.

There was a brief conversation during which the sheriff went a strange grey colour, as though he'd eaten something disagreeable.

When Scrivener leant away from the sheriff, he turned to the sergeant and said, "I do believe the Sheriff has realised the seriousness of the situation and wants you and your men to assist us in restoring law and order. Isn't that right my lord?"

The sergeant looked incredulously at his master who slowly, grey faced, nodded his agreement. He murmured, "I really must lie down. I feel quite nauseous, it must be something I've eaten."

Scrivener bowed. "My lord, we'll leave you to retire. Osbert, sergeant we've work to do, let's make haste."

20

REVELATIONS

The anchorite's attendant, Maud, was indignant. "She's sleeping my lord, you can't disturb her."

The bishop said matter-of-factly, "I'd be surprised if she doesn't wake up with the noise we're about to make. Tear that wall down lads."

The mason and his men began to hack away at the wall next to the opening into the anchorite's cell. Maud started to wail. The cathedral was still busy with pilgrims and the noise of the woman and the chisels soon attracted attention. De Ward appeared from somewhere and came hurrying towards them. The bishop's guards who'd fanned out in a rough semicircle in front of the anchorite's cell, stopped him before he got too close.

"Is Dame Dorothy unwell my lord?" he cried out.

The bishop gestured to his men to let de Ward past. He approached and with a horrified look on his face watched the widening hole into the anchorite cell.

"Listen to me de Ward. Once we're through the wall, you're to take Dorothy and that bloody pigeon of hers to my quarters. Oh, and the wailing Maud as well. I'll send two of the guards with you. Lock yourself in, make the old girl comfy and let no one else in until you hear it's me outside."

"Is she in danger my lord? I don't understand what's happening."

"You wrote down the prophecy yourself. Do you not believe your own words?"

He said, "This seems somewhat extreme my lord. There are many ways to interpret Dame Dorothy's visions."

"Well this is my way and you'll do as I say. Tell me de Ward, do you know where Ralph of Shrewsbury resides in the precinct? No one I've asked has a clue."

"Ralph of Shrewsbury," he sputtered, "I've no idea, is it important?"

Before the bishop had time to answer a familiar voice boomed out from far down the length of the great building.

"My lord bishop. The traitor is known to us."

"Ah Bernard," murmured the bishop.

Bernard and Will came hurtling up the length of the building, scattering pilgrims, canons and guards before them.

They arrived fighting for breath.

Will gasped, "It's Ralph of "

"Shrewsbury. Yes I thought as much," said the bishop.

Bernard still wheezing said, "How?"

The bishop shrugged. "A very perceptive pigeon amongst other things."

The bishop stuck his head through the gap the mason had just hacked in the anchorite's cell wall. He jerked back as Dame Dorothy barged through and stood ruffled but dignified besides the gaping hole.

Will said, "My lord, there's a riot taking place in the marketplace. I think Mudstone might be with the mob there."

The bishop swivelled around. "I'll be damned! A riot and Roger Mudstone you say? That bloody pigeon is right again. Even more reason to move you for your own safety Dame Dorothy."

"I know Ralph's lair," said Dorothy as she brushed plaster and bits of broken stone from her hair. She glared at Maud and said, "Stop wailing woman, you're giving me a headache."

The bishop jerked his head at the hole in the wall and said, "De Ward, get in there and secure our feathered friend."

The thin canon slipped through the hole and vanished, only to appear moments later with the pigeon cradled in his hands. It cooed softly and regarded them with a beady eye.

Dorothy said, "It's been many years but I remember still. Go down into the undercroft in the bishop's palace. In the long passageway you'll find a small door in the side wall. Behind it is a stone staircase that winds up and up. Ralph occupies the rooms above the great hall in the south corner."

"I didn't know there were any rooms up there. You mean to tell me he's been sat up there above our bloody heads all this time?" the bishop said indigently. "Do you know these rooms exist de Ward?"

"No my lord. I'm not sure I've ever heard Ralph mutter more than a few words. He's just, well, here I suppose, then he isn't. I think he was a canon before I was even born my lord."

"Does anyone know where Scrivener is?"

Will said, "We sent Osbert to fetch him and bring him down to Saint Mary's abbey. Mudstone has murdered the abbot and prior."

"Christ's bones! Bernard, Will. Go find Ralph, I don't

care where he is, in his lair or not. Drag him back here if you have too."

"But Mudstone my lord, he's here," said Bernard.

"Do as I say. I'll deal with the mob, if Mudstone is with them he'll rue the day he ever set foot back in Draychester. Now go. De Ward, to my chambers with Dame Dorothy."

Ralph looked down on the scene from a window high in the bishop's palace. The thought he might actually be in danger sent a thrill through his old bones. He broke wind noisily and smiled as the mob spread out across the precinct. He doubted they would steal from the great cathedral itself, fearful of divine retribution, but everything else was fair game. The bishop's palace would provide rich pickings. His own chambers were hard to find even for those who knew the palace well, for now he was confident he could watch the destruction with detached amusement. Of course it was always possible they could torch the precinct when they tired of looting. He'd instigated a few riots in his time, they were unpredictable.

He spotted two of the bishop's officials, Bernard and Will heading directly for the palace with two of the guards. The mob, now apparently leaderless and chaotic, was milling on the cathedral green. Bernard led his party straight into them. The big man cracking heads and knocking over anyone who got in his way with a swipe of his huge arms. Discouraged, those who remained began streaming back towards the cathedral, unwilling to tackle such a force of nature. They were aided by the guards who pushed and prodded them at sword point away from the palace.

Ralph watched Bernard and Will progress towards the

main door, which he had no doubt was barred from the inside. They went out of sight directly below. Ralph heard a hammering. "Open up, damn you. It's Bernard and Will you idiots, open the door."

He narrowed his eyes in puzzlement as de Ward, Dame Dorothy and even more guards crossed the green and began making their way towards the palace. She looked straight up at the window and raised an arm as though to point. The crowd had thinned considerably, and upon seeing more of the bishop's men they scattered at a run. He ducked back from the opening, although he was fairly confident he couldn't be seen properly. He'd not laid eyes on Dame Dorothy outside her cell in twenty years, but she looked much the same as he remembered. He shivered with excitement. Perhaps after all he'd let things go too far.

The boy led Sir Roger down through the kitchen door of the bishop's palace and on into the passage that led to the undercroft. Half way along, a small inconspicuous oak door was set into the wall. An iron ring served to open it.

Sir Roger gestured at the door. "Is this some trick boy, his chambers are here, above the very heads of the bishop and his men?"

"I swear it. He once told me he's lived here since before old bishop Thorndyke took office."

Sir Roger grunted. "It's clever, I grant you that. Close to the heart of power and what better place to see but not be seen." He tried the iron ring, the door was firmly locked. "You have a key?"

The boy shook his head. "No, the woman has always led me to his chambers."

Sir Roger took his sword and jammed it in between the edge of the door and the surrounding stonework. He grabbed the iron ring with the other hand and heaved on it as he levered the door with the sword. The door groaned under the force but otherwise didn't budge. "Damn it boy, there must be another way up there?"

The boy shrugged. "Probably, but not one that I know of."

"Grab hold of the iron ring and pull while I use the sword." This time with both hands on the sword and the boy pulling on the ring there was a tortured sound of breaking wood and iron. The door popped open suddenly, throwing the boy to the floor.

"Don't hang about boy. Get in there." He hauled the boy to his feet and pushed him through the broken door. A narrow spiral stairway with worn stone steps led upwards. Sir Roger pulled the broken door closed behind them. The boy started to climb with Sir Roger close behind. The way was dimly lit by narrow window slits set at every two or three turns of the stairway. They climbed higher and higher and Sir Roger started to drag his injured leg at the exertion.

He sucked air in through his broken front teeth and hissed, "Christ's bones boy, if your master is as old as you say, how does he manage these stairs?"

The boy slowed and looked back at him. "He's stronger than he looks."

Sir Roger grunted again and urged the boy upward with a shove. The stairway came to an abrupt halt at a small stone landing with another door with an iron ring. Sir Roger coming up the stairs fast almost ran into the back of the boy.

"Fool," he said, gasping for breath. He gestured to the door, "Try it."

The boy turned the iron ring, but the door was locked.

Sir Roger was getting increasingly irritated. "Damn the man, does he sit up here like some hermit all day, locked away from the world."

The boy said, "He's a secretive man."

Sir Roger roughly shoved the boy out of the way and put his shoulder to the door. It groaned, and he felt it move slightly, but it wasn't going to open easily. Forgoing any pretence at stealth he placed one hand on the wall for balance and using his good leg he stamped down on the edge of the frame with his booted heel. He heard something creak, and he did the same again with more force. The frame splintered and the door burst inwards revealing a narrow whitewashed stone corridor, punctured with shafts of light from a row of narrow windows spaced about ten feet apart.

"This must lead the entire length of the great hall, we're in the very walls of the palace."

The boy said nothing. Sir Roger drew his sword and brought the tip close to the boy's throat. "You go first, if anyone is going to get a dagger in the guts from the old man it won't be me."

The boy reluctantly stepped through the door and Sir Roger followed with the sword a hairsbreadth from the boy's back.

"What's at the end of the passageway?" asked Sir Roger.

"The door to his chambers."

Sir Roger prodded the boy onwards with his sword. As they shuffled along the narrow passageway, Sir Roger glanced out of one of the narrow unglazed windows that pierced the thick walls. He hissed through his broken teeth at the sight of Bernard, Will and the bishop's guards striding across the courtyard towards the main door.

Sir Roger's broken teeth throbbed as though red-hot

pokers were being driven into the roof of his mouth. Wiping a thin film of sweat from his brow, he found he was in two minds whether to go back down and confront them or deal with the old man first. Better to go on.

"Boy," he hissed. "When you get to the door, knock. If anyone answers, it's only you out here."

There was an eyehole in the door. As the boy knocked Sir Roger stood ready with a dagger. There was the sound of movement from the other side of the door. The wooden cover moved aside and Sir Roger ruthlessly plunged the dagger through until the hilt jammed on the edges of the hole. He dragged it back out, fully expecting to see the gory aftermath. But there was nothing. He pushed the boy out of the way and tried to shoulder the door open with his full weight. In the event it wasn't locked and the door smashed into the wall with a sound that must have been heard throughout the bishop's palace.

Sir Roger advanced with his sword drawn. The room before them was almost bare apart from a large and expensive looking rug and a chair positioned by the one window, the shutters open. There was nobody there.

Sir Roger could feel his anger growing by the second. He swung around and pointed the tip of his sword once again at the boy's throat. "I grow tired of this. Where is this man you call master?"

"I've only ever met him to receive instructions in this room. I swear it."

Sir Roger strode over to an archway set in the wall on the right. It was another stairway leading down. There was an opening directly opposite where they had entered. It had evidently been a door at one time. Now it was set with thick iron bars about two feet apart preventing access. They were deeply embedded into the stonework. Sir Roger warily stuck his face up to the bars. It was a room much the same size as the one he stood in. The space was richly furnished, hangings hung on the walls and a rug covered the floor. There was a large desk scattered with papers and a fireplace against the far wall with a low fire burning. A man dressed in a black cloak sat in a chair, his back to the open window. Through another doorway a woman entered and came to stand by the chair. Sir Roger recognised her, she was the same plain faced woman who had brought them to Saint Mary's Abbey.

The old man turned his gaze on Sir Roger. Even the hardened knight flinched as the dull lifeless eyes contemplated him like some raven viewing a worm. Sir Roger grasped the iron bars and hissed, "You've led me a merry chase old man. I'm tired of it, you'll give me some explanation before I kill you."

A pungent smell wafted towards the opening, and Sir Roger recoiled, swearing. He quickly covered his nose and mouth. Ralph laughed softly. "I'd be lying if I said it was a pleasure to finally meet you Sir Roger. I knew your father and brother of course, half wits at best. I'm somewhat disappointed, you don't really live up to your reputation."

Sir Roger grasped the iron bars, his knuckles turning white with the force. "Insult me behind your iron bars old man. I dare say if I follow the stairs from this room I'll find another way to you. I'll gut you like the hog you are and hurl your lifeless corpse out of that very window you sit in front of."

Ralph cackled. "At least it's true what they say about your temper. You let your anger drive you too far. Look what's become of you. I've used you to my own ends and you don't even realise it."

Sir Roger pushed his face through the bars as far as he could and hissed, "Why old man, why all this? Tell me!"

"You're very good at stirring up trouble. It follows you like flies to dung. Unpredictable, but I have used you, amongst others, to discredit the bishop."

"You can't hate him the way I do."

"Perhaps not. I like to play games because I can. To influence behind the scenes, that's a real power to have. Call it the whimsy of an old man, but it gives me pleasure. Gifford is an unusual man, he can't be bought or corrupted, but any man can be disgraced in the eyes of others, whether it be deserved or not."

"You're mad," said Sir Roger.

Ralph cackled and slapped the arm of his chair. "No more than you Sir Roger. The difference between us is that I know it."

"You talk in riddles old man, I think you've lost your mind. I hope you can still get out of that chair because you'd better start running."

"Oh, I don't think you'll find yourself in any position to make threats."

Sir Roger sensing danger swirled around but was too late to stop the boy driving a dagger deep into his thigh. The boy released the dagger and stepped back wide eyed. The old man chuckled deeply. "It's always the quiet ones you need to watch out for."

"You little bastard," hissed Sir Roger, his eyes never leaving the boy. He reached down, grasped the hilt of the dagger and pulled it out. The blood flowed freely down his leg from a deep wound. He brought up the sword and levelled it at the boy's chest. "I should have done this days ago."

The boy backed away slowly and suddenly dived through the archway and down the stairs. Sir Roger roared but didn't pursue him, instead he turned around slowly and looked at Ralph still sitting in his chair. The woman stood at his side smirked, then turned her back and ducked down to crouch in front of the fire. The boy suddenly burst through the door behind them and stood by the fireside gasping for breath.

Ralph smiled indulgently at the boy. "Ah, so all the sheep have returned to the fold. Boy, take a look out of my window, tell me what you can see?"

The boy moved over to the opening and looked out. "The bishop's guard's, everywhere. I can see more men, the sheriff's I think."

Ralph nodded and said, "Good, predictable but good." He felt the overpowering need to break wind noisily at the excitement of it all. The smell was overpowering and the boy coughed, almost retching. Sir Roger winced at the stench and turned his face away from the bars and said, "God's teeth. You must be rotting from the inside out old man."

Ralph chuckled again. "I do believe you may be right. I'm dying of course. Another month, maybe two at the most. I felt it in my bones this winter and I'm seldom wrong. It comes to us all, even me and I've lived longer than I have any right to."

The woman stood up, a look of shock on her face, "Father?"

"Don't look so surprised girl. I'm sure you must have wished for it often enough."

"He's your Father?" blurted out the boy looking between Ralph and the woman.

"Yours too," said the Woman harshly.

The boy looked to Ralph and he nodded slowly in confirmation. A single tear trickled down the boy's cheek.

Sir Roger rattled his sword between the bars. "Far be it from me to break up this touching family reunion but we have a score to settle old man. You'll be dying on the end of my sword, not in some soft feather bed."

He backed away from the bars, intending to go through the arched doorway and to the stairs beyond.

Ralph smiled at him and simply said, "Daughter?"

The woman swiftly turned back to the fireplace, there was a strange hissing sound, she whirled around and sent a pot trailing smoke and flame skidding across the floor.

Sir Roger watched in horrified recognition as the pot of Greek fire hurtled under the bars separating the rooms. It travelled between his booted feet and smashed into the back wall, releasing a sheet of flame that singed the hairs on the back of his head. He turned to face it. The heat was suddenly intense and he shielded his face with an arm. With no other options Sir Roger dived through the archway, stumbling and sliding down the steps on his front, his sword ripped from his grasp. He howled with rage and frustration as he collided with another locked door at the bottom of the stairs.

21

A RECKONING

"This must be the door. Looks like someone couldn't find the key," said Will gesturing at the splintered wood. Bernard pushed the broken door aside, drew his sword and started up the narrow stairway. "You coming or not?" he said without looking back.

Will sighed. "What else would I be doing?"

Bernard's bulk filled the narrow stairwell and he was half crouched as they ascended with Will close behind. "God's teeth, this must be designed for the court dwarfs, I can't even stand upright."

Will panting with exertion at the speed of the climb paused at one of the narrow windows and said, "We're inside the exterior wall, these windows look out on the courtyard."

Bernard grunted. "No time for sightseeing, come on."

They finally emerged from the top of the stairwell onto a stone landing. A broken door hung from a splintered frame that gave entrance to the long passageway that led to Ralph of Shrewsbury's chambers.

From the far end they could hear shouts and a crackling

sound. Bernard picked up speed and Will struggled to match his pace. As they approached the open door at the far end of the passageway, a tongue of flame shot out and a billow of smoke rolled towards them.

Bernard stopped dead in his tracks and Will ran into his back.

"There's a fire," cried Bernard, backing up quickly, nearly crushing Will. They both coughed and their eyes watered with the smoke. Will recognised the smell. It was the same acrid burning stench they'd encountered in the anchorite's cell at Snertherhide weeks before.

"Back, go back," roared Bernard, feeling the heat coming from the open doorway.

They hastily beat a retreat down the corridor. The heat diminished, but the smoke was now thick and rapidly advancing down the passageway after them.

"Hurry lad," said Bernard pushing Will onwards. He tried to pull some fresh air into his lungs as they charged past one of the window openings. There were ominous sounds of crashing coming from the far end of the passageway. A blast of hot searing air shot past them carrying burning embers, making them both gasp. Bernard flailed at the back of his tunic as it smouldered. He bellowed, "Faster for Christ's sake, faster."

They entered the stairwell and half ran, half fell until they burst out of the door at the bottom.

Gasping for breath, hands on knees, Will said, "Do you think Ralph set that fire on purpose? He can't hope to escape the flames."

Bernard leaning against the wall for support wheezed, "God knows, but we need to raise the alarm, the whole palace could burn."

The two of them made their way up from the undercroft

into the main hall. Will gasped. High above smoke was already gathering in the rafters. In a far corner, they could see the glow of fire and flames licking the roof timbers. Bernard cursed. "At that height it'll be damn near impossible to save the roof."

Will said, "Let's look from the courtyard, it may not be that bad."

Outside, far above the heads of the watching crowd, smoke and flames were billowing from the window openings which lined the passageway in the walls.

They found the bishop, sword still in hand, gazing up with a horrified expression on his face. They came to stand beside him.

Will said, "That's not good is it?"

The bishop shook his head. "No, it's bloody terrible. We need to get everyone out of the building and now. Move anything we can and organise a water bucket chain, not that'd it'll do much good. Where the hell is Scrivener?"

Bernard said, "What about Ralph of Shrewsbury my lord?"

"You didn't find him?"

Will said, "We got up there but the fire was already burning my lord. It was impossible to get to his chambers. He may well have started this."

The bishop grim faced said, "Well if he's still in there I hope the old sod burns all the way down to hell. Right now I have other concerns." He turned away and starting barking out orders that sent men running in half a dozen different directions. Will started to follow.

Bernard grabbed him by the arm. "Leave them to it, there are already too many men running around. I want Mudstone, he has to be here somewhere. He sparked that riot, I'd wager a year's wages on it."

"What makes you think he didn't go up there as well, perhaps to meet Ralph himself? De Ward took Dame Dorothy to the bishops chambers, shouldn't we make sure they're safely out?"

Bernard hesitated, in two minds as to the course of action. "Come on then, back in we go, but we'd better be quick, there's a breeze, at that height it's going to fan the flames."

They entered the great hall again. Flames were spreading across the far end of the roof and hot embers were raining down. The fire was taking hold rapidly. A steady stream of servants and guards came rushing the other way carrying everything that wasn't physically fixed down.

Reaching the bishop's chambers, they found the door locked. Barnard hammered on the wood, causing it to bounce in the frame. Will cried, "De Ward open up at once. The palace is on fire. You and Dorothy need to come out now."

There was no response, so Bernard began kicking the door. Finally, de Ward's nervous voice said, "The bishop told me to open up for no-one but him. How do I know I can trust you?"

Bernard bellowed, "Don't be a fool man. Open up now or by God we'll leave you to burn. Make your mind up."

The door opened a crack and de Ward could be seen peering out. Bernard jammed his foot in the door and forced it open. Dorothy was on one of the stools in front of the bishop's fire. The pigeon of perception sat in one of her hands whilst she fed it crumbs of bread from the other. There was an ominous rumble, then an ear-splitting crash from the direction of the great hall.

De Ward jumped. "What is that?"

Bernard said impatiently, "That's the roof of the great hall collapsing. I told you, there's a bloody great fire."

Will stuck his head through the door, "Dame Dorothy, please, for your own safety you need to come out into the courtyard. The flames have taken hold, I fear the whole palace will be consumed."

Dame Dorothy sighed and fed the last of the bread to the bird. She stood, the pigeon still sat on one hand and said, "The palace won't be completely destroyed, but I want to go out into the courtyard; there's something to see. Come de Ward, I'll be perfectly safe."

"Forgive me, but how do you know this Dame Dorothy?" asked Will.

She gave him a piercing look. "I just know it."

Bernard said, "There's no time for this, de Ward lead her to safety. Avoid the hall, go out via the undercroft if needs be."

De Ward nodded, and accompanied Dame Dorothy out into the corridor and hurried her away.

"Let's find Mudstone," said Bernard drawing his sword.

Will slapped his forehead. "Why not, the building is only burning down around our ears, what better time?"

"I'll not let him escape again. Are you with me or not?"

Sir Roger leant all his weight on the door at the bottom of the steps. The heat coming from the room above was intense. The sweat streamed down his face and made his eyes sting. The door groaned, but it didn't give. He pulled a dagger from his boot and hacked frantically at the wood of the frame. He jammed the dagger deep into the crack, placed his foot at the bottom of the door on the same side and gave it his all. Something splintered and the door gave way, sending him sprawling down more steps onto a stone landing. There were two choices, more steps led down or he could go through another open doorway from the landing which presumably led up to Ralph's chambers. Sir Roger crawled over to the doorway and looked up. The heat could be felt even from here and the stench of the smoke and the super-heated air made him cough.

"I hope you're still in there old man," he bellowed up the stairs. "Roast like the hog you are and then burn some more in hell. I'd like to hear you squeal and watch the fat boil off your old bones, but it's time for me to leave." Sir Roger thought he briefly heard laughter over the roar of the fire and a faint voice shouted, "What would the devil do for company if it was not for such as I?"

Sir Roger clawed himself upright using the wall and slowly and painfully, one arm against the stonework of the stairwell, made his way down.

Ralph of Shrewsbury stood by the open window, his black cloak wrapped tightly around him, shielding his body some-what from the heat. His thin hair was already burnt to a crisp, his head a soot-covered skull. The room was a mass of flame, smoke and destruction. There was no way out now. He could have left with his children while he had the chance. They'd looked at each other for a moment while there was still time and he'd shaken his head and then they were gone.

Sir Roger's last bellowed curses were already passing from his thoughts. Ralph knew he would die, had planned for it, and now he embraced the moment, welcomed it even.

He looked down into the square which was a heaving mass of figures, some helping to remove valuables from the palace, others gawping up at the fire that was rapidly destroying the roof and upper floor.

"It's a long way down to the courtyard," he said out loud, "I suppose I'd better make haste as my path lies further still, all the way down to hell." He climbed with difficulty up onto the window ledge, the opening not quite large enough for him to stand fully, so he crouched. For those down in the square he had no doubt that he looked like a big black raven ready to take flight. He grinned to himself and swayed backwards and forwards on the very edge of the ledge. The thought made him break wind loudly and gloriously. With a whoosh of flame, his cloak caught on fire and he dived gracefully from the ledge. He dropped swiftly, his cloak flapping around him, trailing smoke and flames until he landed abruptly on the hard cobblestones below. Ralph of Shrewsbury lay a bloody and broken mess at the feet of the watchers.

The bishop prodded the smouldering body with the end of his boot. It left a wet red mark on the leather. "Well, it saves a trial I suppose, but we're denied the pleasure of stringing the traitorous old bastard up by the neck. Who knows what secrets he would have revealed with some suitable persuasion?"

Osbert, stood beside his uncle Scrivener, looked at the bloody bundle before them, shivered and crossed himself. "A demon sent straight back to hell my lord."

Scrivener drew his cloak tighter around him and pursed his lips in thought. "Perhaps it's better he takes some secrets

to the grave my lord. His is a tale I wager was stranger than
ever we've heard. The man by any normal standards had
lived two lifetimes, and I'm not sure I want to know how he
achieved it."

The bishop grunted. "You know I'm not normally of a
superstitious persuasion old friend but I have to agree."

They gazed up at the roof of the palace, now blackened and collapsed over the length of the great hall. The
wind had dropped and the fire had mostly burnt itself out.
The remaining roof beams still smouldered, but the
bishop judged the rest of the building was safe. Half the
contents of the palace were scattered around the courtyard, piled in untidy heaps. The bishop's guards kept the
merely curious and those with more opportunist interest
at a distance.

The three of them moved to the doorway of the great
hall and surveyed the interior. Across the floor lay a jumbled
mass of burnt beams, broken stone, plaster work and dark
black ash. Thick acrid smoke drifted up through the open
roof.

Osbert was dismayed. "It's a disaster. The palace is
ruined."

The bishop leant against the doorway and folded his
arms. "Such pessimism Osbert. Still, I agree, it is a bloody
mess in here and we'll need a new roof. As for the rest of the
place, it's going to smell of smoke for weeks." He signed
resignedly. "I suppose it could have been worse, if the palace
had burnt to the ground we could now be seeking hospitality with that idiot the sheriff or the half-wit the coroner.
And Scrivener, should I even ask how you got the sheriff's
men to come to our aid?"

Scrivener smiled weakly. "Best that you not know the
full details my lord. Suffice to say I reminded him of a few of

his more unsavoury activities. After which he was more than happy for his men to help disperse the riot."

The bishop grinned at his old friend. "I bet he was. You're a devious sod Scrivener."

Scrivener nodded graciously. "Thank you my lord, I'll take that as a complement."

Sir Roger reached the bottom of the stairs and found another door, this time barred from his side. Without opening it he rested against the thick boards. His leg was still streaming with blood and he cursed out loud. From what he could see it wasn't fatal, but neither was it painless.

"God's teeth, that boy will rue the day our paths ever crossed," he muttered with vicious intent. He reached inside his tunic and with difficulty tore a strip from his linen undershirt. Folding it several times in a rough square, he used it as a pad to absorb the blood. From the top of the stairs he could hear various rumblings and groans. The actual stairs shuddered as something far above in the walls gave way. A cascade of dust and small stones came bouncing down the steps towards him.

Sir Roger slid back the wooden bar and eased the door open a crack. He saw another corridor that looked remarkably similar to the one the boy had guided him along on first entering the bishop's palace. It was full of servants carrying valuables away from danger. Sir Roger waited until there was a brief lull in activity, with only one man in the corridor. He stepped out in front of him. The surprised man stopped dead and Sir Roger took the opportunity to punch him hard in the face. The man dropped the basket he was carrying to clutch at his broken nose and Sir Roger followed up with another blow. The man slumped unconscious to the floor and Sir Roger half dragged, half pushed him back through the doorway to the stairs and pulled the door closed on him. He picked up the basket and with it held up in front of his face he limped off up the corridor.

Sir Roger kept his face pressed close to the basket and had to navigate by taking sidewards glances as he hobbled along. Eventually he managed to run into the back of another servant. They were at the foot of the stairs leading up from the undercroft into the courtyard.

"Have a care you clot, I've got a pile of cooking pots."

Sir Roger couldn't help himself, he kicked out which elicited an angry yelp from the man in front. He kept the pressure on the man's back using the basket and eventually they moved upwards into the bright sunshine. He clutched the basket tightly, not daring to reveal his face. To one side he recognised with a jolt the warrior like figure of the bishop and Scrivener, his secretary. They were stood over the body of a man, sprawled bloody and broken on the cobbles. He risked a look upwards at the burnt out windows of the upper story of the palace. Sir Roger realised with grim satisfaction it was probably Ralph of Shrewsbury's corpse, the old man had jumped to his death. His only regret was he hadn't killed the old bastard by his own hands.

"Oy, you man, put that basket down over there and get yourself back in there. Plenty more to bring out yet."

Sir Roger ignored the call which was directed at him. He did a shuffle to the left and right as he tried to align himself in a direction that would take him out of the courtyard.

The bellowing voice came from behind him this time, "Are you deaf man? Put that bloody basket down somewhere and go fetch something else."

"Damn it!" he hissed and sped up, his wound hurt like

hell and he could feel the blood starting to flow down his leg towards his boot.

A hand clamped on his shoulder and dragged him to a stop.

"What the hell is wrong with you man? Have you lost your wits? Give me that..."

Sir Roger turned around slowly, forcing the man to break contact with his shoulder as the basket came between them.

"Want this do you?" hissed Sir Roger. "Then take it." He shoved the basket as hard as he could at his pursuer, who toppled over with the basket on top of him. Sir Roger half walking, half limping with his head down moved as fast as he could away from the man. He headed between the randomly positioned bishop's guards who were facing the other way, holding back the hordes of onlookers. He disappeared into the crowd.

∽

Back in the undercroft Bernard and Will, exploring the other end of the passageway, came across another door.

Will said, "This has got to be another way up to Ralph's chambers." There was a groan from behind the door. Will grabbed hold of the iron ring and pulled the heavy door open. A man with a bloody nose sat groaning on the bottom step of some stairs. Bernard briefly stepped around him and peered upwards. He could see smoke and feel the heat of the fire from above. "If anyone's still up there they'll not be coming down alive."

Will crouched down before the injured man. "What's happened to you?"

The man peered at Will through two fast blackening

eyes. His nose was bloody and obviously broken. He said, "I was fetching valuables from the undercroft, as I'd been told. Some miserable bastard thumped me in the face and stole the basket I was carrying. Woke up here. Does my face look bad?"

Will patted him on the shoulder and said sympathetically, "Couple of black eyes and a broken nose. You'll live. What did this man look like?"

"Only saw him for a moment. Broken teeth. Odd scar on his cheek."

Bernard said, "Like a letter?"

The man nodded painfully, "Cant write myself, but yes."

Will swore softly. "Mudstone no doubt of it."

Bernard said, "He must have gone back out."

Leaving the man groaning on the steps they ran back down the passageway and up onto the green. The bishop, Scrivener, de Ward and Dame Dorothy stood around a body lying on the cobbles.

Bernard and Will hurried over. Will said, "My lord, Mudstone was here, down in the undercroft. We think he's come back out of the palace now."

The bishop scanned the courtyard and the crowd being held back by the guards. "He may have slipped past us unseen." He gestured at the corpse at his feet. "I fear we may have been distracted by Ralph of Shrewsbury. He took an unfortunate tumble."

"He was on fire as he fell," said Scrivener grimly.

They looked up to the burnt upper floor, smoke still rising and back to the broken body. Bernard nodded impatiently. "Nasty fall. He does look a bit crispy too. Mudstone my lord, can we set the guards to search?"

The bishop nodded. "Find him. I believe the sheriff's men are still in the marketplace, make use of them as well as our own men. And now I need to deal with this mess." With that he hurried back towards the entrance to the great hall and was immediately besieged by a sea of servants and officials demanding his attention.

Dame Dorothy entered the cathedral alone, except for the Pigeon of Perception, which she cradled in her hands. In the confusion of the courtyard, she had given both de Ward and her servant Maud the slip. She made her way to the cell she had so long inhibited. It had been a tumultuous day and her body was tired. Her legs ached, unused to walking any distance. The entrance to the open cell was surrounded by the broken stone and plaster work that once filled it. Dorothy slipped inside. After being so long confined in the space, there was nowhere that she felt more at home. She just wanted to be alone again, to contemplate the day in peace.

The cell was dim, and she set down the pigeon on a low stool as she fumbled about trying to find a candle. The pigeon cooed softly.

She murmured to it. "We're home now my love, settle down and I'll find you some bread crumbs."

Out of the dark a voice said, "Perhaps you'll offer me something as well old woman, and it'd better be more than some bread crumbs."

Dorothy jumped at the voice. Before she could move away a hand shot out and grabbed her around the wrist.

"I know who you are," she hissed, trying to pull away.

The voice laughed and said, "Well, it didn't take the Pigeon to work that one out for you."

"Roger Mudstone," she said.

"Guilty," said the voice.

"What do you want?"

From out of the gloom, Sir Roger's face loomed into view. The letter shaped scar on his cheek catching what little light there was.

"I was going to kill you, and I still may. For now you're going to be the guarantee I get out of here alive."

Those who didn't reside in the precinct or had no good reason to be there were slowly herded back towards the main gate, many protesting bitterly at missing what remained of the spectacle. Scrivener and Osbert had positioned themselves next to the gate. They cast an eye over each person passing out in the hope that Mudstone would be spotted trying to escape.

As the afternoon wore on towards evening, Will and Bernard met Osbert and his uncle at the gate. Will said, "Nothing. We've been through the palace as best as we can. The outbuildings we've combed through twice. No sign of him, or the boy for that matter."

Scrivener said, "All the gates are closed. Mudstone must be within the precinct somewhere. I'm confident he hasn't escaped yet. I've set men watching the walls, both inside and out."

Will scratched his head in frustration. "We've got men ringing the cathedral as best we can. It must offer a hundred different hiding places. We could search for hours."

Bernard snorted angrily. "He must be in there. If it takes days to find him, then so be it. I won't rest until he's on the end of my sword."

Scrivener put a hand on the big man's arm. "We have to

be practical my friend. We can't lockdown the cathedral or the precinct itself for days on end. There's a hundred or more pilgrims through the gate before noon each day, and countless others who have business here of one kind or another."

Will nodded in agreement. "We need to resolve this quickly.Mudstone doesn't know the building well, he's been away for years. I'd wager he's not set foot in there since he was a boy. We need to look at the problem through the eyes of a desperate man."

"If I was Mudstone, God forbid, I would first seek the almighty's forgiveness before the altar. He's committed a multitude of sins," said Osbert piously.

Scrivener frowned. "I very much doubt a man like Mudstone is looking for forgiveness Osbert. But the cathedral would offer the best chance to keep somewhere out of sight and then escape when things are quiet."

De Ward suddenly appeared. "I can't find Dame Dorothy anywhere."

Scrivener sighed, "What do you mean you can't find her? I saw you with her in the courtyard not above an hour ago."

De Ward wrung his hands, "She's nowhere to be found. I took my eyes off her for a few moments to speak to the bishop. When I turned back, she had gone."

Bernard shrugged. "She's a formidable woman, tough as old shoe leather. She'll come to no harm. We've more important matters on our minds de Ward. We're trying to catch a killer."

Will trying to console the nervous de Ward said, "She's not been out of that cell in twenty years. Don't worry my friend, she won't have wandered far."

Osbert nodded. "Perhaps she has returned to her cell. She's a pious woman, she won't break her vows for long."

Bernard said, "We're just wasting time. Lets start a search of the cathedral for Mudstone."

Scrivener gestured to the guards and the sheriff's men, who were close by, to follow them to the cathedral.

There were two men standing guard at the great west door.

"You seen anything at all?" queried Bernard before they entered.

"Nothing," said one. They were about to go in when the other guard said, "Apart from the old woman, Dame Dorothy."

De Ward who had followed them said eagerly, "You let her in? Where is she?"

The man nodded, then scratched his head. "Don't rightly know, went to her cell I suppose."

Scrivener said in frustration, "Why did you let her in?"

"You never said anything about letting people in, just out. It was only the old woman anyway."

"Idiot!" said Bernard, shoving the man out of the way with a huge hand.

Sir Roger set off down the nave towards one of the two candle lit shrines that were at the opposite end of the great building. His hand still about her wrist, he dragged Dame Dorothy after him. So far she'd managed to contain herself but she let out a muffled cry as she stumbled and fell painfully onto her knees. Sir Roger didn't stop but dragged her along the smooth stone floor of the nave. "On your feet old woman or I swear it'll be the worse for you."

The sound of pounding feet came from behind. He looked back into the gloom and saw a dozen dark figures pursuing them. He crossed the transept at the centre of the nave at a semi-run. Dorothy was now back on her feet, knees bloody but still in his grip.

"Mudstone," bellowed Bernard angrily and charged forward.

Sir Roger glanced behind at the big man fast closing on him. Grabbing Dame Dorothy around the throat he held her in front and slowly backed up, dragging the old woman with him. He shouted, "Stay back or I swear I'll break the old woman's neck like a twig."

"Ignore him, his time is drawing to a close," said Dame Dorothy in a steady voice that held absolute conviction.

"Shut up, you revolting old hag," he hissed in her ear and shook her so hard she saw stars.

Sir Roger continued to move backwards at a fast pace until he crashed into the side of one of the saint's shrines, scattering burning candles and wax figures across the stone floor. Losing his grip on Dame Dorothy, she scuttled off to one side, out of his reach. The pursuing bishop's officials and guards came to a stop in a rough semi-circle behind Bernard, who drew his sword. De Ward, who had retrieved the Pigeon of Perception from the cell, rushed over to Dame Dorothy's side and gently helped the old woman out of further harm's way. When she had gained her feet again, she reached out and took the pigeon from de Ward.

She whispered to the bird, "There, there, my dear, settle down now, there's nothing to fear."

"Come, I'll accompany you outside Dame Dorothy. It's not safe in here," said de Ward.

"No," she said forcefully. "I need to see the end to this."

Sir Roger brought his sword up, the tip pointed at Bernard and said, "You'd do violence in a holy place like this; in front of one of the saint's shrines?"

Bernard grinned without humour and held his sword ready before him. "You jest with me. My conscious would be clear if I dispatched you on top of the very altar, let alone here in front of the shrine."

Scrivener said, "There's no escape from this place now Mudstone, we're too many, even for you. See sense and lay down your weapon."

Sir Roger shrugged and said, "Perhaps I'll claim sanctuary, we're in a cathedral after all."

Scrivener snorted in response.

Sir Roger said angrily, "You'd deny me my rights?"

Osbert who had now taken refuge beside one of the huge pillars of the nave hissed, "He has no rights, he forfeit those long ago. Finish him."

"Ah, the little clerk," mocked Sir Roger, eyes briefly coming to rest on Osbert. "I wondered where you'd gone. Ever ready to offer advice but never to take action yourself. And the other one, the ginger haired fool, is he with you too?"

Will came out of the shadows behind Bernard and stood beside his friend, sword at the ready.

Sir Roger nodded. "Ah, excellent. So we're all here. Let's finish this once and for all."

He suddenly lunged at Bernard, the big man only just stepping back in time to avoid Sir Roger's blade, which continued on to rip the front of Will's tunic.

Will stumbled backwards, looked down in horror at his chest, but the blade had miraculously only torn the fabric and not broken skin.

Bernard never taking his eyes off Sir Roger murmured, "You all right lad?"

Will nodded and croaked, "Yes."

Bernard smiled grimly. "Then stay well back. Leave this turd to me."

Scrivener grabbed Will's arm and pulled him back. Bernard suddenly pressed forward in a vicious attack. There was a clash as blades came together. Sir Roger retreated as Bernard made a flurry of thrusts and lunges. In a burst of speed that defied his bedraggled appearance, Sir Roger turned and darted out of sight around the edge of the shrine and made off into the gloom of the nave, heading towards the high altar.

Bernard bellowed, "Coward!" and charged after him.

The rest followed at a safe distance, de Ward and Dame Dorothy bringing up the rear.

There were two candles burning on the altar, casting a yellow glow that illuminated the end of the cathedral.

Sir Roger, with few options left, cast around for some advantage he could use. Towards the high altar itself, on a side wall, was the tomb of Bishop Thorndyke. The elaborate effigy of the former bishop, carved in alabaster, was still in the process of being installed atop his tomb.

Sir Roger limped over to wall. The effigy hung in a harness of ropes, some two feet above where it would eventually rest, supported by a large wooden trestle. Tools, coils of rope and bits of timber were next to the trestle. A pile of stones and broken mortar was heaped against the wall, debris waiting to be removed.

Sir Roger scrabbled in the pile and grabbed a stone, which he hurled at the approaching men. Bernard in the lead ducked, and the stone passed over him and hit one of the guards full in the face. The man dropped to the floor like a sack of grain. Sir Roger laughed manically and rained debris at the bishop's men. They held off approaching any closer as he exhausted the ammunition, hitting no one else.

"You're finished man," shouted Bernard. "I'll make it quick if you lay down your sword now."

Sir Roger gleefully replied, "If you think a stinking turd like you can take me, then by all means approach. Try your luck."

He suddenly reached down and grabbed a mason's hammer and hurled it with such force that he nearly fell over when releasing it. The hammer sailed high over the bishop's men's heads and smashed into one of the pillars, gouging a chunk from the stonework before falling down with a metallic clatter.

De Ward peered up and tutted. "He's damaged the stone work. Who will pay for the repairs?"

"Christ bones man, be quiet," muttered Scrivener.

"You'll have to do better than that," spat Bernard advancing with menace.

Sir Roger reacted by slashing out in fury, Bernard ducked, and the sharp sword edge sliced through several of the ropes holding Thorndyke's effigy above the tomb base. The figure dropped with a jerk, one end now within a foot of the flat surface beneath. The heavy stonework swayed and there was an ominous groan from the wooden trestle as the other ropes took up the strain. The effigy of the bishop now hung at a forty-five degree angle, his feet higher than his head. Sir Roger pressed forward again, and Bernard found himself forced against the stone base of the tomb.

"Let's hope the old bastard will be more useful now than he ever was in life," hissed Sir Roger. He deliberately slashed through more of the ropes holding the alabaster effigy. The figure, suddenly unrestrained, swung wildly around. The bishop's stone head struck Bernard a heavy blow which sent him staggering away, bloody and dazed. He dropped to his knees and Sir Roger gleefully moved in, raising his sword arm for a killing blow.

Will dived forward and caught Sir Roger's brutal downward stroke with his own sword It deflected the blow but the weapon was forced from his hands. Sir Roger turned to him in a fury.

"You are about to die dimwit," he hissed.

The pigeon suddenly struggled in Dorothy's grip and in a whirl of wings and feathers flew straight at Sir Roger's face. He flailed at the bird as it flapped madly at his head, all thoughts of Will forgotten. He tried to bat at the pigeon with his sword arm, but it was too close and his sword crashed into the stonework of the tomb, raising a shower of sparks.

Bernard recovered his senses enough to crawl away from the enraged man. Sir Roger dropped his sword and tried to protect his face from the clawing bird. Driven into the swinging effigy, he lost his footing and reached up, grabbing the figure to stop himself from falling. There was a groan and shudder as the remaining ropes gave way and the figure dropped directly down on top of the falling man. With a last desperate cry from Sir Roger, the heavy effigy crashed to the floor, crushing him against the flagstones in a gory spray of blood which splattered the onlookers. He lay spread eagled directly under the stonework, his head no longer visible but his broken limbs sticking out from the sides. They gave a brief twitch and then all was still. A growing pool of blood began to spread from underneath the effigy.

"I never thought it'd be old Thorny himself lending a hand," said Bernard, blood splattered and looking on in fascinated horror.

"It's a miracle," said Osbert, grey faced.

"Is he dead?" said de Ward.

"If he isn't it really will be a bloody miracle," Will observed.

"It's God's justice, plain and simple," said Dame Dorothy. The pigeon, still in the air, fluttered back to Dorothy's outstretched hands and landed gently.

There was the sound of running feet behind them and a large contingent of men came to a juddering stop led by the bishop himself with sword drawn.

The bishop looked down at the man crushed under the reposed figure of Bishop Thorndyke, his palms together in prayer.

"God's teeth, that's as nasty a sight as I've seen in many a year. Is that Mudstone under there?"

Bernard, still kneeling on the floor, said wearily. "It's him all right my lord, Roger Mudstone, sent to hell with the help of old Thorny himself."

"And the Pigeon of Perception," said Dame Dorothy.

The bishop shook his head in wonderment and sheathed his sword. "And to think I wasn't even going to have a ceremony for the completion of the old goat's tomb."

De Ward said matter-of-factly, "I hope Mudstone hasn't damaged the effigy. The chapter will be most upset at any further expense."

Will said, "I think you'll find the damage was all the other way around. I'd swear that's a smug expression on old Thorny's face"

They all turned to look at the bishop's head, resting on his stone pillow. In the flicking light of the candles from the high altar, Bishops Thorndyke's effigy did indeed look to be smiling.

22

AN ENDING

A cart left the city by the small gate situated behind the bishop's palace, its driver whistling a cheerful tune. The cart trundled along the rough track beside the city wall until it joined the main road leading from one of the great gatehouses. Travis's eyes affixed on the grinning head of his former master impaled on top of a long spike by the side of the road. Mudstone gazed down on him, a blackened, squashed and shrunken skull, with a few tufts of hair remaining. The letter M still clear for all to see branded on his sunken pickled cheek. Mudstone's head was one of a half a dozen set up either side of the road. They were a grisly reminder to the inhabitants of the city of the power of the law.

The man driving the cart slowed and turned back to look at his passengers. He grinned at Travis. "They done a nice job on him don't you think? Had to patch his head back together first. Last a few years he will now. Parboiled and coated in tar. Some of those lads have been up there longer than I've been in the hanging business."

The other passenger in the back of the cart, a guard

Scrivener, looking directly at Tom the Stretch, said, "Make it quick lads, no funny business."

Tom nodded his understanding.

Travis ran a hand over his grimy face and said, "I wasn't all bad, was I?"

Scrivener sat on his horse, shook his head slowly. "No man is all bad. I remember that girl Annie you rescued once. And Bernard said you saved his life. As for the rest, you made your choice. You chose Mudstone over a life. I don't pretend to understand why."

"I've helped him do terrible things. They haunted my dreams. I've not slept properly for years. I'm so tired Master Scrivener."

Tom the Stretch reached out and gently dropped the noose around Travis's neck. "Don't worry about that. Let us take care of things and you'll soon be sleeping."

He quickly threw the rope around the gallows, pulling the slack tight, tying it off around the main post with practiced ease.

Travis stood in the back of the cart. Tom hurried back to the horse. The guard still sat in the cart, his arms folded, expression neutral, taking in a scene he'd witnessed a hundred times before.

"I'm sorry," said Travis.

"I know," said Scrivener and nodded at Tom.

Travis mumbled a prayer, "Lord have mercy upon my soul..."

Tom slapped the horse on its rear and it jerked forward, Travis was pulled backwards across the floor of the cart and then dropped and left twitching in midair on the end of the rope clutching at his throat, eyes bulging from his head. The guard jumped off the cart, ran back and put his arms around Travis's legs and hung his full weight off them, breaking the man's neck and ending the struggle.

Tom sniffed and ran a hand under his nose. He looked up at Scrivener sitting on his horse. "It looks like we'll miss the rain after all. A quick tidy up here and we'll be back to the city and an afternoon in the Pope's Head. And you Master Scrivener, fancy a drink?"

Scrivener gave a humourless smile. "It's tempting Tom but I believe I'm shortly expected at Saint Mary's Abbey." He pointed at Travis's lifeless body gently rocking in the wind and felt the bile rise in his throat. "You'll take care of the business with the head?"

"All part of the job, we'll do the honours and he'll be up on his pole soon enough."

The guard, who was already removing Travis's worn-out boots, shouted across, "All depends on how long it takes to boil his head of course."

Tom nodded. "Very true. Some have to boil longer than others, and it takes a fine eye to know when to stop."

With a shudder, Scrivener nudged his horse into motion and without another word rode off down the hill.

The bishop and Scrivener were shown into the abbot's chamber at Saint Mary's. They found Brother William sitting on a stool before the fire. He rose to greet them, a guilty look on his face. "My old bones, I find the warmth is the only thing that soothes them," he said apologetically.

The bishop smiled. "Don't apologise Brother, a man should be able to relax once in a while, even a monk." He gestured for William to sit down again. The bishop sat down with a sigh in the abbot's comfortable padded chair.

Scrivener leant against the wall behind the bishop and folded his arms.

Brother William looked between them, unsure of what was to come. Finally the bishop said, "So, I believe Scrivener spoke to you soon after the death of Abbot Richard about the future of the abbey?"

Brother William nodded nervously. "He did my lord. These last few days have set the abbey in a turmoil. He said you might be able to assist?"

The bishop leant forward and put his hands together. He studied the old man and nodded as if coming to some inner decision. "How would you feel William if I said you should be abbot of this place?"

William looked bewildered for a moment before understanding of the bishop's question dawned. "Abbot of Saint Mary's. No, God forgive me my lord, this is not what I would wish for. I'm not worthy of such a task," the old monk said pleadingly.

Scrivener said, "Which is exactly why you're by far the best man for the position. If you think of the task as a burden, then I suggest you treat it as your penance Brother, or should I say Abbot William."

William ran a hand over his tired eyes and shook his head. "But the rest of the brethren would have to vote on such a matter. There is no guarantee they will choose me, even if I was willing to agree to such a thing. I'm far too old; my years are numbered."

The bishop rested back in his chair and smiled indulgently. "Nonsense, with age comes experience, isn't that what they say? I will be most generous in agreeing to become a patron of the abbey and our many friends in the city will be as forthcoming with their donations and bequests. I'm sure the good brothers, cloistered life or not, know which way the wind is blowing. The future looks bright my friend. Would you and your brethren rather be cast out and see this place a ruin?"

William shook his head sadly, "No my lord, it would be a betrayal of all the good men who came before us. But I'm not sure I can carry on the affairs of the abbey as they have been conducted in the recent past."

Scrivener said, "I believe the previous abbot and prior were the type of monks who do much business outside the monastery?"

Brother William nodded. "Yes, it's true. Abbot Richard and the prior did much arranging of contracts and sales with lay people."

Scrivener probed further. "Perhaps they acquired too much of a taste for life outside the monastery? Hunting, fine horses, good living, good drinking, perhaps a fat swan on the table once a week?"

"All those things. I fear they strayed far from the path Master Scrivener. Pride and greed were their downfall."

The bishop pointed at the old man. "But you William, these aren't things that should tempt you I think. You don't strike me as that type of man. You'll live by the rule and perhaps allow us to guide you occasionally on business outside the cloisters."

The old man contemplated his fate, accepted it, looked the bishop in the eye and said firmly, "If this is God's will my lord, then it will be so. I have always tried to follow the rule as Saint Benedict ordained. A monk without rules is like a fish without water."

The bishop nodded, satisfied. He smiled graciously and said, "Then I believe we understand each other well enough, Abbot William."

The boy had waited each morning outside the decrepit alehouse in Codlingham for the last three days. A dirty leather hanging, through which he would periodically scuttle when someone with the look of authority passed by, covered the main door. Three miles north of the city, Codlingham was a place where one could shelter from the authorities without too many questions being asked. Of course that anonymity lasted only as long as did the coins in your purse. He'd slept in the rank smelling smokey interior of the alehouse for two pennies a night and felt himself lucky not to have had his throat slit. If the woman didn't come for him today, then he judged he had enough money left to eat or sleep in the alehouse, but not both. The prospect of taking his rest under a hedge didn't appeal, but hunger won out. He took a quick look up and down the road. The track was busy with travellers but he saw no one who remotely resembled the woman, even in disguise, so he went back into the alehouse. There were no windows, just a small hole in the turf roof that let a minimal amount of smoke vent upwards from the fire. His eyes stung, and he half choked as he breathed in the hot stale air.

Out of the gloom came the sour faced serving woman. She wiped her hands on a filthy rag and scowled at him. "You still here?"

"For now."

"Can I give you a piece of advice boy?"

"Can I stop you?"

"You're a miserable bugger for one so young. But that's not my advice, you already know that. I don't know who you're waiting for and I don't care. I do know that you can't rely on anyone else in this life other than yourself."

The boy slapped down one of his last pennies on the rough tabletop. He said, "That's it, is it, your advice? Fetch me some pottage and leave me alone."

The serving woman scowled at him, then shook her head and snapped, "Some never learn." She snatched the coin up and disappeared back into the gloom.

The boy was spooning the last of the thin pottage into his mouth from a wooden bowl when the leather hide over the doorway of the alehouse was suddenly pulled roughly aside. He looked up, but the light was blinding. Someone moved inside and let the hide fall back behind them. When his eyes readjusted to the gloom he saw that it was the woman.

"Still here then?" she said, more a statement than a question.

Licking the last of the food from the wooden spoon he said, "You're the second person to ask me that question today."

The woman came and sat opposite him. "So, do you wish to come with me or not?"

He shoved the empty bowl aside and in a low whisper said, "No, but what choice do I have? Between that madman Mudstone and the old man, my prospects are ruined."

She mocked him, "And you're blameless in all this are you? Do you forget the death of the abbot and the prior?"

He flinched and replied, "Mudstone killed the prior not me and it wasn't I who started the fire at the palace. The bishop's men will string us both up if they lay their hands on us."

The woman looked around cautiously then pulled a bulging bag of coins from under her cloak and held it so he could see before swiftly concealing it again. The boy's eyes grew wide. She said, "We are far from destitute. I have coin enough for the both of us. Enough for a few months at the very least. I suggest you stop moaning and start thinking."

"Why would you help me?" he said suspiciously.

She laughed softly. "God only knows, I'm not sure I do. We're hardly a family are we? Don't think me a sister to you, and you know better than to think me sentimental. Ralph saw something of value in you, perhaps you'll be useful."

The boy said, "We can't stay in Draychester. Where would we go?"

"To London. I've long prepared for this day, the old man couldn't live forever. I have two horses outside and supplies for the journey."

The boy's mouth hung open. "London, and what will we do there?"

The woman said, "I have plans. I know people there."

"What sort of plans, what people?"

She sighed, "You ask far too many questions boy."

"That's what he used to say."

"Who?"

"Our father, Ralph of Shrewsbury."

"He never acted as a father to me, to you either. I served the old man well and look where that led."

"God's teeth, I won't miss that smell or rubbing his boney old toes," said the boy.

"So, decide. Are you coming?"

After a moment the boy nodded and said, "When do we leave?"

"Now," she said, getting to her feet.

looking over his shoulder as the big man stood with hands on hips watching them with a scowl.

Osbert hunched his head down further and speeded up. "I threw a rock at him."

"Should I ask why?"

"No." said Osbert firmly.

The streets were still busy as the pair made their way down towards the marketplace. Outside the Pope's Head two men were drunkenly brawling with each other, rolling in and out of the gutter that ran down the middle of the street. Several bystanders stood watching with interest and offered encouragement or insults, it was hard to tell which, to one of the filth splattered brawlers. The bishop's men side-stepped the fighting couple without breaking pace. Further down the street, from a dark alleyway, a red-haired strumpet stepped out and tried to block their way. She grinned at them through blackened teeth and flicked her tongue. "Business is slow, fancy a tumble lads, a penny each?" She looked closer at Osbert and revised her price, "I'll give you a discount love, a half penny."

Osbert stopped and spluttered in outrage before a laughing Will shook his head at her, and grabbed his friend's arm and pulled him away. They could hear the woman cackling as she disappeared back into the alley.

At the marketplace the day's business was over, most of the awnings had been taken down and the last of the traders were packing up. Two men using buckets filled from a water butt were trying their best to sluice away the filth from the cobbles. One sent a cascade of water shooting over the stones towards them. Will expertly skipped out of the way, leaving Osbert's boots to take a soaking.

"God's teeth, can you not be more careful," he hissed at the man.

The man shrugged and said with little interest, "I could, but I don't get paid to," and quickly moved off to soak some other unfortunate passerby.

The two of them stood next to the gate of the cathedral precinct while Osbert tried to shake the water from his boots.

Will couldn't help but laugh. "You seem to attract misfortune like a bee to honey."

The gatekeeper, who'd seen the incident, ambled out and stood beside them chewing on some sort of meat pie.

"Evening lads," he said, mouth half full. With gravy running over his hand and heading down towards his grubby sleeve, he gestured to the square.

"Not been the same since the market clerk got clobbered. Nasty afternoon that were. Mind you, no one ever had a good word to say about him. He were an evil bugger at the best of times."

Osbert sniffed. "My uncle Scrivener says it wasn't a great loss. A fresh man is to be appointed, this time with the consent of the stallholders."

The gatekeeper nodded and crammed half the pie into his mouth. He helped the last bit in with a shove from his finger, chewed once and appeared to swallow the lot. He belched and said, "Good luck to him. It's not a job I'd want."

Will, sniffing the aroma from the pie suddenly felt pangs of hunger. He said to Osbert, "I'm off to the great hall, I need some food and perhaps I'll find Bernard there. He's sure to know more about this mysterious messenger of yours."

Osbert shaking the last drops from his boot replied, "Well I suppose I'd better come with you. There's no chance of us not being involved anyway."

Will clapped him on the shoulder and chuckled. "As I said, misfortune loves you my friend."

The great hall of the bishop's palace was still under repair from the damage caused by the fire. Outside there was a jumble of stonework and timbers ready for use. A huge mound of debris that had fallen from the roof and walls had been removed from the interior and deposited on a corner of the cathedral green. The muddy tracks that had been worn into the manicured grass over the last weeks were still visible as Will and Osbert crossed the space. A forest of scaffolding and wooden ladders both inside and out rose up the blackened stone walls to allow access to the masons and carpenters.

As they entered the hall itself they both instinctively looked up to check on the progress, Osbert almost tripping on a trailing rope attached to a pulley fixed far above their heads.

"God's teeth, take care or we'll have half the roof down on us," said Will.

Osbert removed the rope from around his feet and said, "I wish they'd hurry up and fix the roof. Not only is it cold but it's wet."

Half of the space was back in use, and the long tables and benches were crammed into it. The roof itself now had temporary timbers in place that held an awning to keep the rain off. The awning was only partially successful, and much to the annoyance of those sat below, it allowed water to drip or more often cascade down on them if the rain was heavy.

Despite the conditions the hall was still the central hub of the bishop's palace and was as crowded and noisy as ever. Will smiled as he took in the scene. It was his favourite space in the whole precinct. It was a place where people could mix freely. There were servants, officials, canons, guards, workmen and anyone else who had good reason or no reason to be there. People were eating, drinking, laughing, arguing, shouting and sometimes even sleeping. The bishop's favourite hounds roamed free, searching the floor for scraps and shamelessly begging from those who were eating. A constant stream of servants brought in food and drink from the kitchen, dodging the dogs, the odd drunk and piles of building materials.

Will scanned the crowd and saw the unmistakable bulk of Bernard in deep discussion with Scrivener. Will caught his eye and the big man beckoned them over.

Will and Osbert settled down on the bench next to Bernard. Scrivener was opposite, a jug of ale between them.

"Drink?" said Bernard.

"Always, but I'm hungry too," replied Will.

Bernard grunted. "Always thinking of food you youngsters. Still you're both thin as rakes, you need some meat on your bones I suppose."

Will didn't point out Bernard's own prodigious food intake but let it go with a smile.

"Anyway, before you both stuff your faces we need to talk. The bishop has some business for us."

"What again?" said Osbert, looking up at the roof suspiciously as a water drop landed on his face. "It seems we have only just finished dealing with one madman. Please tell me we don't seek another."

Scrivener said, "Nothing stays the same for long Nephew. You know that by now, alliances shift, men die, others rise up in their place. Other things may need investigating. That's the nature of the game the bishop plays."

"I know it Uncle. It doesn't mean I like it. We're obviously doomed," said Osbert.

Will grinned at his friend. "Ever the optimist Osbert. That's what I like about you, we always know exactly where you stand, and it's not the sunny side, is it?"

Osbert shrugged. "My views, it's true, are generally consistent."

Bernard sighed and shook his head, "Truly you'd try the patience of the angels."

"To business," said Scrivener looking at Bernard.

The big man sighed, ran a hand over his stubbly chin and said, "In the countryside there is a thing the county folk believe in. A Shuck, have you ever heard of such a thing?"

Will shook his head.

"A hellhound," said Osbert with a shudder. He crossed himself and continued. "The name is associated with a large black dog mostly. Some say it can shape-shift into other forms as well."

Will laughed. "An old wives' tale to frighten the children, surely."

Scrivener nodded grimly. "You'd think so, wouldn't you? I've heard the term myself of course. A good tale, told on a dark night in front of a winter fire. It seems perhaps it's not all together a fiction of the storyteller."

"I'm not sure I understand," said Will curiously. "Is this to do with the messenger who arrived the other night?"

Scrivener and Bernard exchanged a look. "In a way. He brought dispatches down from the north. One from Lady Matilda the bishop's sister, the other from the officials of one of the bishop's northern manors. It was rather disturbing."

"In what way disturbing?" asked Osbert, not sure if he really wanted to know the answer.

"It seems the town of Ditton is plagued by a sighting of a Shruck, and all manner of strange occurrences have been happening. The wakeman and mayor of Ditton seek the bishop's help."

"I don't even know what a wakeman is," said Will

"Never mind that. I know where this is leading. You mean to send us to investigate?" said Osbert angrily.

"Exactly so," said Scrivener.

AFTERWORD
FROM THE AUTHOR

Dear Reader,

Thank you for reading one of my books. I've always been an avid reader of historical fiction but also harboured the thought, like so many of us do, that I'd try and write something myself. What you have been reading was the third book I published. It took me a long time to finish the first one and have the confidence to put it out into the world. I worked in the IT and Telecoms Industry here in the UK for many years, ended up running my own company, and inevitably life and job got in the way. I'd do some research, make some progress on the book, then leave it again.

In early 2018 a close family member became seriously ill. Writing offered me an escape from some of the stress and worry involved and gave me the motivation to get the first book over the finishing line.

After I'd completed that first book, I wrote the next two in the series in a just over a year. I learned a lot writing them. What I got over that period was validation from readers they enjoyed my work, which in turn encouraged me to keep on writing and improving.

The writing process can be both uplifting and disheartening in equal measure. I really appreciate every review you guys give my books. Every time you leave some feedback, good or bad, it helps validate that at least someone is out there reading them. I look at each review posted and take your comments to heart and hope to become a better writer because of them.

On Amazon, I've found it makes a huge difference for independent authors like me when prospective readers can learn more about a book from others who post a review. So, if you can spare a minute and share your impressions of the book that would be amazing.

Did you enjoy the book? What did you like about it? Who were your favourite characters? Should the series continue? Give me your thoughts via a review or rating on Amazon.

Be the first to receive the news of upcoming books in the series, exclusive offers and free downloads. Join my newsletter and...

Get your free copy of
Death Of The Messenger
The Prequel to the
Draychester Chronicles

You can sign up at this link:-
www.westerbone.com/newsletter

* For lots more information visit my author website,

www.westerbone.com

* You can also connect with me on Facebook,

www.facebook.com/mjwesterbone

*and on twitter,

www.twitter.com/westerbone

@westerbone

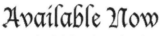

Available Now

Book 1 of the Draychester Chronicles

Death Of The Official

Available Now

Book 2 of the Draychester Chronicles

Death Of The Vintner

Hope to see you soon,

M J Westerbone,
Hindley Green, England, U.K

COPYRIGHT

Printed in Great Britain
by Amazon

58218044R00161

A mysterious killer is on the rampage. Make no mistake, the countryside can be a deadly place in late 14th century England, but who would dare target the village anchorite?

Wouldn't it be a deadly sin? Harm those devoutly religious women, walled up for life inside a cell in the village church, and face eternal damnation…only an angry, desperate man could be persuaded to carry out such evil…

In the local cathedral city of Draychester, Bishop Gifford is angry and baffled. Events are spiralling out of control. Young Will Blackburne, bishop's official, and his companions Bernard and Osbert are swiftly dispatched to investigate.

But perhaps all isn't quite as it seems. A shadowy figure from within the city guides the killer's actions, bringing events closer to home than anyone can predict …except perhaps the cathedral's own anchorite, Dame Dorothy, famous for her visions of the future. She dreams of death and destruction. The killer must be stopped, his evil master thwarted and Dorothy saved…

The third book in the Draychester Chronicles series plunges the reader head on into an immersive tale of humour, murder and intrigue set in a gritty depiction of medieval England that's not for the fainthearted.

ISBN 9798598519813